Sugar Spinelli's
Little Instruction Book

I can hardly believe that Flynn Morgan showed up at the Lost Springs Bachelor Auction. Now, there was a boy riding for a fall. But I heard he turned himself around. Started up his own business. Went straight. Became a stand-up guy. I guess his appearance at the auction is proof of that. One look at him and I knew. *Flynn Morgan was a changed man.* Now I'm just fussing over who he's going to hook up with. That boy deserves a good woman. A woman who will appreciate all the fine qualities Flynn tries so hard to hide. Yeah. That boy deserves a break.

Dear Reader,

We just knew you wouldn't want to miss the news event that has all of Wyoming abuzz! There's a herd of eligible bachelors on their way to Lightning Creek—and they're all for sale!

Cowboy, park ranger, rancher, P.I.—they all grew up at Lost Springs Ranch, and every one of these mavericks has his price, so long as the money's going to help keep Lost Springs afloat.

The auction is about to begin! Young and old, every woman in the state wants in on the action, so pony up some cash and join the fun. The man of your dreams might just be up for grabs!

Marsha Zinberg
Editorial Coordinator, HEART OF THE WEST

The Perfect Solution

Day Leclaire

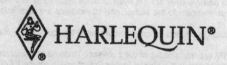

HARLEQUIN®

TORONTO • NEW YORK • LONDON
AMSTERDAM • PARIS • SYDNEY • HAMBURG
STOCKHOLM • ATHENS • TOKYO • MILAN • MADRID
PRAGUE • WARSAW • BUDAPEST • AUCKLAND

If you purchased this book without a cover you should be aware that this book is stolen property. It was reported as "unsold and destroyed" to the publisher, and neither the author nor the publisher has received any payment for this "stripped book."

Day Leclaire is acknowledged as the author of this work.

ISBN 0-373-82594-3

THE PERFECT SOLUTION

Copyright © 1999 by Harlequin Books S.A.

All rights reserved. Except for use in any review, the reproduction or utilization of this work in whole or in part in any form by any electronic, mechanical or other means, now known or hereafter invented, including xerography, photocopying and recording, or in any information storage or retrieval system, is forbidden without the written permission of the publisher, Harlequin Enterprises Limited, 225 Duncan Mill Road, Don Mills, Ontario, Canada M3B 3K9.

All characters in this book have no existence outside the imagination of the author and have no relation whatsoever to anyone bearing the same name or names. They are not even distantly inspired by any individual known or unknown to the author, and all incidents are pure invention.

This edition published by arrangement with Harlequin Books S.A.

® and TM are trademarks of the publisher. Trademarks indicated with ® are registered in the United States Patent and Trademark Office, the Canadian Trade Marks Office and in other countries.

Visit us at www.romance.net

Printed in U.S.A.

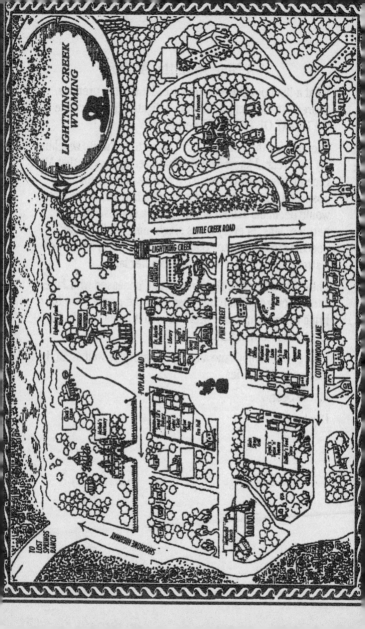

A Note from the Author

What a fun book this was to write! I loved the premise, adored the characters and was delighted to participate in the HEART OF THE WEST series.

The idea for the heroine, Jane, came to me while watching my son. Yeah, I know. Weird. What I really mean is that Matt recently discovered chemistry, and he became instantly obsessed. The world could grind to a halt and there Matt would be, in his school lab, glued to a microscope. My heroine, Jane, is every bit as single-minded. She also needs a strong man to complement her. Heck, she needs a strong man to drag her away from her lab!

Enter Flynn Morgan. He's irreverent, obsessed with Jane and has overcome a tough past. He's the perfect one to bring romance into her life—though it takes a while for him to realize that fact.

I hope you'll enjoy Jane and Flynn's story, as well as all the stories in this series.

All the best,

Day Leclaire

Many thanks to Dr. Joseph Gardella, Professor of Chemistry at the University of Buffalo. He generously offered his time and expertise and was of immense help (as well as being a really nice guy). Many thanks, also, to Dr. George Preti of the Monell Chemical Senses Center. Any lab or pheromone errors are strictly my own.

PROLOGUE

*Lost Springs Ranch for Boys outside of
Lightning Creek, Wyoming*

"CAN'T BELIEVE YOU SHOWED UP," Zeke Lonetree said.

Flynn Morgan flashed that grin, which either charmed the hell out of people or got him in more hot water than he could handle. "Can't hardly believe it myself," he drawled.

Once upon a time, he wouldn't have made an appearance at the Lost Springs bachelor auction, in spite of his promise and regardless of the fact that Lost Springs Ranch had been his home, along with all the other lost boys, after his parents abandoned him. He would have stood them up. When the time came, he would have conveniently forgotten—an accident of deliberation that wouldn't have surprised those running the event one little bit. A few years ago, he wouldn't have given it a passing thought. He'd have done it. Period.

But at some point between then and now, all that had changed. *He'd* changed. He grinned, his mouth pulling to one side. And he continued to change. The latest growth spurt was thanks to a painful right hook from his business partner, Paulie. Flynn rubbed the bruise that still darkened the side of his face and winced. Damn, that man could hit.

What had his partner said that had been so helpful? Oh, right.

"You're dead, Morgan!"

A fist had followed on the heels of Paulie's declaration.

Flynn couldn't even claim it caught him by surprise, mainly because it didn't surprise him. Not only had he expected the blow, he deserved it. Maybe he should have ducked. He could have. But something had made him stand there and take it on the chin. Or in this case, on the side of the mouth.

He'd needed a minute to recover enough to attempt a cocky grin. "Paulie. Something got your shorts in a twist?" That had earned him a second fist, one he'd ducked. Hell, he wasn't a total moron, just an idiot.

"You had to help her out, didn't you?" his partner had ranted. "Despite what we'd agreed, despite the background check I ran, and despite the fact that your brains seep into your pants whenever there's a woman in trouble around."

"What can I say?" Flynn retorted with a shrug. "I'm a sucker for a damsel in distress."

"I warned you getting involved with her was a mistake. It was all a scam to entrap her husband, and you—" Paulie jabbed his index finger into Flynn's chest. "You of all people fell for it like some ignorant, peach-fuzzed, apple-cheeked mark fresh off the bus. We're supposed to install security systems, Flynn, not help disgruntled wives exact revenge on wayward husbands."

"Aw, hell, Paulie. I didn't know what she'd planned. And she *cried.*"

"Yeah? Well next time some dame starts up the water-works, you just remember I have another right hook waitin' for you. Got it, Morgan?"

Of course, that wasn't the only painful experience he'd recently suffered. Returning to Lost Springs Ranch had proved almost as bad as Paulie's fist. There were too many unfortunate memories and too many wary faces. Faces who remembered him, remembered the scamming, sassy-mouthed asshole he'd once been. How did you explain that the boy they'd known was nothing like the man he'd become, especially when it had taken so many years to achieve that change?

Flynn took a vacant chair in the line of bachelors waiting to be sold and slouched down, his gaze wandering over the others, automatically pigeonholing them. It was an occupational hazard, one he couldn't quite seem to get past. He sighed. Maybe he should get out of the security business. He'd spent his entire life reading people, figuring out what they wanted in order to see where they fit in the general scheme of things and how that scheme involved him. He'd made a living reading people. He'd also come within an inch of destroying his life thanks to that particular talent. And he'd disappointed more people than he could count, including a few he'd bumped into, right here at Lost Springs.

There'd been puny Robbie Carter, not so puny anymore, now bought and paid for by a couple of little old ladies. What had Carter become? A doctor? Figured.

Then there was that snot-nosed kid, Shane Daniels, now a hotshot rodeo star. His was the next head to roll on the auction block.

Then there was Zeke. Flynn had once scammed the kid out of twenty bucks. Hell, Zeke hadn't even caught on, he'd been such an innocent. But Flynn remembered. And for the first time in his entire life, it weighed on him. Damn it to hell! Life changes sucked right up there with tax audits, crooked lawyers and humorless judges who thought a little innocent fun deserved the death penalty.

He drummed the arm of his chair for a full five minutes, trying to convince himself that life changes did not necessitate atonement for sins committed. After all, the past was the past.

He wasn't convinced. Giving in to the inevitable, he leaned forward and offered his hand to the man he'd scammed.

Zeke eyed him with deep suspicion.

"Feel free to count your fingers afterward," Flynn offered. "I promise, they'll all still be there."

Zeke reluctantly returned the handshake, staring in surprise at the twenty dollar bill that lined his palm afterward. "What's this for?"

"Owed it to you." Flynn shrugged, not cutting himself any slack. "I took it off you years ago when you didn't know better than to trust me. Thought it was about time I paid you back."

Zeke's brows drew together. "Can't say as I remember."

"*I* remember."

Comprehension dawned. "Got it." Zeke grinned. "Thanks, Flynn."

It was a small gesture, but one that made him feel better, one in a long string of gestures to help even out a very lopsided scale. After he'd fulfilled his obligation to Lost Springs he'd have plenty of time to contemplate the latest error of his ways—an error that had been punctuated by Paulie's right fist.

"Morgan! Didn't you hear me? Flynn? You're up."

Flynn got to his feet with a sigh. He was dreading this next part. Some wide-eyed, dewy-mouthed woman would buy him. She'd want a weekend of romance. Dinner. Dancing. Sweet, meaningless conversation. Hell, with his reputation, she might even expect more. After recent events, he didn't think he could handle that. Paulie's fist had proved a potent deterrent.

Following the whispered directions, he stepped forward, surprised by the number of people in the audience. Most of them were women, and a few feminine shrieks rang out as he stood for their inspection, like a bull up for stud.

"This is Flynn Morgan," the auctioneer announced, checking his clipboard. "And it says here he's a partner in a home-and-business security firm. Hey, folks. That's quite a deal you could have here. Need advice on keeping your valuables secure? Flynn's your man.''

"Just keep your women locked up!'' someone shouted from the audience.

"Sorry, friend,'' Flynn hollered back. "There isn't a lock I can't pick. Especially if there's a woman on the other side.''

Laughter followed, and once it died the auctioneer resumed. "Flynn's thirty-four, and when asked about his ideal woman, he claims there's not a woman born he hasn't taken a shine to.''

"Now, that I'd believe,'' came another voice from the audience. If Flynn didn't know better, he'd swear it was his fourth-grade teacher. Back then, he'd been a bit more obvious in his affections. Before he'd learned better. "And they shine right back.''

The auctioneer grinned at that. "I guess that means you can find Flynn wherever there's trouble abrewin' or a woman in need.''

"And where there's one, there's usually the other,'' Flynn joked. "But what's a man to do? I go where I'm needed.''

"And he was needed right here tonight and we appreciate his helpin' us out. Flynn says his greatest achievement is sticking to the straight and narrow, even when that straight and narrow wobbles a bit. If he were to describe himself in five words, he'd say…'' He checked his notes again. "He'd say he's a changed man.''

"Hey, Morgan. That's only four words,'' Zeke joked.

"So it is.'' Flynn rubbed a hand across his jaw and came up against his bruise. "In that case, make it a *forcibly* changed man.''

That drew more laughter and the auctioneer held his clipboard in the air. "So, ladies, what am I offered for this forcibly changed man? Any bids to start us off?''

Determined to give the ranch their money's worth, Flynn

flashed his patented grin. Slowly, he unbuttoned his jacket and shrugged out of it. His small act met with instant approval, whistles joining the feminine shouts. Aw, what the hell? It was for a good cause, right? He reached for his tie and yanked at the knot, sliding the silk from beneath his collar. Balling it up, he tossed it into the crowd. It ribboned into the audience and disappeared from view beneath a bevy of eager young women. Next, he flicked his shirt buttons through the holes, one by one, until he reached the belt of his trousers. The shirt gaped.

"Take it off!" someone shrieked.

His grin widened and he whipped the tails out of his trousers. Maybe he hadn't changed. Not totally. He didn't want to spend the weekend with a strange woman, but he found the situation mildly amusing. And if his current antics helped line the ranch's coffers, then his actions weren't all that bad. He thumbed his cuff links free and flung them high into the air. A scramble ensued. Then he ripped his shirt off his shoulders and tossed it aside. Folding his arms across his chest, he waited.

"A hundred dollars," a woman shouted from the crowd.

"Five," shrieked another.

"A thousand," came a third bid.

Okay, not bad. That should help the ranch. He smiled in the general direction of the third bid. Maybe he'd luck out and she'd be a granny, like Robbie Carter's buyers. He'd always been particularly good with grandmothers. It was their granddaughters he had problems with.

"Five thousand dollars!" came a roar from the back of the crowd.

A very loud, very male roar.

A stunned silence descended. Everyone turned, craning toward the bidder. Flynn shielded his eyes, struggling to see who'd spoken. Three men stood close together—a huge, hulking brute, a small fluttering cherub and a long-haired gentleman holding a gold-tipped cane.

"Five thousand dollars," the one with the cane repeated.

The cherub waved, grinning happily.

Flynn closed his eyes and groaned.

The auctioneer finally stepped forward, taking control. "I have a bid for five thousand dollars. Do I hear anything more?" He scanned the crowd with a hint of desperation. "Fifty-five hundred?"

Silence.

"Say sold!" shouted the cherub.

Flynn looked on in horror. Choked laughter came from the direction of the bachelors still waiting to be sold. This was *not* good. Bending, he snatched up his shirt and put it back on, buttoning the damned thing to his chin. Then he shoved the tails into his trousers and snagged his suit jacket.

"Fifty-one hundred?" the auctioneer prompted.

More silence.

"Sold!" the cherub shouted again. "Say sold!"

"Five thousand, fifty dollars?"

The crowd began to shuffle uneasily and Flynn decided he'd had enough. His sense of the ridiculous kicked in and laughter rumbled through him. Never in all his born days would he have thought he'd be purchased at a bachelor auction by three old men. Fate just loved to kick him in the teeth. He began to chuckle, his chuckle growing to a flat-out roar of laughter.

"Five thousand, once…!" the auctioneer reluctantly called.

Flynn cut him off. "Give it up, friend," he managed to say. "Sold to my friends in the back for five thousand dollars." He grinned at the crowd. "This should make for an interesting weekend, don't you think?"

Laughing applause escorted him offstage.

CHAPTER ONE

Salmon Bay, Washington

"THEY ALL BACKED OUT of my research study?" Jane Dearly asked in dismay, her hand tightening on the phone receiver. "Every last one?"

"I can probably round up another bunch of students at the University of Washington at the start of the fall semester. There's always a new crop eager for a way to earn a few dollars."

"But I need help now."

"I'm sorry, Jane. Unless you want to drive down here to Seattle and scoop some volunteers off the street, you're out of luck. You sure you can't find anyone in that cute little town of yours?"

"Positive. They're sort of experimented-out around here. They have been since I was about fifteen."

It was not her favorite memory and she closed her eyes, fighting to control her disappointment. Some birthday this had turned out to be. She'd been trying for so long to make her big breakthrough and time was running short. Failure had dogged her the past few years, as did the knowledge that she wasn't the only one working on this particular project. Competition was fierce. She couldn't afford a single day's delay, let alone several weeks.

"Isn't there any chance of changing their minds about participating in the study?" Jane asked.

A tiny silence followed her question. "Apparently they balked when they read your questionnaire," came the hesitant explanation. "You might want to consider toning down some of the questions for the next group."

Darn. "I see. Thanks for your help."

"I'll be in touch as soon as I have more volunteers."

Offering her appreciation a final time, Jane hung up the phone. Dipstick, her huge Saint Bernard, whined, lumbering back and forth between her and the door.

"Time for the mail?" she asked. "Maybe there'll actually be some good news for a change." A brisk knock sounded at the door and Jane opened it to the mail carrier. "Hello, Mr. Keenan."

"Happy birthday, Jane."

It didn't surprise her a bit that he'd remembered her birthday. Salmon Bay retained all of its small-town characteristics, despite its proximity to Seattle. The residents knew one another as intimately as their own family members, something she'd always appreciated about her hometown. "Why, thank you." She gave the box a hopeful glance. "Have you brought me something for my birthday?"

"Sorry. It's for your uncles. Since they weren't home, I thought I'd drop it off here." At her crestfallen expression he asked, "Were you expecting a package?"

"Not really. Just hoping I'd get something to brighten my day."

"Ah." He nodded sagely. "Another experiment gone awry?"

She leaned against the doorjamb and grimaced. "My test subjects took a walk. Can you believe it? So now I have my latest series of formulas ready to go and no one to test them on."

"Scared them off, did you?"

Her smile turned wry. "Don't I always?"

"Okay. Tell you what. This once—and just this once—you can test me."

That brightened her right up. "Really? You'd do that for me?"

"People in Salmon Bay would do anything for you, Jane." He gave a self-conscious shrug. "Well... Anything but participate in your experiments. Since it's your birthday, I'll make an exception this time. It's nothing dangerous, is it?"

"Not a bit."

He handed her the box and tapped the receipt taped to it. "Okay. You sign for the package and do whatever experiment you have to on me. But don't take too long. I have the rest of my route to complete."

She gave the mail carrier a quick hug. "Thanks, Edward. I owe you one. Now, stand right there, okay?"

"Right here," the mail carrier confirmed, planting his size twelves firmly on her doormat.

She rushed back inside and closed the door behind her, looking hastily around. "Darn it all. Where did I put that spray?" She frowned at Dipstick. "I don't know what's wrong with me. Do you suppose it's because I turned twenty-nine today? I thought I'd have until at least thirty before I became an absentminded professor."

The dog nudged her pocket and she plunged her hand into it, coming up with a glass atomizer. "There we go. Thanks, Dip."

Hastily spritzing herself with a bit of perfume, she glanced in the mirror to make sure her hair was right. It hadn't budged from the impossibly tight knot she'd twisted it into this morning. She slipped her glasses from the crown of her head to the tip of her nose and smoothed the lapel of her lab coat, checking to make sure nothing untoward had spilled on it. She wanted to look businesslike, not grungy.

And she wanted to make sure her appearance wouldn't in any way affect the results of their encounter.

Crossing to the door, she pulled it open and greeted the mail carrier with a professional smile. Not too much teeth. Heaven forbid she taint her experiment by being too friendly. "Hello, again," she said casually. At least, she hoped it sounded casual. She'd never been terribly good at pretense.

Edward Keenan fought back a grin. "Hello again, Miss Jane."

Dipstick shoved his huge head between the two of them, snuffling loudly. Darn it all! The silly dog had probably sucked up all of her perfume. "Phew. Sure is warm today." She leaned over the Saint Bernard and gently fanned the air in the mail carrier's direction. Nothing. Maybe she hadn't been generous enough with the spray bottle. No doubt another squirt was in order, if only she could find a way to do it without Edward catching on.

"Sure is." The mail carrier shifted from foot to foot. "Er, Jane?"

"Yes, Edward?"

He gestured toward the box she still clutched. "I need you to sign the receipt on that package I brought, remember?"

Inspiration struck. "Let me get a pen," she said. That way she could give herself another dousing of perfume.

To her dismay, he pulled one from his shirt pocket and offered it. "No need. I have a pen right here."

"Don't be ridiculous, Edward. Why would I want to use up your ink when I have plenty of my own?"

The mail carrier groaned. "Okay, okay. Time out."

"Already?" She checked her watch before regarding him with a frown. "Thirty-two seconds. I seriously doubt that's sufficient time for my experiment to take effect."

"Come on, Jane. Spill it. What witch's brew have you cooked up in that lab of yours? Doggy love drops? Won't help." He stared glumly at Dipstick. "No offense, but I hate dogs and not even one of your concoctions can change that."

She grabbed for Dipstick, covered her poor baby's ears. "Mr. Keenan, I think very highly of you, you know I do. In fact, I can honestly say your attitude toward dogs is your one-and-only failing as far as I'm concerned, though it's a serious one. But please don't say such things where Dipstick can hear. And it's not doggy love drops."

"Right. Let me guess. Mind-altering address labels. You switched the labels, right?" He reeled around, staggering ever so slightly. "I'm hallucinating as we speak, aren't I?"

She didn't know what to say to that one. "I suppose that depends on what you're seeing," she offered after a moment's consideration. "Since it's impossible for me to make a specific comparison between your perception and mine, we can only attempt to match—"

He staggered again. "I'm sure my mind is altered."

Oh, dear. She'd hoped for a reaction to her perfume, had, in fact, felt an unsettling emotion akin to desperation. But this would never do. Not in a million years. Who'd want a perfume that drove men postal? "I just wanted your reaction to my perfume," she hastened to explain. "That's all."

He paused mid-stagger and winked at her. "Your perfume doesn't affect my sanity, does it?"

"No— Oh. You're teasing," she realized.

"Yes, Jane. I'm teasing." His expression gentled. "Sorry, I was just trying to make you smile on your birthday."

She sighed. "Thank you, but if you really want to make me smile, you'll sniff me."

"Come again?"

"Sniff me, Edward!"

"Your perfume."

"Yes."

"Not doggy love drops?"

"Goodness, no." She gave the Saint Bernard a quick hug. "Dipstick is lovable enough without them."

"Not mind-altering address labels?"

"You know... That's an interesting concept." Glimpsing a return of his earlier amusement, she hastened to add, "But, no."

"Just perfume."

"It's a very special perfume. Does that help?"

"I'm afraid not." He checked his watch. "Sorry, Jane. I have to be off now. If I'm not reacting the way you hoped, then I guess your perfume doesn't work any better than that bug spray you invented for Sheriff Tucker." With a friendly wave, he started down her porch steps.

"My bug spray worked just fine," she retorted, stung. "The sheriff simply forgot to mention—" Edward disappeared down the sidewalk and Jane sighed. "He forgot to mention that he wanted it to *kill* the bugs. Though, why he'd want to kill something so fascinating is beyond me."

Returning inside, she picked up the atomizer she'd left on the hallway table and regarded it with a frown. "Well that didn't work too well, did it, Dipstick?" The dog wagged his tail in agreement, as if he understood everything she said, which she secretly thought perhaps he did. "I have to find a man I can test this perfume on. It's vital."

More important, she had to prove herself as a bona fide chemist. Prove that the years of effort and training she'd received from her uncles—brilliant chemists every one— hadn't been an utter waste of resources. Time was running out, and with each passing day her desperation grew. This experiment was her life and nothing, absolutely nothing, would prevent her from finding a successful formulation for her perfume.

Dipstick butted her with his head, and she scratched the dog behind his ears as she thought. "A man. I absolutely have to find a man for a test subject. Now, where am I going to find someone? It's not like I can just order one through the mail."

She slumped onto the floor next to the Saint Bernard and shoved her glasses from the tip of her nose to the top of her head, ticking off on her fingers. "No students available. No townspeople willing to help. No men, period. Hell. Too bad I can't just buy one." She ruffled Dipstick's ruff and chuckled. "Hey. Now, there's an idea. I'll run out to the corner store and buy myself a man. Wouldn't that be a great solution?"

FLYNN STUDIED THE THREE MEN who had "bought" him. A ponytailed, silver-haired sorcerer, a hulking brute whose hangdog expression would have done Walter Matthau proud and a blushing-pink cherub. Just great. Now what the hell was he supposed to do? He dreaded the first question he'd have to ask....

Folding his arms across his chest, he cocked an eyebrow. "So, gentlemen. What's your pleasure?"

The leader of the group, the one he'd privately dubbed "the sorcerer," matched him, lifted eyebrow for lifted eyebrow, his pale blue eyes glittering with frank enjoyment of the situation. "Why, now you get to help save a beautiful young woman." He tapped the massive chest of the brute with his gold-tipped cane. "Bring him, Dogg."

The brute—Dogg—made a growling noise deep in his throat while the cherub shifted from foot to foot in front of Flynn.

"He means, he wants you to come," the cherub explained. Chubby hands danced in the air. "Come along."

Flynn sighed. "Look... Why don't I just—"

"We don't want our money back. We want you," Dogg interrupted.

"—give you the money you paid and we'll call it—" Flynn broke off, disconcerted for an instant before managing to hide it. "Cute trick."

"Come along, Mr. Morgan." The sorcerer's voice drifted back to him. "Time is wasting."

Flynn gave in. What would it hurt to hear what they had to say? He could always refuse. They'd demand a refund from Lost Springs Ranch and he'd reimburse the loss, while, once again, having lived up to his reputation for being a no-good troublemaker.

Yeah, right. That would work. A few years back, maybe. But not now. Which meant he gave these three their money's worth as he'd promised.

A large stretch limo waited outside the auction area, incongruous in a lot filled with pickups, rentals and more practical sedans. The sorcerer gestured for Flynn to enter. Eyeing the three purchasers with a combination of suspicion and resignation, he climbed into luxury. He'd thought being purchased by a pair of little old ladies or giggling young girls was laughable. But at least those fellow bachelors had been purchased by women. Hell, these three had to be bottom of the barrel, worst of the worst, god-awful *bad*.

"Why don't we introduce ourselves?" the sorcerer suggested. "I'm Hickory."

"And I'm Rube and this is Dogg," the cherub hastened to add. "And you're Flynn Morgan."

Flynn closed his eyes. Crazy. They were clearly crazy and he'd gotten into an enclosed space with them. "Look—"

"Scaring him," Dogg announced.

"Are we?" Hickory planted his cane between his legs and leaned on the gold handle. "We're chemists, if that helps at all. Perhaps it also helps explain our...oddness."

It was only then that Flynn realized the crisscross of gold lines of Hickory's cane formed some sort of atomic model, like an explosion of elements. Perhaps if he'd paid closer attention in chemistry class, he'd have been able to decipher it. But at least it gave him some badly needed insight. It suggested the wizard appreciated science on some level and that he might employ reasoning and logic in his thought processes. Flynn settled back against the leather seat, forcing himself to utilize that possibility in his response to his three "purchasers."

"Fear is a natural fight-or-flight instinct," he explained, projecting a calm he was far from feeling. "In my case, it's a product of my early environment."

"How fascinating." Hickory tilted his head to one side. "And what in particular about us causes this reaction?"

"Your reason for purchasing me."

Wicked amusement flickered to life in Hickory's eyes. "Did you think we wanted you for ourselves?"

Flynn fingered the tender bruise at the corner of his mouth and winced. "I sincerely hope not."

Rube busied himself unwrapping a lemon sour ball. "Don't have to worry about that. We're not interested in you. Nope. Not at all. Want you for Jane."

"Rube."

The cherub blushed as pink as the wisps of faded red hair floating around his shiny pate. "Sorry," he muttered. "Got ahead of myself."

Flynn sighed. If the last few minutes were any indication, it was going to be a very long weekend. "I don't suppose you'd care to explain what this is about?"

The three exchanged quick glances. "No," Hickory replied, apparently having reached a consensus of opinion from that single look. "We wouldn't. At least, not until we're sitting down and enjoying a leisurely lunch. Then my brothers and I will be happy to explain everything." His eyes glittered with amusement again, his focus uncomfortably intense. "Or almost everything."

They drove from the ranch, straight into wilderness, leaving a trail of dust in their wake—a dust Flynn had done his level best to shake from his boots years ago. The irony hit hard. It would seem he couldn't escape this place any more than he could escape the past that had molded him. Though he appreciated how all the counselors and instructors associated with the ranch had helped him, encouraging him to set his feet on a different path through life, those years had been painful. Almost as painful as the events leading up to his stay at Lost Springs.

When his parents had dumped him here, they'd neglected to release their parental rights. So though they were happy to forget all about him—never once visiting him—they refused to release him, to allow him to start over with a new family. Not that anyone had been terribly anxious to adopt him. He'd been far too much trouble for a sensible couple looking for an openhearted child. He'd been as closed-down as they came.

But he'd dreamed of a real life, yearned for it, thirsted for it...and buried those desires deep inside where no one could find his vulnerability.

It didn't take long to get to Lightning Creek. Flynn slouched lower in his seat and thrust out his long legs, staring at sleepy roads and Old West buildings that hadn't changed a bit since he'd left. Hell, the bustle from the auction had probably stirred up the most traffic they'd seen around this place in the last couple of decades. A traffic jam on Main Street. Who'd have thought?

He could guess where they were headed for lunch, not that there were many choices in Lightning Creek. The Main Street Grill—or the Roadkill Grill, as the locals called it—was part restaurant, part bar and general hangout during his less-than-illustrious youth for the horny and hopeful. Of course, at this hour, it would be filled up with families intent on lunch.

Walking in the door with his purchasers, Flynn did a quick scan of the place. There were a few bachelors from the auction scattered around, none of whom paid him any attention. He sighed. Well, what did he expect? He'd been a con artist all those years ago, not someone who'd have made an enduring friend. He'd also been one of the ranch's most spectacular failures, so when they'd contacted him about the auction, he'd been amazed. The very fact that they'd be willing to solicit his help just proved the desperation of their financial situation. But then, perhaps they knew how hard he'd worked at redemption these past few years and that was why they'd called on him.

There wasn't much of a wait for a table. The minute they were all seated, Hickory spoke up. "You've been very patient, Mr. Morgan."

Flynn regarded the ringleader with an impassive expression. "Did I have a choice?"

"None." He tapped his cane against the floor, like a conductor signaling for the attention of his orchestra. "Shall we begin?"

"We bought you for Jane," Rube announced in a rush. "There. I said it. Phew! Now that we have that out of the way, we can enjoy our lunch."

"Who's Jane?" Flynn asked mildly.

Hickory reprimanded his brother with a look, before returning his attention to Flynn. "Jane Dearly. She's our niece..."

"Her parents died when she was five. We raised her." This from Dogg.

Rube nodded. "And she needs a man."

Flynn held up his hands. "Whoa! Time out. What do you mean, she needs a man?"

Hickory smiled. "Why, just what we said. She's in need—desperate need in our opinion—of a man." He tapped Flynn with the handle of his cane. "We chose you."

JANE STRAIGHTENED her lab coat and frowned. Maybe the coat had been a mistake, especially on her birthday, but donning it had become second nature to her, so she sometimes forgot she'd put it on. Perhaps no one would notice. She perked up. No. No one would notice anything out of the ordinary. They'd just conclude she'd been in a hurry and forgotten to take it off. That happy assumption lasted right up until she reached the outskirts of town.

One look at her apparel and everyone smiled and shook their head. They also gave her a wide berth.

With a tiny sigh, she shoved her glasses onto the top of her head and unbuttoned the coat, hoping it would make her look more casual. After all, she was heading into town for a drink at the local bar on her birthday. What could be more casual than that? Surely Mr. Keenan had been too busy delivering mail to spread word of her latest experiment. She didn't want to give people the mistaken belief that her presence had anything to do with work.

Pushing open the door to the Guy's Place, she smiled at the bartender. "Hello, Milton. Could I have a diet soda, please?"

"Happy birthday, Jane." He filled a glass with ice and

hesitated. "Sure you wouldn't like something a little stronger? Maybe some rum in that soda?"

"No, thanks."

"Heard your latest experiment isn't going well."

Just great. She should have known word would spread within five seconds of Edward's departure from her front doorstep. "Not too well," she admitted. "Between that and my birthday…" She trailed off with a shrug.

With an understanding nod, he fixed the drink, thumping it onto the bar in front of her. "It's on the house. Just don't scare away my customers again with one of your experiments, okay?"

She chuckled. "I'll try not to, but I make no promises."

Two of the Henderson boys lounged at one end of the bar, and she offered a friendly nod. They were a bit younger and had once had an ongoing bet to see who'd be the first to date her. Neither had won. But she'd never held it against them. She understood all about competition and achieving goals.

A whispered conversation ensued and then the oldest of the two, Glenn, joined her. "You here on business or pleasure, Janie?"

Uh-oh. She leaned out of his air space as unobtrusively as possible so he wouldn't accidently inhale her perfume, or this could very well turn into business. "As long as you can't smell me, it's pleasure."

"Business. Hell." He shook his head in disgust. "You've gone and cost me fifty bucks, Jane Dearly."

"Excuse me? I said I was here for—"

"Forget it, Jane. You look as guilty as the day is long. That means it's business. I told Billie you'd dropped in because those three nutty uncles finally let you off your leash. That maybe you wanted to be human for a change and have a little fun on your birthday. But Billie said no way. Said it didn't matter what today was, you were here doing another of your crazy experiments." He eyed her hopefully. "Any chance Billie's wrong despite that nervous look you have going?"

"Every chance in the world." She took a quick sip of soda, studying Glenn over the rim of the sweat-moistened glass and thinking fast. She still wore her perfume and if he expressed any interest... "But if there was an experiment, would you want to participate?"

Glenn held up his hands and backed away. "Thanks, but no thanks."

She hopped off her seat and took a step toward him, attempting to explain. "I just thought—"

"That's your problem. You think." He jabbed his finger at her, than snatched it back as though fearing contamination. "Well, 'scuse me for buttin' in when you're conducting business. Next time you're working on one of your warped experiments, try visiting someplace we're not."

"But, Glenn... I'm testing a perfume. That's all. And I'm not asking you to participate. I just offered in case you were interested."

"Hey, I said no, okay?"

"Fine. I just wondered how you liked it."

"Put the drinks on our tab, Milt," Glenn said. He glanced at his brother, Billie, and jerked his head toward the exit.

Jane looked from the bartender to the Henderson boys, thoroughly perplexed. "I don't understand what all the commotion's about. It's just a perfume. And I agreed not to experiment on any of you, if you didn't want."

Billie shook his head. "You really don't get it, do you? Can't you just be a regular person for once? Even when you're not working, you're working. It puts people off. Especially men. Not that you seem to care."

The door slammed closed behind them and Jane swallowed hard, turning to face Milton. "I'm sorry. I didn't mean—"

"Forget it, Jane. I know you can't help it." He swiped the counter with a cloth. "Mind if I make a suggestion?"

Politeness combined with a twinge of guilt forced her to nod. "Not at all," she lied. She'd never been particularly good at social fibs, but apparently she'd managed this one with some level of success, since Milton immediately offered his opinion.

"You promised folks a number of years back that you wouldn't use Salmon Bay as your own personal laboratory."

"I know, but—"

"It makes them feel like lab rats, honey. So when people suspect that's what you're doing again, they get a bit tetchy."

She released her breath in a gusty sigh. "People don't like it, huh?"

"No, Jane. They don't. You're a nice lady. You're smart, and I'll bet if you didn't run around trying so hard to look like a scientist, you'd be downright attractive."

Milton thought she was attractive? She stared in astonishment. She couldn't remember the last time a man had said that to her. In fact, she had a strong suspicion no one ever had. Could it be... *The perfume!* She leaned across the bar toward him, waiting while he inhaled once or twice. "Milton?"

"Yes, Jane?"

"Do you think maybe it's my perfume that makes you think I'm attractive? It's a new formula."

The bartender sighed. "Honey, have you heard a word I've said?"

"Oh, yes." She beamed. "You said I was attractive."

"Jane?"

"Yes, Milton?"

"We all love you. We truly do. But I want you to try something, even if it's just for today."

"What do you want me to do?"

"Be a woman, Jane. Give it a shot for just twenty-four short hours. Be a woman first and a scientist last. Do you think you can do that?"

Her mouth twisted. "You don't understand, Milton." She plucked her glasses from the top of her head and slipped them on before pulling her lab coat tighter around her. "I've never been very good at being a woman. Being a scientist is all I know."

"Then for your sake, I hope someone comes along who recognizes the woman." He gazed at her in concern. "She's there somewhere. She just needs to get out from behind that coat and those glasses. But she's there and, whether you realize it or not, she's special as hell."

CHAPTER TWO

Lightning Creek, Wyoming

"LET ME GET THIS STRAIGHT..." Flynn said, struggling to make sense of what he'd been told. "You just paid over five thousands dollars because you want a man for your niece? Because she needs one—what did you say—*desperately?*"

"Yes," Dogg rumbled.

Flynn shoved back his chair and stood. "Gentlemen, it's been interesting. Now, if you'll excuse me, I'll be on my way."

"But we bought you," Rube protested. "You can't leave."

"Watch me."

"Sit down, Mr. Morgan." Hickory fastened his pale blue eyes on him. They were odd sorcerer's eyes that looked too old and saw too much. "Please."

Gut instinct urged Flynn to run. Now. He'd learned at an early age to listen to his instincts and it bothered him that he couldn't react as promptly as he would have once upon a time. "I'll write you a check to cover what you paid Lost Springs."

"Sit *down,* Mr. Morgan. At least do us the courtesy of hearing us out."

It was, unfortunately, a reasonable request. He swiveled the chair around and straddled it, resting his arms along the back. It made a statement, as he intended. "Talk fast," he advised.

Before they could, a waitress approached, a tall, voluptuous woman in her early twenties. She caught one glimpse of Flynn and flashed him a hungry look that promised she'd eat him alive while at the same time offering him the opportunity to return the favor if he were so inclined. "Well, hello, darlin'. What can I get for you?"

He shot her an appreciative smile before his bruise helped tweak his memory. Not so long ago, he'd have indulged in a mild flirtation and enjoyed it immensely. Too bad those days were behind him. Turning over a new leaf could be a royal pain.

"Coffee, please," he requested.

"Aw, come on, sugar. Sure there's not anything else you want?" Lashes fluttered and her mouth glistened. "Anything at all?"

"He's already spoken for," Rube interrupted. "We bought him and he's ours."

The waitress's eyes widened and her lush mouth formed a perfect O. "Yours?"

Flynn closed his eyes and Rube struggled to explain. "We're giving him to Jane, you see."

"Let it go," Hickory advised. "Our waitress isn't interested."

"But she—" Rube's gaze skittered to Flynn. "He—"

Dogg cleared his throat. "They aren't interested. Not now."

The waitress leaned closer, offering a peek of her ample charms. "Look, boys... As amusing as this has been, I have other tables to take care of. Now, do you want something or not?"

It was time to take charge, Flynn decided. Otherwise, he'd never get out of here. "Four coffees. Four house specials."

"You got it." She scribbled something on her order pad, muttering, "And that's all you get."

Now, why didn't that surprise him? Flynn remained silent until the waitress had disappeared in the direction of the kitchen. "You were saying?" he prompted the brothers, a wave of exhaustion washing over him. Right now, all he wanted was to finish this nonsense and get back to San Francisco so he could make amends with Paulie. Was that so much to ask? He had a business to run and he couldn't do it from Wyoming.

Hickory contemplated the ball of exploding atoms decorating his cane. Then he lifted his gaze and fixed it on Flynn. "I believe I mentioned that we're scientists." He made the comment matter-of-factly. "We've worked as a team for over thirty years. If we strike you as somewhat eccentric, you'll have to excuse us. We've spent so much time in our lab, we've never quite acclimatized ourselves to the real world."

"Don't get out much," Dogg interrupted.

"When we run out of lemon sour balls," Rube offered. "Or when Jane makes us. We get out then. Don't like it, though. Don't like it much at all." He lowered his voice, adding significantly, "And people don't like it when we do."

Flynn was willing to bet good money on that one. "Jane is the woman I'm supposed to—"

"Help," Rube explained, responding defensively to Flynn's sardonic tone. "Today's Jane's birthday. She's a clever girl. Very clever. And she works hard. She's the sweetest, smartest, most generous girl in the world."

"Forgot awkward," Dogg inserted.

Hickory nodded. "And that, I'm afraid, is part of the problem. You see, Jane's our niece. She's as close to us as a daughter. And why wouldn't she be? She came into our care when she was only five.''

Flynn found the wizard's phrasing interesting. "What happened to her parents?''

"They were killed in an accident. They...left her to us.''

"Were they insane?'' Flynn asked politely.

A humorless smile flickered across Hickory's mouth. "Probably. Jane's mother, Laura, was our little sister and the fourth member of our team. Besides adding immensely to our research, she did her best to socialize us—with only limited success. She also trusted us implicitly, which is how we became Jane's guardians. We raised our niece and trained her. She's a chemist, as well. In fact, she shows signs of becoming a quite brilliant scientist. Unfortunately, she doesn't enjoy a social life, and we've realized, a bit late, that she's followed our less-than-stellar example.''

"She's a hermit.'' Flynn sighed. And a geek, no doubt.

"Not a hermit. I suppose you'd call Jane...socially inept.''

Definitely a geek. "And you expect me to do something about it as a birthday present?'' Aw, hell. Why him? "In one weekend?''

Dogg shook his shaggy head. "No.''

"As for the weekend—'' Hickory glanced at his companions. "We'd like to purchase your services for a full two weeks. In exchange, we'd be happy to renegotiate our contribution to Lost Springs Ranch.''

"You've already paid five grand for me and you're willing to renegotiate?'' Flynn asked incredulously.

"Yes.''

"I sure picked the wrong line of work.'' Flynn shook his head. "I didn't realize chemists made out so well.''

"Successful chemists 'make out,' as you phrase it, extremely well, Mr. Morgan. Patents can be very lucrative items to own. And my brothers and I own quite a number of popular patents. Considering that the ranch is in such dire financial straits—"

"Yes, yes," Rube said, jumping in. "And considering how much we need a man for Jane—"

"We can afford to please ourselves, please Lost Springs Ranch, please Jane and even please you."

Please him? Forget it. Once upon a time he could have been bought. But not any longer. He'd cover the loss to Lost Springs out of his own pocket before he'd regress to the sort of man he'd once been. "I don't care how much you pay the ranch, I'm not making love to your niece."

Three sets of eyes stared at him in shocked confusion.

Flynn cleared his throat, suddenly realizing he'd taken a right turn while these three had gone left. "You don't want me to seduce your niece?"

"No!" Indignation made Rube look like an outraged pink teddy bear. "We most certainly did not ask you to...to..."

Flynn gritted his teeth. "You said—"

Hickory cut him off. "I do believe we're talking at cross purposes." He chuckled softly. "When we said we wanted your services, we didn't mean romantic services."

"Then what do you want?" Flynn dreaded hearing the answer to that one.

"For one thing..." Hickory exchanged quick glances with his fellow chemists. "We want you to protect Jane."

"Protect her from what?"

"It's a whom. From a man named Mick Barstow. He was Jane's former partner and...and they had a personal involvement, as well."

"Now, there's a surprise."

"Mr. Morgan, we had you investigated very carefully."

That gave Flynn pause. What would their investigation

have turned up? More than he wanted them to know, he'd bet on that. "And?"

"And we know about your background—" Hickory waited a beat before adding significantly "—all of it. We know about your past. We know how you've changed your life around as a result of that past. We know you have an extremely successful business with a Mr. Paul Richardson. And that you install security systems. And we know why you're so good at your job."

"And?" Flynn repeated, his tone like ice.

"We need your expertise. As we mentioned, we can also provide a substantial donation to Lost Springs Ranch over and above what we paid for you."

"I'm still sitting here." Just.

"We received the literature about your auction and instantly understood what we needed to do."

"Which was?"

"We needed a man who's capable of saving Jane from Mick Barstow. Now that they're no longer partners, he's determined to steal from her. Hurt her. She needs a protector."

"Then you bought the wrong man."

"We disagree." Hickory's pale eyes grew more intent. "We needed a man for Jane. A very special man. A man we deem safe, and who's capable of looking out for her."

Flynn shook his head. "Trust me," he informed them in a low voice, desperate to do the right thing. "I'm not the least bit safe, whatever that means. You don't want a man like me anywhere near your niece."

Hickory leaned forward. "On the contrary. You're precisely the sort we do want. Charming. Good with women. A bit of a con man. And temporary. Very temporary."

Ouch. "In and out, is that it?"

The scientist didn't rise to the bait. "We require your

services for two weeks. We want you to install whatever security system my niece requires for our laboratory complex. We'll pay separately for that, of course. And we have one other small job for you.''

Hell. "What job is that?''

"You're a con man. We want you to con Mr. Barstow.''

"I *was* a con man. I'm not any longer.''

"It's for a good cause, Mr. Morgan. This man is trying to steal my niece's research work, work she's invested years of her life developing. We have no way of stopping him.'' Hickory fixed his pale eyes on Flynn. "But you do.''

"Why hasn't your niece hired someone to take care of this already?'' The three scientists exchanged quick glances and he knew what that meant. "She doesn't want help, does she?''

"No,'' Dogg said.

"We'd have to do this on the sly,'' Hickory explained. "Come with us to Salmon Bay. Knock on Jane's door. Tell her we hired you to install a security system in the lab. Use some of that charm you possess in such abundance to gain her cooperation. You're a reformed man, we know that. You won't let anything or anyone harm her. Catch Mr. Barstow in the act of stealing Jane's notes, turn him over to the cops and you can go on your merry way. You can accomplish that much with a modicum of success, can't you?''

"If I'm so inclined.'' Flynn waited a beat. "Which I'm not.''

"Then do it for the sake of the ranch, if not for yourself. Prove that you really are a changed man.''

Flynn swore beneath his breath. This was some sort of sick joke, the universe's way of taking his good intentions and throwing them back in his face. He'd sworn off cons, regardless of how well-intentioned they were. But here sat these three, offering him a damsel in distress—his greatest weakness—and the chance to save her. The only problem was he'd have to lie to achieve his goal. As for being safe, who were they kidding? If they'd really had him investigated they'd know better.

He began to laugh, the cynical sound edged with exhaustion. "You're serious? You want me to save your niece?"

"Yes," Rube said with a big, happy smile. "If you wouldn't mind."

Flynn shrugged. Why the hell not? Maybe this would present a way to get back into Paulie's good graces. If he showed that he could resist seducing the woman he'd been hired to help, it would go a long way toward easing Paulie's anger. Besides, he wouldn't be lying to Jane. Not exactly. He'd install a security system, as promised. And if he caught Barstow in the process, she'd be grateful, right? As for his being safe around Hickory, Dickory and Dock's precious niece... How had they described her? Awkward, a workaholic, socially inept. How tough would that be to resist? She'd be safe enough.

"Okay, fine," he agreed. "Double your donation to the ranch and I'll do it."

"Excellent." Hickory stood and tossed some money onto the table. "Shall we go?"

Flynn lifted an eyebrow. "What? No lunch?"

"No time," Hickory said, shoving back his chair. "We have a private plane waiting to take us to Washington State. Salmon Bay, to be exact, an hour north of Seattle. We have plenty of food onboard, if you're hungry."

"And lemon sour balls," Rube added happily.

Hickory's amused blue eyes held a wealth of secrets, and Flynn realized in that moment that he'd just made a bargain with the devil. A bargain he suspected he'd spend a very long time regretting.

"THIS HAS *NOT* BEEN a good day," Jane announced to Dipstick. "Maybe I should relabel this particular sample. I think Irritation Potion number one would be more appropriate, don't you?"

The dog whined in what she chose to take as absolute agreement.

The doorbell rang and Jane reached into the pocket of her lab coat for the atomizer. Should she, or shouldn't she? So far, she wasn't doing too well with this particular sample. After spending most of the day in town being avoided by all and sundry, she'd returned home to write up the unspectacular results of her initial trial with Mr. Keenan. Calling the day a total bust wouldn't come close to describing it.

She tossed the bottle lightly in her hand, nibbling on her lower lip as she considered whether or not to give it one last try. Oh, what the heck? Another attempt wouldn't hurt. That way she'd know for sure whether this first batch had any redeeming features. She hastily sprayed herself while Dipstick circled, whining in dismay. Shushing him, she opened the door.

Edward stood there, another box in hand. Jane blinked in surprise. "Hello again, Mr. Keenan. Is there something else I can do for you today?"

"Found this just as I was locking up the post office. Since it's your birthday, I thought you'd want to have it."

She blinked at the unexpected rush of tears. "Thank you, Edward. That's very kind of you."

"Any luck with your experiments?"

"Not unless it's considered lucky to annoy people."

"Would you like my advice?"

"To be perfectly honest, I'm a bit advised-out today."

"I heard the Henderson boys didn't take your perfume test too well."

"But I didn't—" She gave up. No one would believe

her, anyway. And why would they? Milton was right. People only saw the scientist because that's all she ever showed them. No wonder they went out of their way to avoid her. "No. The Hendersons didn't care for my perfume at all."

Mr. Keenan nodded in sympathy. "Well, maybe they'll send up some more students from Seattle."

"Someone who doesn't know me, right?" They shared a grin. "Thanks, Edward. I appreciate your bringing this by."

"My pleasure."

Returning inside, she closed the door. Dipstick regarded her with an expression she interpreted as saying, "I told you so."

"Okay, so I shouldn't have tried the perfume again." She dropped the glass bottle into the pocket of her lab coat. "If I'd known it was Edward, I wouldn't have. And if it makes you feel better, I doubt anyone will have any use for this particular perfume. Considering how frank everyone's being, I'd say this scent works almost as well as my truth spray."

Dipstick tilted his head to one side, his tongue hanging out of his mouth, his nut-brown eyes filled with doggy sympathy she almost believed he understood everything she said. "Come on, boy," she said with a sigh.

She proceeded through to the kitchen with the box, dog trailing at her heels, and opened a drawer containing a pair of scissors, a neatly wrapped ball of twine and an extra set of keys to her lab. The items were all arranged in a tidy row. She removed the scissors and carefully cut through the packaging tape before returning them to the drawer. Opening the lid, she removed the card.

"Happy Birthday, Jane. Love, Hickory, Dogg and Rube." She carefully pushed aside the protective packaging material and removed the hand-blown glass globe inside. It was perfect, absolutely perfect, she thought, smiling in delight.

Carrying the gift into the living room, she straightened a perfectly centered vase and set the huge glass globe next to it, flicking away an imaginary speck of dust from the surface. Both the vase and globe had been created by Josh Simpson, and collecting his artwork was the only bit of whimsy she allowed herself in an otherwise clean-cut world. How sweet of her uncles to add to her collection.

Stooping to examine the globe, she lost herself in the imaginary "planet" Simpson had created from blown glass. Green, brown, red and yellow swirls formed the land portion of the planet, waving fronds of glassy grass almost seeming to drift in an unseen breeze. Surrounding the land formations was a vast sea, the color ranging from a brilliant azure to the palest robin's egg blue. Sometimes when she was puzzling through a problem, she'd meditate on her dilemma while studying the intricate whirls and colors of the various globes she owned, like some long-ago alchemist searching for answers in a crystal ball.

The glass atomizer weighted her pocket, turning her thoughts to work. Where had she gone wrong with this particular sample? Perhaps she'd put too much perfume in the potion and not enough formula. Or perhaps it was as simple as getting the balance of ingredients wrong. If LP-1 caused anger, at least she was successfully affecting emotions. Now all she had to do was find the one that would inspire love.

Assuming such an emotion existed.

Dipstick released a loud bass woof an instant before another knock sounded at the door. Jane carefully straightened away from the table. Maybe Edward had returned. The thought brightened her right up. Perhaps the perfume had a delayed reaction and he was standing on her doorstep, consumed with love.

The dog galloped to the door ahead of her, skittering on the waxed floor. He was two hundred pounds of shedding hair that she spent hours vacuuming. But she didn't care. He was the most loving creature she'd ever known—aside from her uncles, that was. He looked over his shoulder at her, eagerly waiting for her to answer the door.

She turned the knob and tugged it open. Taking one look, she realized her birthday had just taken a turn for the better. A man she'd never seen before stood there and she grinned.

The perfect test subject had just arrived on her doorstep.

FLYNN CAUGHT ONE GLIMPSE of the most beautiful smile he'd ever seen and knew he was in deep, deep trouble. *This* was Hickory's awkward, workaholic, socially inept niece? Just one look warned that this succulent bit of femininity was about as safe from him as a nerdy lamb from a not-quite fully reformed wolf. So much for his assumption that he'd be dealing with a Plain Jane.

She was of average height. If he held her in his arms, her head would nestle perfectly beneath his chin. And her hair, though plastered back from her face, was dark blond, highlighted with pale gold streaks. It made him wonder what it would look like if she ever released it from the prison of her various pins and clips. To his amusement, she wore two sets of glasses, one perched on the end of her nose, the other propped on top of her head. The fading sunlight reflected off them and all four huge plastic lenses winked at him, one after the other. For some odd reason he found her protective mask of glasses both vulnerable and endearing. It also made him realize that this woman was far too attractive for his peace of mind.

Only one possibility offered a shot at salvation. Maybe the woman standing in front of him wasn't Jane, the niece. It was a long shot, considering the uncles had shoved him up onto the front porch of this very house. They'd then hidden behind a huge laurel bush that divided their property from their niece's. Still, he could hope.

"Jane Dearly?" he asked, praying she'd deny it.

"Yes?"

Damn. "I'm Flynn Morgan. Your uncles sent me."

"Fantastic. Stand right there," she ordered.

Hell, who was he to argue? "Okay."

"I mean it. Don't move."

"Not a muscle."

The door slammed in his face and the uncles, muttering among themselves, shoved through the bushes. Swiveling to glare, Flynn signaled them to return to their hiding places. Hickory and Dogg caught on instantly. Rube took a bit more convincing before he fluttered back behind the greenery, sour ball wrappers floating in his wake.

The door opened again and Jane stood there, her mouth set in a regrettably straight line. It was then that Flynn made a decision. He might be a changed man, but that wouldn't stop him from doing his level best to coax free another of her incredible smiles.

Far from smiling, disappointment further dimmed her enthusiasm. Apparently, standing there and staring wasn't what she had in mind. "Hello," he said, offering a broad grin of appreciation.

Her eyes widened behind the lenses of her glasses and he realized they were a dark green, a color similar to the one that haunted the cool depths of a pine forest. Isolated, untouched, primitive and wary of intruders.

"Hello," she replied cautiously.

Still no smile. Once they got to know each other a little better, he'd have to explain the importance of lips and teeth on a man. "I'm Flynn Morgan."

"You mentioned that already. I'm Jane Dearly."

"I think I mentioned that your uncles sent me. I'm supposed to make an appointment with you to install a security system in your lab, but I heard it's your birthday today, so..." He whipped out the box of chocolates and bouquet of roses he held behind his back. When she failed to smile, he prompted, "These are for you. Happy birthday."

"I'm not interested in a security system."

"Your uncles are. That's why I'm here."

Her frown deepened. Definitely bad news. "Let me get this straight. My uncles hired you?"

"Right."

"For security?"

Her eyes had grown so dark he could barely make out the color. It would seem night had come to the forest. "You can't be too careful these days," he said.

Somehow the situation had taken a nosedive, though he couldn't figure out what the hell he'd done wrong. Most women on the receiving end of chocolate and flowers not only smiled, they tumbled into his arms and thanked him with a full-blown kiss. The sort of full-blown kiss he'd like to experience with Jane. The sort he doubted he'd receive from her any time in the near future. The sort he *shouldn't* receive from a client unless he wanted to become reacquainted with Paulie's fist.

"That's why you were being so friendly? Because my uncles hired you?" She took a step closer, fanning her hands back and forth as though suffering from a hot flash. "No other reason?"

"It's your birthday, right?"

"So?"

"So..." He gave the box and flowers a little shake. Rose petals rained downward, settling at his feet. "So, I thought I'd bring you these."

"Why?"

He fought to enunciate through gritted teeth. "For. A. Birthday. Present. Are you familiar with that custom?"

"Yes." She eyed the flowers and grimaced. "For hothouse roses, these sure have a strong odor. Here. Let me get these out of the way." She grabbed the bouquet and held the flowers behind the door. "Now, stand there and take a deep breath."

"Right." Flynn made a hasty reassessment of the situation. Tightly wound scientist, gut-wrenching smile, gorgeous eyes—most of the time—and nutty as a sack of almonds. Damn.

"Are you breathing?"

"It's sort of automatic with me." She planted her hands on her hips and he released a sigh. She reminded him of the nun he'd suffered as a young schoolboy right before his days at Lost Springs Ranch—a tough old teacher who'd done her best to reform him with the painful end of a ruler. "Yes, I'm breathing."

"And?"

It took him a full sixty seconds to realize that the truth might actually work to his advantage. "And I like your smile."

Unfortunately, the truth didn't work. Pink flared into her cheeks. At a guess, it wasn't because she had a tendency to blush. She confirmed it the instant she opened her mouth— the same mouth he'd have loved to explore in intimate detail. "You can't fool me. You're just saying that because you're hoping to sell your security equipment to my uncles."

"Not really," he said with absolute honesty.

"Tell my uncles I'm not interested in fooling with a security system right now. It's inconvenient. If they really want to help, they can get me a man. A *real* man."

With that she whipped around him and into her house, slamming the door behind her.

CHAPTER THREE

FLYNN ADDRESSED the door knocker. "That went well, don't you think?" He turned his attention to the trio watching from the massive laurel bushes. "Looks like your plan backfired. You better get on up here and explain the situation to her."

A whispered consultation followed and he began to suspect it was their normal mode of operation. He filed the information away for future use. It might come in handy at some later time.

Rube emerged from the bushes. "Try it again," he encouraged in a stage whisper. "Only this time start talking before she slams the door."

"Use some of that infamous charm of yours," Hickory suggested caustically. "If that doesn't work, try sticking your foot in the door."

Flynn scowled. The hell he would. He was rather partial to his toes right where they were. Damn it all. Why had he agreed to their harebrained scheme, anyway? *Because he was a changed man.* His mouth pulled to one side, tugging at the bruise, and he winced. Great. Just great.

Setting his jaw at a more aggressive angle, he glared at the door. So how did he win over a logical, emotionally stunted scientist? A scientist, moreover, who had her hair twisted into a knot so tight it gave *him* a headache, who kept her lab coat on in the privacy of her own home and wore not just one but two pairs of glasses. Those she'd perched on the tip of her slightly upturned nose had huge, red-trimmed plastic frames incongruous against the setting of her delicate features. The secondary glasses—a violently purple-rimmed pair—sat on top of her head, the tips of the earpieces somehow embedded in her tightly bound hair. Maybe she couldn't get them off. Maybe they'd gotten stuck up there. He closed his eyes, thinking he should ignore the damn glasses and get to work.

He didn't have to look over his shoulder to know the uncles were huddled in whispered consultation. The humor of the situation struck him and he chuckled softly. This had to be a first. He'd never had a woman reject him before. Not once in all his thirty-four years. The adulation had begun at an early age and continued throughout what had passed as his existence to date. And he'd gotten used to it, had accepted it. Hell, he'd come to expect it as his due.

But now, with one look from eyes as rich and fertile and lush as a tree-shrouded meadow, he had been put firmly in his place by a woman who, he didn't doubt, most unobservant men tended to overlook. She'd seen through the teeth and the boyish sincerity and the practiced charm and the arrangement of features that had never failed to please, despite the fact that they currently sported a walloping bruise.

At least… They'd never failed to please until now.

And the most amusing part of all was that he'd genuinely enjoy getting acquainted with this particular woman. For reasons he couldn't explain, he was curious to discover what she had hidden beneath her crisp white lab coat. He wanted to know why she felt the need to wear her hair in such a tight twist and why three old men were so worried about keeping her safe that they'd hire a man like him to take care of the situation. But most of all he wanted to know why she kept those mind-drugging smiles all to herself.

Okay, fine. So she didn't find him appealing. He still had

a job to do and an obligation to fulfill. Only this time, he'd do it his way.

Confirming his suspicions about small towns, he twisted the knob and pushed open the door. The dog—what had she called him? Dipstick?—greeted him with an enthusiastic whine and wagged his tail so hard, it threatened the safety of the few pieces of furniture the house contained. With a happy wriggle that left bits of hair spinning around the excited animal, Dipstick launched himself in Flynn's direction.

Beneath the dog's exuberant attention, Flynn crashed back against the front door, the animal's huge paws planted squarely on his chest and an enormous tongue threatening to do serious damage to his face. The dog regarded his new-found friend with golden-brown eyes full of unmistakable mischief, and his huge mouth parted in a big sloppy grin.

Takes one to know one, Flynn decided, returning the grin. "You're a friendly fella," he said, giving the dog's ruff and ears a thorough scratching. "Too bad your mistress isn't more like you." The dog emitted a human-like groan of sheer pleasure.

Jane appeared in the hallway. "What...?" She stared in disbelief. "What do you think you're doing?"

"I'm petting your dog."

"I can see that. Dipstick! Get down."

A tiny frown gathered on her brow and he decided he didn't like it one bit. Last time that expression had appeared on her face, he'd almost kissed wood. She planted her hands on her hips, her glare moving from man to dog. Both lost their big, happy grins beneath her withering reprimand, and Dipstick—the coward—actually tucked tail. Thank God *he* didn't have a tail, Flynn decided. How humiliating would that be?

Apparently satisfied that she'd brought them both to heel,

she asked, "I meant, what do you think you're doing in my house?"

"You didn't lock the door." He nudged the dog and whispered, "Buck up, buster. Be a man." To his delight, the dog's tail reappeared and smacked his thigh with renewed enthusiasm.

Jane's pretty mouth dropped open, outrage suiting her far better than her earlier frown. "Don't encourage him. He's undisciplined enough as it is."

"Most males are," Flynn explained very gently.

Aside from a deepening of the rosy color tinting her cheeks, she ignored his observation. "An unlocked door does not give you the right to barge in."

"No. But it certainly makes it easier for a thief to gain access when you're not around."

"A thief," she repeated, lifting an eyebrow.

He suddenly realized she'd removed her glasses. At least she'd removed the red pair on the end of her nose. The purple ones in her hair remained. Without the huge frames swamping her face, her delicate features were even more apparent. She had softly rounded cheekbones, a firm, stubborn chin and large, almond-shaped eyes, the thick, gold-tipped lashes setting off the unusual color. He could also make out a faint dusting of freckles across her upturned nose. And then there was her mouth, so sweet when it curved into a smile.

Not that she was currently smiling. He sighed. "You don't think that's possible, do you?"

"For a thief to ply his trade here? In Salmon Bay?" She dismissed the suggestion out of hand. "No, I don't think it's even remotely possible."

Dipstick, realizing they weren't going anywhere anytime soon, collapsed onto his haunches. His massive head swiveled between them as though keeping track of their verbal tennis match, and he gave Flynn an encouraging whine.

Flynn winked at the dog, pleased to see the animal was on his side, even if his mistress wasn't. "I know this may come as a shock to you," he said. "But there's nothing to stop a gang of bad guys from visiting your little town, robbing the residents blind and then going along their merry way. That's how burglary works, in case you're interested."

"I'm not. Besides, a stranger would be noticed."

"And what if it wasn't a stranger?"

If anything, she looked even more outraged. "The children of our town are quite well behaved."

It was his turn to lift an eyebrow. "You're accusing the children of your town?"

"No! I—"

"Not very nice of you to suspect innocent young tykes of breaking into your house."

"*Oh!* I never once said—"

Her anger faded as she caught on to his teasing and a glimmer of answering amusement appeared in her eyes. Then her mouth quivered and he waited for it. Finally, she gave him the ultimate reward. A smile blossomed across her face and she laughed. If he'd thought her smile did odd things to his physiology, her laugh sealed his doom. It wasn't in the least what he'd have expected, given her rigid hairstyle, professional lab coat and reprimanding frown. The sound was deeper, rich and full-bodied and generous. She possessed a woman's laugh, filled with ancient mystery and feminine allure.

He linked his laughter with hers and even Dipstick joined in, racing around and nudging them toward each other. Flynn allowed himself to be propelled into Jane's orbit. After all, how could he resist two hundred pounds of determined matchmaking? "I'm serious. I know this is a small town and your crime rate is low, but you should still lock your door.''

"Are you really a security expert?''

He winced. "*Expert* might be a small exaggeration. But I'm qualified to take a look at your setup and make suggestions. And I have a partner who can install whatever you need.''

She considered his comment, her gaze assessing. He returned her look, waiting her out. If she turned him down flat, he'd tell the uncles he'd given it his best shot and failed. They might not like it, but Flynn couldn't force Jane to accept him or use his services. If she wouldn't play, he'd reimburse the uncles' money and take a walk. Of course, he'd feel a few regrets—among them, not having an opportunity to sample Jane's full, lush mouth. But he'd walk, anyway.

She wavered, her expression suggesting he'd have an opportunity to get to know her better over the next two weeks. Then her gaze cooled, her eyes dimming to the darkest of greens. "First answer a question.''

Uh-oh. "Sure.''

"And I want an honest answer.''

Dipstick released a groan and Flynn knew he was in trouble. "No problem.'' He hoped.

"My uncles hired you, right?''

"They paid for my services.''

"And they asked you to look at our security needs.''

Among other things. "Yes.''

"*Just* our security needs?''

Aw, hell. "No.''

"I knew it! What else did they want you to do?''

Honesty or a lie? Flynn looked at the roses she'd tossed onto the hall table—the ones he'd given her at her uncles' insistence—and frowned. No matter how awkward, he wouldn't lie any more than necessary. And this wasn't a necessary lie. "They asked me to do whatever it took to obtain your cooperation. I guess they're serious about wanting this security system."

Jane wasn't quite certain what she'd expected Flynn to say, but that wasn't it. How mortifying! "Whatever it took," she repeated stiffly. "So once you found out it was my birthday, you assumed candy and flowers would get you the contract?"

His mouth tilted to one side in a tempting smile. Of course, everything about the man tempted her, from the way his black hair curled across his forehead, to the beauty of his features, to the expression in his unusual gold eyes—eyes that seemed capable of reading her every thought. Even the intriguing bruise at the corner of an equally intriguing mouth appealed. There was something compelling about him, something that drew her. If it hadn't been for his charm, she'd have found him incredibly attractive. But that charm made her wary.

"The candy and flowers were for your birthday. I already have the contract."

She shook her head. "Only if I agree—which I don't. That's my lab we're talking about and I decide who messes with it."

"Look... I'm not trying to buy your favor, if that's what you're suggesting. And I apologize if I've offended you. To be honest, I'd have done the same thing for any of my clients once I'd discovered it was their birthday."

"Candy and flowers." She lifted an eyebrow at that. "Even your male clients?"

He laughed, holding up his hands. "Okay, you got me there. A bottle of Scotch and front-row seats to their favorite sporting event for my male clients. I guess that was rather sexist of me to assume you were a candy-and-flowers woman. Would you rather have some whiskey and Sonics tickets?"

She folded her arms across her chest. "I can't be bribed."

"I'm not trying to bribe you," he retorted in exasperation. He studied her for a moment, and for the first time she knew what it felt like to be on the wrong side of an experiment. His scrutiny weighed and analyzed, reaching a conclusion in those few short seconds. "This isn't getting us anywhere. I'll tell you what. Let's start over. You want to stick to business? Fine. Your uncles have asked me to look over your lab and recommend a good security system. When would it be convenient to drop by? For *business* and only business."

"There won't ever be a convenient—" Wait a minute. *Business!* She eyed him assessingly in return, an idea occurring. Why hadn't she thought of it sooner? This might provide the perfect opportunity to expand the parameters of her perfume tests. If she could get him to agree to help... "How do you feel about scientific experiments?"

The question didn't alarm him anywhere near as much as it did the residents of Salmon Bay, despite Dipstick's warning bark. "Fine, I guess. Why?"

"This is a business arrangement, isn't that what you said?"

"Yes."

"Which means that our business can go both ways, right?"

Even bewildered he exuded charm. "If that would make you more comfortable, I don't see why not."

"So if I conduct business while you're conducting business, you wouldn't mind?" She gave him a hopeful look. "Would you?"

The second she saw the crinkles appear at the corners of his eyes, she knew he'd agree. "You're the boss. As far as 'm concerned, that gives you the right to make those types of decisions. I can work around your schedule.''

"That's not what I meant." Oh, dear. She'd never been terribly good about tiptoeing around an issue. Unfortunately, her directness had the distressing tendency to scare people off. She plunged her fists into the pockets of her lab coat and fixed Flynn with her most professional look. What the heck? She'd go for broke. "I'd be willing to give my uncles the go-ahead if you'd be a test subject for my latest study."

Dipstick collapsed fully onto the floor, burying his head in his massive paws. Flynn lifted an eyebrow, apparently taking the warning seriously. His amusement faded. "Test subject? What would that involve?"

At least he hadn't beat a hasty retreat out the front door. "Not much," she said. "You'd have to answer some general questions. And then I'd need to test your reaction to a formula I'm working on."

"This formula... What does it do?"

"I can't tell you that." At his narrow-eyed look, she hastened to explain, "It would skew the results if I told you too much."

"I'm not supposed to drink it, am I? I'm not the best person for any Jekyll-and-Hyde experiments." A wealth of memories gathered in his eyes, bleak memories that tarnished the odd gold color. "You wouldn't like the results."

"You won't come into direct physical contact with the formula. Does that help reassure you?"

He rubbed a hand across his jawline. Accidently clipping his bruise, he winced and Jane couldn't help wondering what—or who—had given it to him. "Let me get this straight. If I help with this study you're doing, you'll agree to my firm installing a security system, right?"

"Right."

"You'll give me free access when I need it, where I need it."

"I—" She frowned. Somehow he'd managed to turn the tables on her. He was calling the shots, and she didn't like it one bit. "You can't interfere too much with my work. I'm at a rather crucial phase in my experiments."

"I'll do my best, that's all I can promise. But there will be times I'll need you out of the lab. How about this..." His brows drew together as he thought. "Once I've determined what sort of system you require I'll have my partner fly up from San Francisco. While he's installing the hardware, you can conduct your experiments. Would that work?"

"It just might." She held out her hand. "Are we in agreement?"

He took her fingers in his. "It's a deal."

She could scarcely contain her excitement. "When do we start?"

His mouth curved into another slow smile and he regarded her with lazy amusement. "Hell, darlin'," he drawled. "I'm a generous man. Pick the time and place and I'm all yours."

"HEY, PAULIE. IT'S FLYNN."

"You son of a bitch! You have a hell of a nerve calling me before I'm done bein' mad at you. I have a mind to hang up on your ass."

Flynn held the receiver with an uplifted shoulder as he worked the buttons of his shirt. "Yeah, well. Normally, wouldn't interrupt your temper tantrum. But I have a problem."

"You think that comes as a surprise? Hah!" A full minute passed while Flynn waited him out. Finally his partner released a gusty sigh. "Okay. What's the problem?"

"There's this woman—"

Paulie groaned. "No. Please tell me you haven't found another woman in trouble."

"'Fraid so." Flynn tried to sound contrite, but suspected he failed rather spectacularly.

"What happened to that good deed of yours? Wasn't it an auction or something? I'd have thought that was enough to keep you occupied."

"That's how I got into my current predicament." Flynn tossed his shirt toward the hotel room chair and kicked off his shoes. "These fellas bought me and—"

"*Fellas?*" Paulie's laugh ripped down the phone lines. "Now, *that* I'd have paid serious money to see."

"Yeah, well. You'll laugh even harder once you meet them. Which brings me to the reason I called. I was hoping you'd come up here and lend me a hand."

"Keep you out of trouble, don't you mean?"

Paulie knew him entirely too well. "That, too."

"So, where's here?"

"A little town north of Seattle. It's called Salmon Bay. Ever heard of it?"

"I've barely heard of Seattle."

Flynn chuckled. "It's not far from Vince Martelli's place. Remember that job?"

"Installed the Lockdown 986. 'Course I remember."

"That's the one. Will you come?"

"I don't know. I'm still pissed off."

"I don't doubt it for a minute." Now for the tricky part. "I need you to work on this place while I keep the owner preoccupied."

"And why's that?" Paulie asked suspiciously. "You scammin' again?"

"Maybe a little. I gather she doesn't want anyone fooling with her precious lab—"

"Lab?"

"She's a scientist. A chemist, to be exact. We need to secure her lab so her research doesn't fall into the wrong hands."

"Got it. So it's a good sort of scam?"

"If any scam can be considered good." Which Flynn seriously doubted. No matter how well-intentioned, someone always gets hurt in a scam. "Catch the first plane out, will you? I'll fax you directions."

"I'll be there." Paulie sighed again. "A woman chemist, huh?"

"Yeah. Oh, and Paulie?"

"What?"

"She's got a killer smile."

"That's just what it'll be if you take advantage of it," Paulie warned tartly. "A killer."

"Might be worth it." With a soft chuckle, Flynn hung up.

JANE HURRIED OUT TO HER LAB early the next morning. The building was a large single-story concrete-block structure that spread across half of the enormous lot behind her house and half of her uncles', as well. Long before she was born, her parents and her uncles had bought adjacent residences and built the laboratory complex she currently used. When she'd turned twenty-one, she'd moved into her parents' home, a decision that had helped establish a small measure of independence. Not that her uncles had minded. She smiled. They supported all her choices, in everything.

She checked her watch, aware she had precious little time left. For some reason, getting ready for her appointment with Flynn Morgan was taking far longer than she'd anticipated and she still had a lot of organizing to do before he arrived. She yanked at the door to her lab, just as someone pushed from the other side.

"Watch it, Jane. You almost ran me down."

"Mick?"

Jane fell back so quickly, her glasses slid from her hair. In a practiced movement, Mick caught them before they hit the ground and returned them to her. "Maybe you should put those things on a string. Then you wouldn't lose them all the time."

She started to reply, but caught herself at the last second. She'd learned long ago that arguing with Mick entailed an incredible expense of energy, all of it wasted and further discussion proved fruitless. He reminded her of a pit bull. Once he bit down, he didn't let go.

"What are you doing here?" she asked.

"Looking for you."

She glanced past him toward the open door of her lab. "I was over at the house. Why didn't you try there?"

"I didn't think you'd be in. You rarely are." He checked his Rolex. "Perhaps I should be asking why you're *not* where you should be."

"Don't try to turn the tables on me, Mick. My lab is off-limits to you and you darn well know it."

"Oh, come on, Jane." He regarded her with outright disdain. "What the hell do you think I'm going to do? Steal some of your precious perfumes? Why would I want them? They don't work."

She folded her arms across her chest, hoping she didn't appear too defensive. "You have no way of knowing that."

"As a matter of fact, I do."

Outrage rippled through her. "Only because you went through my research notes!"

"*Our* research notes."

"*Mine.*" She thrust her glasses onto the bridge of her

nose and glared at him. For some reason she felt safer behind the bulky purple frames, more logical and better equipped to deal with Mick. "Somehow they became ours while we were dating. And somehow my research project became ours about the same time. Right up until—"

"Old news, Jane."

Had she sounded hurt? She unwrapped her arms and thrust her fists into the pockets of her lab coat. Her right hand curled around the perfume atomizer she'd deposited there from yesterday's experiments. If this particular scent truly did cause irritation, what effect would it have on someone already irritating? Without thinking, she pulled it out and squirted it on herself. If nothing else it should distract him.

He reacted just as she'd expected. The mouth she'd once found so kissable sagged open, which pleased her no end since it looked downright repulsive. And the thick-lashed brown eyes she'd once dreamily compared to chocolate fudge switched from aggressive to alarmed. How nice to know that the last of the romantic fog he'd once conjured had fully dissipated. Now she could look at him without feeling the least bit of hurt. Or better yet, the least bit of desire.

He took a quick step backward and covered his nose with his hand. "What the *hell* was that?"

"Nothing," she said, blinking innocently. "At least... nothing much." She waited a second for that to sink in and then asked, "How are you feeling, Mick?"

"Fine!"

She sidled a little closer and fanned the perfume in his direction. "Fine? Are you sure? You're not experiencing any sort of reaction at all?"

"What have you done, Dearly?"

Once upon a time, he'd called her Dearling. She couldn't

believe she'd found it cute. What an idiot she'd been. She knew it was spiteful, but she couldn't seem to help herself. "Any ringing in your ears? Any odd cravings? You're not drooling, are you?"

"I... No! You're pulling my leg." Big brown eyes pleaded with her. "Aren't you?"

She drew herself up. "I don't pull legs or play games or steal other people's research. I'm a scientist."

"You're crazy. As crazy as those uncles of yours. If you've done anything to me, I swear I'll be having a word with Sheriff Tucker."

"Go right ahead. You'll never be able to prove a thing." She held up the spray bottle again. "But if I find you've fooled with any of the equipment in my lab, I'll be the one talking to Tucker. Of course, that won't be a problem much longer. I'm sure you'll be pleased to know my uncles have decided to install a security system."

"It won't do you any good." He edged around her. "It's not like you've discovered anything new. You've been working on your little experiments for years and what have you come up with?"

His comment hit and hit hard. "At least I can say the work I've done is all mine," she managed to return.

Mick grinned at that. "Don't you know? Ownership is the least of it. It's the one who gets the contract who wins."

He was right and they both knew it. She silently stewed as he tromped across the grass toward the side of her house. Unable to stand his having the last word, she shouted, "Hey, Mick!" He threw her a quick look over his shoulder. "You will give me a call if anything vital signs of falling off, won't you?"

She could see his mouth move and suspected whatever he'd said didn't bear repeating. Chuckling softly, she tossed the atomizer into the air, caught it, then made her way to the lab. She reached automatically for her safety goggles. Slipping them on before entering, she wound her way around rows of lab benches to the locked cabinet containing her current samples.

Inside the temperature-controlled environment were twelve plain glass bottles. Each was marked with LP and a number. It wouldn't take any time at all to mix up a new perfume sample. She reached for LP-2, since it was next in line. Minutes later, a new atomizer rested in her lab coat pocket and she crossed to her computer to type up a few notes.

The only emotional reaction to her first "perfume" had been annoyance. Of course, she couldn't say for certain whether the spray had prompted the reaction or the experiment itself. It was too early to tell if Flynn had reacted unusually to it—she didn't know him well enough to make that determination. Perhaps she'd try it out on him at some point in the future and see whether he found it annoying. But not on their first—

Her fingers slipped on the computer keys and her eyes widened. Good grief! She'd almost called it a date. Where in the world had that come from? Well, wherever it had emanated, it better go right back. After Mick, the very last thing in the world she wanted was another romantic relationship.

Love affairs were messy and hurt like hell when they came to an end. They engaged emotions that were impossible to analyze or control and usually involved lies. Her mouth tightened. Many lies. Keeping her energies and emotions focused on her work wasn't just smart, at this point in her career it was vital. She didn't need a man like Flynn in her life, a temporary distraction that promised long-term pain. No. She'd use him for her experiments and nothing more. She certainly wouldn't allow any sort of romantic entanglements. She sighed.

No matter how kissable a mouth Mr. Flynn Morgan possessed.

CHAPTER FOUR

"YEAH, YEAH. I'M COMING." Flynn yawned, snatching up a T-shirt. He thrust his arms into the holes and yanked it over his head as he opened the door to his hotel room. A man he'd never seen before stood there. "Sort of early for a social call, isn't it?"

"It's almost noon."

Flynn thrust a hand through his hair, tumbling it out of his eyes. "Really? Haven't slept this late in ages. Guess that's what a clear conscience does for you." If his visitor caught the underlying irony, he didn't let on. Flynn sighed. "What can I do for you?"

The man threw a quick, nervous glance over his shoulder. "Could we discuss this in the privacy of your room?"

Flynn stepped back with a shrug. "I guess. Mind telling me who the hell you are?"

"Oh, right." The man looked surprised, as though common courtesy hadn't even occurred to him. "Mick Barstow."

Flynn's eyes narrowed. There couldn't be two Mick Barstows in a town as small as Salmon Bay, which meant this had to be Jane's Mick. "Flynn Morgan."

"I know who you are," Barstow claimed, striding into the room. "What I haven't figured out is what you're doing here."

That was direct. And none of his damn business. Flynn summoned up the energy to say as much. "That's none of your damn business. Are we through talking now? I wouldn't mind catching a few more hours of shut-eye.''

''Not even close.''

Mick made himself comfortable in the nearest chair, and Flynn wondered what the hell Jane had seen in the man to convince her he'd be a welcome addition as both a partner and a lover. Granted, he wasn't too bad-looking. A bit weak-jawed, perhaps, but he made up for it by being tall, blond and decently built. Unfortunately, he had a serious attitude problem. Worse than that, his bristly mustache covered up lips too thin to do justice to Jane's generously proportioned mouth.

A piss-poor match there.

Flynn planted his backside on the low-topped dresser and thrust his legs out in front of him. He yawned again, wondering if the room had a coffeemaker somewhere. Better yet, maybe he'd wander over to Jane's and beg a cup off her. Maybe she'd have slept in, too. Would she open the door to him, all tousled and flushed with sleep, her eyes still filled with misty dreams of sweet romance? Or would she already be bespectacled and trussed up and wearing her lab coat like a suit of armor? It might be interesting to find out.

But first he had to take care of business. He leveled his visitor with a jaundiced eye. ''What do you want, Barstow?'' he asked. ''You're intruding on my sleep time and I don't take kindly to that.''

''Then I'll get right to the point. You're here to install a security system for Jane Dearly, right?''

Flynn cocked an eyebrow. ''So?''

''So, I want to know what else you're up to.''

''Got it.'' Flynn straightened and grabbed Barstow by the arm. ''This is where you leave.''

''Wait a minute! You can't throw me out.''

''Give me one good reason.''

"I've had you investigated."

That gave him pause. "How? I just hit town yesterday."

"I have sources," Barstow warned. "Excellent sources."

Flynn sighed. "What is it with people around here? I thought small-town folk were supposed to be trusting. First Jane's uncles and now you." He eased his hold. "What is it you think you know about me?"

"I know that you're not all you claim. I know if you're involved in something, there's a scam going on."

Flynn didn't like the expression glittering in Barstow's eyes. "Let me rephrase the question. *Why* are you telling me this?"

"You're a security expert, right?"

"I can find my way around most systems."

Mick smiled, a cold, calculating twitch of mustache and lips. "And I know why, too."

"Get to the point or get the hell out."

"I want you to get my notes from Jane. They're locked up in her computer. I have access, but not knowledge. You have both."

"This is where you leave."

"I'm willing to pay, and pay big."

Flynn gave him a quick shove toward the hotel room door. "Out."

Mick held up his hands. "I'm not asking for anything that doesn't belong to me. I can give you the specific file I need. You can even read the information before you hand it over to prove to yourself it's mine."

"Why me? Why haven't you taken your complaint to a lawyer?"

"There's no time! I need that file now, before her findings become known."

"I'm not interested."

"Think about it, Morgan. That's all I'm asking."

"Fine. I'll think about it." Flynn yanked open the door and tossed Barstow on the far side of it. "But it would take a lot to make me betray a client. A lot more than you have, I'm willing to bet."

With that, he slammed the door closed.

"ANYBODY HOME?"

Flynn's call came from the foyer and Jane hastened from her lab to join him. He must have recently climbed out of a shower. His dark hair had been combed into submission and he had that fresh-scrubbed-and-shaved look about him. She found it entirely too distracting. Perhaps a hint of formality was in order.

"Good afternoon, Mr. Morgan."

"Make it Flynn, if you don't mind. Sorry I'm late. I've been working nonstop the past few weeks and I'm afraid it finally caught up with me." He offered an abashed grin. "My first day on the job and I slept in."

She waved aside his apology. "To be honest, I didn't notice."

"Got lost in your chemicals and potions, did you?"

That…and far too much daydreaming. "I enjoy it," she confessed with a shrug, "so it doesn't seem like work."

"You ready to show me around?" His gaze swept the foyer in an assessing manner. "I didn't realize this place was so large. I'm not sure two weeks is going to be long enough to install an adequate security system."

"You can see the facility later. We have more important business to attend to first. Let's go into my office and we can fill out the survey for my study." She didn't bother to wait for his response but pulled open a wooden door with her name neatly etched into the wood, and waved him toward a seat.

"We really need to discuss your security needs. That *is* why I'm here."

"Later. This is more important."

"What's more important?"

She frowned. Hadn't he listened to a word she'd said yesterday? "The informational part of my survey. Don't you remember? You agreed to participate in my experiment."

"Oh, right. I thought we could do that after we'd determined what sort of system you required."

"Low priority, Mr. Morgan." He looked less than pleased with her comment, but she ignored that. She needed to take advantage of the man fate had dropped on her doorstep, and quickly. Heaven only knew when—or if—it would happen again. "We'll start with my study *then* worry about locks and dead bolts."

"Actually, security systems have become a bit more sophisticated than—"

She cut him off briskly. "Yes, well. We can go into all that another time." Opening the drawer to her filing cabinet, she pulled out a folder. She returned to her desk with it and removed a neatly stapled packet of papers. "Do you want anything before we begin? Coffee? A cola?"

"Nothing, thanks."

"In that case, I'll ask my questions. Let me just find a pair of glasses." She opened her desk drawer. To her surprise, Flynn leaned across the desk and plucked a pair off the top of her head and set them gently on the tip of her nose.

"That's the third different pair I've seen so far. How many do you have, anyway?" he asked curiously.

The question bothered her, since Mick had always fussed about her glasses. It wasn't that he objected to her wearing them. He simply objected to the colorful frames, calling them "crass." And the frequency with which she lost them had infuriated him. "A lot. I tend to misplace them. Does it matter?"

"No." He tilted his head to one side, studying her. "Actually, it's kind of cute. I like the yellow daisies."

She took instant exception. "I'm not cute, I'm a scientist." Unfortunately, her comment only served to amuse him.

"Scientists can't be cute?"

"Not this scientist." Fighting to regain control of the conversation, she glanced at her notes. Somehow she'd managed to lose it, an all-too-frequent occurrence around Mr. Morgan, she suspected. He had an uncanny knack for turning her attention from business to personal with one simple question. She found it most disconcerting. "As I mentioned, it's all standard information. Name, age, address, phone number, educational background and vital statistics."

"Vital statistics?"

"Height and weight."

To her surprise, her questions made him wary. Why was that? she couldn't help but wonder. "You already know my name. I'm thirty-four." He rattled off his address and phone number, then hesitated. "I'm six foot one and a hundred eighty-five pounds."

Most of which appeared to be good, lean muscle. "And your educational background?"

"Is that really necessary?"

"I need it for statistical purposes. All the information I gather will be kept strictly confidential, I promise."

He glanced away, his mouth tightening. "I received my GED at age twenty."

She fought to conceal her astonishment. "I see…"

"Do you?" His gaze returned to her and he leaned across the desk. Where once she'd considered him incredibly good-looking, now his features had hardened into taut, uncompromising lines. They spoke of a man who'd ridden long and far and overcome life-altering obstacles. "You want to know the bare-bone facts of my life and record them in some file. Sounds familiar. I've probably had my entire life recorded in various files littering the country."

"Mr. Morgan, it's just a survey—"

"Why don't you get to know me as a person instead of asking a bunch of questions that don't have a thing to do with who or what I am?"

He was overreacting and she couldn't help but wonder why. Slowly, she pulled off her glasses and dropped them to the desk. "I'm sorry, Flynn. I have a regrettable tendency toward single-mindedness when it comes to my work. You're not comfortable with this, are you?"

"No."

"It's simple background information," she explained gently. "What you do for a living, your marital status. That sort of thing. If it would make you more comfortable to make it part of a normal conversation, we could do it that way."

He slouched low in the chair and thrust his feet out in front of him as though he didn't give a damn. But she knew differently. For some reason, a simple, basic survey had thrown him, had touched a painful place, still raw with memories. "You want details?" he asked with a careless shrug. "Fine. Why don't we just get this over with and take care of business? I'm part owner in a company that installs security systems. I'm not married, but one of these days I hope to find a woman who'll take me on permanently. We'll settle down and have a passel of kids. Is that good enough? Are we through now?"

He'd surprised her again. "You want to marry? To have children?"

"I haven't ruled out the possibility. Right now I find the idea a bit off-putting."

For the first time in her entire life she had a glimmer of insight into another person. She couldn't recall it ever happening before, and the fact that it happened first with this man worried her. "Having kids scares you, doesn't it?"

"Right down to my bones."

She flipped the folder closed and rested her elbow on the desktop, cupping her chin in her hand. "Me, too. Why does it scare you?"

He hesitated and she could practically see him fight to get past a lifetime's worth of protective barriers. "I'm afraid I'll follow in my parents' footsteps. I'm afraid I'll make a god-awful father and screw up some poor innocent kid. I've made so many mistakes in my life, I can't even count them. But one mistake I won't be making is having a son who'll spend the better portion of his youth at Lost Springs Ranch for Boys."

She stared at him blankly. "What's that?"

"That, sweet lips, is where I grew up. It's a pretty little spread in Wyoming where they ship kids who've been abandoned or are about an inch away from a life in juvey. I qualified on both counts."

Understanding dawned. He'd mentioned having his life recorded in files. No doubt he'd spent years being probed and surveyed, sitting on the wrong side of a desk answering the wrong types of questions. She couldn't have chosen a worse way of approaching him. But she also couldn't help being curious, a curiosity that had nothing to do with her survey. "Did you hate living on the ranch?"

"No. Though, I didn't take to it as well as some of the others. I can't say why. The other kids were in the same boat I was. They were all in trouble with the law or had been abandoned or had parents who flung them out because it was easier than raising them."

She fought to hide her compassion, suspecting it wouldn't be welcomed. "I gather you were one of those who was flung?"

"You got that right. Flung at a time when I was flirting with jail."

"A time when you needed your parents the most."

"I needed parents." His smile was a devil-may-care, lop-sided twist of his lips. "Just not the ones who brought me into this world."

Oh, Flynn! "So you ended up at this ranch? The people there raised you?"

"Right up until I'd had enough of the good life and de-cided to rip out the few admirable qualities the community attempted to instill." Darkness settled on his face and his eyes grew bleak and flat. "It's taken me a long time to realize the error of my ways. But I finally did and I'm gonna make sure my children have the best possible example to follow instead of the worst."

"Without any help?" she asked gently.

"Damn right. The ranch did their damnedest to save my life. They won't have to save my child's."

It was a telling comment. Whenever he decided to have those kids that scared him so badly, he'd make a wonderful father. "I gather that despite everyone's efforts, you didn't graduate from high school?" She asked the question tenta-tively, waiting for him to shut down on her and end the conversation. To her surprise, he kept talking.

"A prank at the end of my senior year pissed off the principal and he withheld my diploma. That in turn pissed me off enough that I decided I didn't need the damn thing. Two years later, after enduring every sort of dead-end job imaginable, I swallowed my pride and sat for a high school equivalency test.''

''What about college?''

''Do I *look* like a college boy?''

She shoved the folder to one side and regarded him curiously. ''I don't know, Flynn. What does a college boy look like?''

''Prissy.''

Jane couldn't help it. She chuckled. To her surprise, the irritation drained from him and he smiled, too. ''I confess, I've taken courses that have helped with my security firm.''

''But you don't trust organized education, is that it?''

''Got it in one.''

''All right. I'll put down 'some college.'''

''Don't bother prettying me up. I am what I am. I don't need whitewashing.''

''Who's whitewashing?'' He'd revealed so much of himself during their conversation, it seemed only fair to return the favor. ''For your information I never went to school at all. Did my uncles mention that they raised me?''

''They said something to that effect.''

''My parents died when I was five. I was so afraid and so alone. But they—'' She tried to relate years of care and love and devotion with a quick sweep of her hand. ''They rebuilt my world when it had fallen apart.''

''It's obvious they care for you.''

''Yes, they do. When I was little, my uncles educated me at home and hired tutors for the subjects they couldn't cover. They wanted to ensure I had the best education possible. They even made arrangements through the University of Washington for me to receive college credits. Eventually I attended the university and received my degree, but I commuted from here instead of living on-campus.''

''Sounds like a lonely existence.''

He had no idea. "A lonely existence compounded by my preoccupation with science. Maybe if I'd been more outgoing it wouldn't have been so bad."

"I gather nothing's changed since then?"

"The loneliness?" For a brief instant an intense yearning took hold. "No. Nothing's changed."

"Why?" So soft. So tender. So compassionate.

"Because work is my life," she said simply. "And because this current experiment is the most important work I've done to date. Next year I'll be thirty."

Even his amusement was gentle. "And?"

Didn't he understand? What did she have to show for her years of work? Years of failure. Her uncles had been so sweet and understanding—not to mention indulgent. Their attitude had been a balm when she'd been a child of five. At twenty-nine it had grown infuriating.

"And I have to prove myself as a bona fide chemist in order to justify my uncles' efforts. To justify my own efforts, for that matter."

She *had* to. And in order to succeed she had to remain focused on work. She slanted Flynn a quick look. It was time to ignore all distractions and get her priorities straight. Right now her priorities didn't include a six-foot-one security expert with a tumble of raven-dark hair, killer gold eyes and a charming smile she found far too appealing.

Today her goal had been to gather as much information about him as possible. After a few days, once she'd gotten a general feel for him as a person, she'd move on to the secondary part of her experiment and wear the perfumes whenever they were together in order to see if they affected his behavior in any way. A shame. She'd begun to like Flynn, as a person. But if she allowed their relationship to develop any further, she'd have a far more difficult time distinguishing between his reaction to her as a person and a reaction induced by her perfumes.

"It's admirable that you want to justify your uncles' faith in you, that you want to prove yourself in their eyes," Flynn said. "But, honey, you can't live your life for someone else."

"I'm not. I'm living it for myself. It's my success in the lab that will justify my uncles' faith." She donned her most professional mask. "Look at how the time's flown. I suppose this would be a good time to show you around."

Other than a swift mocking glance, he accepted her lead. "Good idea." He waited until she'd circled the desk and started out the door of her office before catching her arm and tugging her close. She inhaled sharply, drawing his unique scent deep into her lungs. "One last point before we move on."

"I don't think—"

"Let's be honest, shall we? You're lonely because you choose to be. Because it's safer than dealing with real life."

She refused to look at him. "You have no idea what you're talking about."

"Honey, I've made a living reading people. When I was a kid, it saved my ass more times than I can count. As an adult… Let's just say it became an occupational necessity. You're running scared, though I don't know why." He slid a finger along the curve of her cheek until he captured her chin. Turning her face to his, he leaned closer. "But I will. Count on it."

He was going to kiss her. She read it in his strangely somber gaze, in the tautening of the lines bracketing his mouth, in the heat that slipped from his body to hers, encasing her in warmth.

"Hey, Morgan! Where the hell are you, you son of a—" A short, stocky man came into view. He took one look at the two of them practically entwined in each other's arms and ripped off a San Francisco Giants baseball cap, flinging it to the ground. A bristle of salt-and-pepper hair stood at military attention as he glared at them. "That tears it. Now I'm really pissed."

Jane tore free of Flynn's arms while Flynn closed his eyes and swore beneath his breath. "Jane, I don't believe you've met my partner Paulie Richardson. He's here to help install your security system."

"Heard you were in trouble," Paulie announced, his scowl landing squarely on his partner. He flexed his fist. "I'd say you were in more trouble than you realized."

Flynn smiled. A charming, endearingly familiar smile that Jane now knew came underscored with bittersweet sadness. "So what else is new?"

"MR. PAULIE, YOU DON'T understand," Jane tried again.

"It's just Paulie. And I understand fine. You don't want nobody messin' with your precious lab. I got that. But how am I supposed to make it secure without messin' with it a bit?"

"That's not my problem. I have work that can't be interrupted. I don't particularly care what you do with the rest of the complex, so long as you leave my lab alone. *And* so long as you don't put in any cameras or other electronic contraptions. Just stick more locks on the doors and that should be fine."

Paulie's cap bit the dust again. "You have got to be kidding me."

Jane whipped a pair of glasses out of her lab coat pocket and thrust them on her nose. "No, I'm not kidding. It's *my* lab." She turned to face Flynn. "Explain it to him."

"Yeah, Morgan." Paulie folded his arms across his chest. "'Splain it so I understand."

Flynn sighed. "Okay. Here's what we're going to do. Jane, you and I are going out for a while."

"I can't leave now!"

"I'm afraid you'll have to. Since Paulie will have the power turned off while he works on other sections of the complex, I don't think you'll be able to get much work done in the dark."

"You can't turn off the power!"

"That's it," Paulie announced. "I give up. Most people come into our office begging for our help. We have enough contracts to keep us busy for years. But do we work on those? Do we help out the clients who say, 'Anything you want, you can have'? Or... 'Spare no expense, just put in the latest gadgets'? No! We're stuck with a crazy scientist who's ripe to be robbed blind and doesn't give a—"

"I hate gadgets." She glared at him. "I also have temperature-sensitive solutions in my lab. And just so you know, there are solvents in there that will sterilize you from stem to stern. But, hey. Anything you want, feel free to poke your nose into."

"Lady, I have a good mind to walk out of here."

"If you had a good mind, we wouldn't be having this conversation!"

"That's enough, both of you." Flynn took charge again. He turned first to Jane. "The power won't be off for long. Pack any temperature-sensitive solutions in ice or stick them in your uncles' refrigerator."

"My uncles' refrigerator? Why—"

"That way you'll have a built-in baby-sitter and won't have to worry about anyone waltzing into a house you refuse to lock and helping themselves to whatever potion you're brewing."

His logic annoyed the heck out of her. "What am I supposed to do while Paulie's interfering with my work?"

"What normal people do when they're not working."

She stared blankly. "What's that?"

Flynn shook his head. "Why aren't I surprised you're asking?" He caught her hand in his. "Paulie? You have three hours. Make the most of them. If you have any questions about building schematics or what goes where, the uncles have the blueprints of the building along with the schematics I've drawn up. You know my priorities."

"I can't be gone for three whole hours," Jane protested. Her brows drew together. "And what schematics are you talking about?"

He opened the door to the laboratory complex and ushered her through it. "The ones I discussed with your uncles."

"You went behind my back?"

"Don't act so outraged." She dug in her heels, not that her stubbornness stopped Flynn. He simply resorted to towing her along. "According to your uncles, they own a good chunk of that building of yours, and they want their investment protected. Since they hired me, I do what my employers request."

"Fine, do whatever they want, but not in my lab. And *no* cameras."

"You have a real problem with cameras." He slanted her a curious look. "Mind telling me why?"

"Yes, I do mind." Time for a change of subject. "Where are we going, anyway?"

"I thought we'd head into town and catch a movie."

A movie? "That sounds like fun. I can't remember the last time I went to the movies."

"Then it's past time. Come on. My car's parked around front."

It was a perfect northwestern afternoon. The sun had begun a gradual descent toward the Pacific Ocean, though it would be well past nine before it fully sank behind the mountains on the Olympic Peninsula. A rainstorm had swept through a few hours before, leaving the air rich with the clean fragrance of recently mowed grass and a dozen different floral scents. The mingling of odors reminded her of her experiment and she glanced at Flynn, first from the corner of her eye, and then more openly since she'd never been one for subtlety.

"What?" he asked, without looking at her.

"I was just checking you out."

"Why?"

"I'm analyzing your reactions to our...to our business association." It wasn't far from the truth. Could she help it if that analysis had become almost as personal as professional?

"Intriguing. Don't think I've ever been analyzed for a chemistry experiment before." He returned her examination with one of his own. "So, what's the verdict?"

She forced herself to focus on business. "You appear relaxed. A bit curious, perhaps, but not worried or nervous."

That seemed to amuse him. "Should I be?"

"I can tell you haven't visited our illustrious town or you wouldn't ask me that question." Her mouth twisted. "You'd already know."

"Meaning?"

"Everyone's nervous around me," she stated matter-of-factly. "They're afraid I'm going to try some new experiment on them."

"And are you?"

She shrugged. "More often than not." Her brow furrowed as she recalled her run-in with the Henderson boys. "They think I treat them like my own personal lab rats. Though I've been pretty well-behaved since I turned sixteen."

His eyebrows shot up at that. "Sounds like I need to make a visit to town and have a talk with some of my fellow rodents."

"Thanks all the same, but I'd be just as happy if you'd avoid any outside contact for the time being."

"Now you sound like a scientist."

"I *am* a scientist." They'd reached his rental car and he opened the door for her. "To be honest, I'd rather take a woman to the movies, than a scientist."

"There's no difference," she retorted.

As she brushed past him, he lowered his head, his mouth hovering close to her ear. "There should be a difference," he murmured, the warmth of his breath eliciting an uncontrollable shiver. "The woman should come first. Always. Maybe one of these days you'll discover that for yourself."

She wanted to argue, to explain that she'd tried that once with disastrous results. Instead, she settled on the seat and arranged her skirt carefully around her legs before focusing her attention out of the front windshield. He took the hint. Closing the door, he circled the car. Without another word, he climbed in and started the engine.

CHAPTER FIVE

"I DON'T CARE WHAT YOU SAY, Flynn. Seven dollars to get into a movie theater is outrageous. It's not like this is a big city."

"Obviously you don't get out much. Wait until you see the price of the popcorn and soda."

Jane folded her arms across her chest, making him realize that she still wore her lab coat. He'd have to remember to strip it off her next time they went out. And there would be a next time—many next times—if he had a hope in hell of getting the security system installed in her lab. "Then we simply won't have any."

Flynn shook his head and released a gusty sigh. "But that's where they've got you, honey. Because it's downright un-American to watch a movie without a bag of butter-soaked popcorn and an eight-ounce supersize soda."

"Eight—" A gurgle of laughter escaped. "Eight ounces is considered supersize?"

"You wait and see."

To his amusement, the buttery popcorn passed her inspection. Apparently, being a chemist didn't rouse any concerns about calories or cholesterol. But the soda drew a triumphant laugh. "Twelve point seven," she announced.

"Come again?"

"Usually I deal in metric volumes, so I'm having to convert liters and deciliters. But I'd guess the supersize drink is twelve point seven ounces.'' She handed him the cup. ''That's less the ice, of course.''

He grinned. ''Of course. My mistake.''

''That's all right,'' she offered generously. ''You're not used to dealing with weights and measures. Why, I'll bet when it comes to locks and bolts and spy cameras, you're an absolute font of information.''

''A font. That's me.'' He dropped the bag of popcorn into her hands, wrapped an arm around her waist and urged her into the auditorium. Plucking her glasses off the tip of her nose, he slipped them into the pocket of her lab coat. ''Front row or back?''

''As I recall, I always sat in the middle.''

''Front row it is.'' He caught her hand and tugged her down to the middle seats in the first row. ''Just in time, too,'' he whispered close to her ear as a pack of preteens charged for the front of the theater.

Within seconds they were surrounded by noisy boys. A flurry of popcorn pelted back and forth over their heads before the group settled down. Flynn slanted a glance at Jane to see how she handled their exuberance. She'd fixed her gaze on the screen, but her mouth curved into a smile.

''Feeling right at home, aren't you?'' she teased.

''Yup.''

She spared him a quick glance. ''Did you sit in the front row when you were their age and throw popcorn at the other boys from the ranch?''

''Not quite.'' He leaned closer, dropping his arm along the back of her seat. ''I threw the popcorn at the cute little Lightning Creek girls.''

''No surprise there.'' She lifted an eyebrow. ''And what did the cute little Lightning Creek girls do when you threw popcorn at them?''

His brow crinkled in thought. ''Let's see.... Mary Louise

screamed. Tracey got mad because she ended up with butter splotches on her dress. But Dana Ann Kenny—'' Flynn broke off, a wide grin spreading across his face. He'd intrigued his lady chemist with that smile, he could tell.

"What did she do?" Jane demanded.

"Nothing right then." He shifted closer, lowering his voice. "That came later, once the theater got dark."

"Like it's doing now?"

"Yeah. Just like this."

"And then?"

"Then I slipped over to where she was sitting and—"

Jane turned to look at him, a smile trembling on her lips. "And...what?"

"I did this...."

He leaned into her and did what he'd promised himself he wouldn't. He captured the sweetest smile on the sweetest lips he'd ever had the pleasure to explore. Her mouth was soft and wide and lush, parting ever so slightly beneath the subtle pressure of his. He could taste the butter on her and the hunger. He would have taken it further if the boys around them hadn't caught on to what they were doing.

Laughs and catcalls broke out all around them and they were instantly pelted with popcorn. He released her with a laugh. "I kissed her and Dana Ann kissed me right back. That was my first ever." His laughter died. "And my last for a while."

"Did you get caught?" A preview flashed across the screen, momentarily casting a soft glow across her face. Although her voice sounded normal enough, her expression revealed that his kiss had found a way past the scientist, straight through to the woman. "Did you get in trouble?"

"I was sent back to the ranch in disgrace." He gave a careless shrug. "Not for the first time, you understand. And sure as hell not for the last."

"Was it worth it?" People around them shushed her, not that she seemed to notice. "Was it?"

"Yeah. It was worth it. I'm not sure Dana Ann agreed, though. I heard she got grounded for a month for messin' with one of those ranch boys." She was going to ask another question, a question he didn't want to answer. One that would force him to consider feelings he'd buried long ago. Catching her chin in his palm, he tilted it toward the screen. "Watch the movie."

She fumbled absentmindedly for her glasses. He lent her a hand, plucking them from her pocket and perching them on the tip of her nose. She murmured her thanks before directing her full attention to the story unraveling across the screen. A few minutes into the movie, she turned to him again. "I don't understand."

"What don't you understand?" he whispered.

"This guy, Dantus, is the villain, right?"

"Yup."

"And he wants to take over the world?"

"You got it."

"Why?"

A man seated behind them leaned forward. "Would you mind not talking?"

Jane swiveled in her seat. "I'm sorry. I just don't understand why Dantus wants to take over the world. Don't you think that's far too much trouble? I mean... Does he have any idea of the magnitude of the task he's proposing?"

"Lady, who gives a damn? It's a movie!"

"Shh!" hissed someone else.

"Okay, fine." She turned back around and murmured to Flynn, "But it doesn't make sense."

"I think it's a guy thing. Fast cars, faster women and taking over the world. We start there and then settle for whatever comes closest—like a van, the girl next door and being king of the couch and remote control. To be honest, even the remote control is iffy." He nodded toward the screen and sighed. "But in our dreams..."

She made a sound of disgust. "That explains it. A woman would know better than to waste her time trying to rule people who have no interest in being ruled. It's not at all logical. Aside from an extremely short life expectancy due to the serious threat of assassination, the sheer volume of paperwork must be—"

Popcorn rained down on them, and to Flynn's amusement she slid down in her seat and curled close. Then she slipped a hand into their bag and surreptitiously tossed a few buttery kernels over her shoulder. It wasn't until halfway through the film that she got them into trouble again.

"Now *that* is ridiculous," she snapped.

"Shh!"

"No, I won't shush. What he's proposing is physically impossible. That little dropper of chemicals wouldn't make a mouse sick, let alone take out the entire city of Cincinnati."

"Would you *please* be quiet?"

Jane whipped around in her seat again. "Don't you care that this film is inaccurate?"

The man groaned. "It's not supposed to be accurate. It's supposed to be entertaining and it's not even that because you won't shut up!"

"This is outrageous." Popcorn pelted them. "Do you realize it would take approximately six hundred and forty-five pounds of that mixture before someone got so much as a bellyache? That's a generalization, you understand, since I've had to convert kilograms to pounds."

"Who gives a—"

"And even then, in order for them to become remotely ill, they'd have to stick a spoon in that mixture and eat it uncut. Now, dissolved in water as he's proposing, you'd need—''

Flynn stood. "Time to go, sweetheart," he announced, yanking her from her seat.

Jane let out a tiny squeak. "What are you doing?"

"Saving your life."

Amid cheers, he snatched her up in his arms, popcorn flying in all directions, and hustled for the nearest exit. An instant later they emerged from the emergency exit into the parking lot. He set her down, ignoring her disgruntled expression. Gently, he removed a stray bit of popcorn from her hair.

"Flynn?"

"Yes, sweetheart?"

"I think I remember why I don't go to movies any longer," she confessed.

"Really?"

"I'm afraid so. Movies are rarely logical and I have difficulty containing myself when I catch the flaws."

"Yeah, I sort of noticed that about you."

Her mouth curved downward. "They weren't too happy with me, were they?"

"Not even a little." Unable to help himself, he chuckled. She blinked at him in surprise. Then her mouth quivered and she joined in. Grabbing her hand, he urged her toward the car. "Come on. We better get out of here before they lynch us."

"YOU CAN'T MEAN I HAVE to leave my lab *again*?"

Flynn shrugged. "That's precisely what I mean."

"After what happened at the movie theater?"

"I have to confess, that did give me second thoughts."

"Exactly." Jane settled her glasses more firmly on her

nose and peered at her computer screen. "Now, stop interrupting me. I have work to do."

"No, you have to come with me. You won't be able to work, anyway, because Paulie has to—"

She groaned. "Let me guess. He has to turn the power off."

"You got it."

Saving the information she'd recorded, she shut down her computer. "Where are we going now?"

"I thought a walk with Dipstick might be safe enough."

She snorted. "He gets into almost as much trouble as I do."

"Then I'll have to find a way to keep you both out of trouble."

He didn't give her an opportunity to argue, and deciding she could use the time to get better acquainted with Flynn for her perfume experiments, she didn't fuss too much. The stroll into town passed innocently enough. Once there, Flynn paused outside of every shop window he passed. Dipstick caught on almost immediately and followed Flynn's example, pressing his nose against each glass pane. At the local five-and-dime, Flynn let out an exclamation of sheer pleasure while Dipstick barked encouragement.

"Wait here," he ordered. "I'll be right back."

Slipping on her glasses, Jane peered closer at the window, trying to see what had caused such enthusiasm for man and beast. A few minutes later Flynn emerged with a small bag in hand. "What did you buy?" she couldn't resist asking.

"This is one of the few true pleasures of my youth." He caught her hand in his and turned his smile on her—one she found more and more impossible to resist. "Come on. I'll show you."

"What? Where are we going?"

"To the park. You do have a park around here?"

"It's in the middle of town across from the police station." She pointed. "That way."

As soon as they reached the tree-lined square, Flynn pulled Jane close. "What...?"

"First thing we do is get rid of these." The glasses were snatched from her nose, neatly folded and deposited in her lab coat pocket. "And next we take this off."

Before she could do more than voice a startled objection, he'd worked open the buttons of her lab coat and stripped it away. With due ceremony, he hung it over the back of a wooden bench.

"Why did you do that?"

"Because you can't play dressed for work."

A smile quivered on her lips. "Is that what we're going to do? Play?"

"Yes." He opened his paper bag and removed a Frisbee. "With this. Ever thrown one before?"

She shook her head. "Not ever. But I have seen it done."

"Then this, my sweet Jane, is your lucky day." He pointed to a spot a good distance away. "Run over there and I'll throw it to you."

"Okay, fine." She headed for the spot he'd indicated.

"I said, *run!*"

The Frisbee skimmed the top of her head, knocking loose a few curls from her hair clip, before sailing ahead of her. With an excited bark, Dipstick gave chase. Bounding across the grass, he made a magnificent leap and caught the disk in his mouth. Then he sat, proudly displaying his catch to Jane.

"Show-off," she muttered.

Removing the Frisbee from his mouth, she threw it toward Flynn as hard as she knew how. It spun in the air and plopped to the ground two feet from her toes.

"It's broken," she complained. "Dipstick broke it."

Flynn jogged over to her, shaking his head in disgust. "Dipstick didn't break it. *You* don't know how to throw." He picked up the Frisbee and handed it to her. Circling around behind, he showed her how to hold the disk. "Start out with a gentle flick until you get the hang of it. Like this…"

Guiding her through the motions, he sent the Frisbee soaring through the air. Dipstick gave chase once again, leaping into the air and catching the plastic disk in his mouth. Trotting back to them, he proudly deposited it at their feet.

"Good boy." Flynn rewarded the dog with a thorough scratching. "Now, let's see if your mistress can do it."

Jane picked up the Frisbee and gave a couple of practice flicks without releasing it. Then she let it fly. It wobbled for an instant before sailing across the park, hooking sharply to the left. Flynn gave chase, catching it just before it hit the ground. Rolling, he flipped it back in her direction all in one smooth motion. She attempted to copy his movements, racing across the grass with outstretched hands. The Frisbee grazed her fingertips before slipping away.

"That tears it." She picked up the disk and sent it cartwheeling back to Flynn. Then she kicked off her shoes, rolled up her sleeves, hitched up her skirt and waited for him to send it back. "Okay, Jane," she muttered. "It's your turn now. We accept no excuses and take no prisoners. We're catching that damn thing, no matter what it takes."

Flynn wound up and let loose. The Frisbee ripped toward her slightly to the right. She scampered after it, leaping at the last possible instant to snag it out of mid-air.

"I did it. I *did* it!"

Shrieking triumphantly, she did her best Rocky imitation, fists pumping the air, half dancing, half jogging onto a nearby picnic table, curls spilling loose around her temples. At the edge of the park, Mr. Keenan stood alongside Sheriff

Tucker, staring at her in openmouthed astonishment. Their expressions made her laugh. She flung the Frisbee back toward Flynn. He gazed at her in smiling approval and Jane tried to convince herself that she didn't need his approval. But it felt good. Too good.

Soon she'd have to don her lab coat and slip on her glasses. Soon she'd have to turn back into the real Jane instead of the strange woman he'd released. Soon she'd have to remember the deal she'd made with Flynn and become the scientist studying her test subject.

But not yet.

"Come on, Flynn," she shouted from her perch on the table. "This time make it tough."

"YOU CAN'T WEAR A DRESS on a bike ride." Flynn objected.

"Do you know how long it's been since I've ridden a bike?"

"Not a clue. How long?"

Jane frowned in concentration. "I'm not sure I ever did. I think I fell off once and the uncles got so upset I never rode one again." She offered an apologetic shrug. "I didn't like doing anything that upset them."

"All the more reason to ride a bike now."

She shook her head. "I can't."

"Why not?"

"I already told you. Because I don't own any jeans."

"Somehow I knew you were going to say that." He handed her a bag with the name of a local boutique scrawled across it. "That's why I bought you these."

"Jeans?"

"Jeans."

"But—"

"No arguments. Go change into them before I'm tempted to help you."

She headed for the stairs in the front hallway. "Okay, I'll do it. But I'm not happy. Not even a little. And I certainly don't understand why Paulie needs to turn the electricity off so often. If I didn't know better, I'd think you were making it up." She rounded on him, shaking her finger in his face. "If I find you've been lying to me, Flynn Morgan, I'm going to be very upset."

He swore beneath his breath. "Even if it's for a good cause?"

"I despise dishonest people, regardless of the reason." She started up the steps. "And don't think I haven't heard that excuse before. For a good cause. For the betterment of science. Because I thought it was what you wanted to hear. Hah! A lie is a lie is a lie...."

She rounded the corner out of view and Flynn rubbed a hand across his freshly shaven jaw. "Damn, but I'm in big trouble. A lie is a lie is a lie. Now what the hell do I do?"

"They don't fit!" she shouted down the steps a minute later.

"Yes, they do."

"They're tight."

"Why the hell did you think I bought them?" he muttered. He raised his voice. "They'll loosen up once you've been wearing them for a while. Come on, the bikes are waiting."

"All right, but don't laugh."

She came into view and Flynn decided laughing was the very last thing he'd be likely to do. He'd definitely been off on the fit, he decided as she trotted down the steps. Of course, he'd deliberately bought them on the small side just to give her a hard time. What he hadn't realized was how incredible she'd look in skin-tight jeans. Jane Dearly had been hiding some extraordinary assets beneath those skirts of hers. Long, endless legs, moderately rounded thighs, hips that weren't the least boyish and a slender waist had turned ordinary denim into the sexiest bit of equipment he'd seen in a long time.

She marched past him to fetch another of her endless supply of lab coats and he silently groaned. His sweet chemist had the prettiest backside he'd ever seen stuffed into jeans. It was a crime against nature that she chose to cover all that up in shapeless dresses.

"Let's get out of here before I do something you'll regret," he said, heading for the door to take in a long draw of fresh air.

For the next hour, Flynn managed to ignore Jane's body, focusing instead on teaching her the rudiments of bike riding. Finally, triumphantly, she sailed down the sidewalk without losing her balance once. He watched with a bone-deep pleasure, aware that he hadn't felt so relaxed or happy in... He shook his head. Forever. He couldn't recall a single other time when he'd been himself around a woman. Natural. Open. Not constantly looking over his shoulder for trouble. He could let down his guard with Jane without fear or suspicion, and the realization scared the hell out of him.

He trusted her. Damn. This was bad. Very bad. First the lies, then the jeans, and now this. What had gotten into him? He'd been acting strangely from the minute a certain red-spectacled, bun-haired, unworldly chemist had slammed the door in his face. Even swathed from head to toe in cotton he'd found Jane difficult to resist. But in tight jeans, with those pretty green eyes lit with excitement, and her cheeks pink from the effort of mastering a simple bicycle, he'd become a man he didn't recognize.

And he didn't like it one little bit.

People couldn't be trusted—not even guileless bits of whimsy like Jane. The minute she found out about his scam, he'd be kissing wood again, her door slammed firmly in his face. Not that it mattered. He wouldn't do for a woman like her. She needed someone who'd take care of her when she lost herself in work, who'd tempt her out of her lab and into the real world, who'd make it his life's mission to tease smiles from her lips and gift each one with a soul-deep kiss. To give her the children she feared so she'd know that she'd been perfectly made for motherhood.

She rode toward him, grinning. "How do I look?" she asked as she whizzed past, pumping hard on the pedals.

"From this angle?" He sighed in sheer pleasure. "Magnificent."

To his amusement, her spine stiffened and she took a quick peek over her shoulder, no doubt to see what he found so magnificent. It was a mistake. She plowed straight into a boxwood hedge and landed magnificence-down in the fragrant bushes.

Flynn sighed, loping down the sidewalk to lend a hand. This had to stop. Time to get himself under control. Time to put their relationship back onto a professional footing where it belonged before Paulie decided to lend him a helping fist.

Time to get to work.

JANE FOUND FLYNN SPRAWLED in the middle of her backyard. She couldn't say what had distracted her from work and drawn her from the lab. After all, it was the first day in ages that he hadn't interrupted her, insisting on one of his crazy outings. Nor had Paulie disturbed her with hammering or drilling or endless questions. The quiet had driven her crazy.

Curious to see what Flynn was doing, she knelt alongside, intrigued to discover him watching a stream of carpenter ants. "Now you've really floored me."

"Every once in a while you have to stop and take a look

around," he explained. "Remember what it feels like to view the world from a fresh perspective instead of with jaded cynicism."

She stared at his bent head, understanding with bittersweet compassion where that comment had originated. She knew, beyond a shadow of a doubt, that he'd never had the opportunity as a child to laze in the grass beneath a summer sky and watch in fascination as a line of ants marched past his nose. She had, thanks to her uncles and their rather eclectic teaching methods. On more occasions than she could count. But then, she hadn't played Frisbee or mastered a bicycle until Flynn had come along.

She flung herself down beside him and folded her arms beneath her chin. "Sheriff Tucker wanted me to develop a bug poison to kill his ants," she offered.

"Sheriff Tucker is a man of keen insight when it comes to his fellow humans," he surprised her by saying. "But he's a bit lacking in appreciation of some of the finer creatures that have been put on this earth."

"I didn't know you'd met him."

"We have a passing acquaintance. But it's enough to realize that he assumes others are on the same wavelength as he is. I imagine it could be difficult to disabuse him of that notion."

"I guess that explains why I was so confused," she murmured.

"Confused about what?"

"Well... He never actually explained he wanted a poison. He just requested bug spray."

Flynn didn't say a word, but when she glanced over at him, she noticed his shoulders were shaking in a rather suspicious manner. "Let me guess," he eventually said. "He had every bug imaginable come crawling."

"Something like that. He wasn't too happy with me."

"I imagine not."

The silence drifted between them for a while, comfortable and lazy. She hated disturbing it, but some things were inevitable. "I thought I should warn you that I'm about to enter the next phase of my experiments."

"You've been experimenting? I hadn't noticed."

"Yes, well. There was the survey." She slanted him a quick, nervous glance. "You might recall that, since you didn't like it much. And I considered having you fill out a questionnaire, too, but decided against it. The last group of subjects didn't take it too well, so I figured you wouldn't, either."

"Subjects," he repeated, without turning his head. "Is that how you think of me? As a subject?"

For some reason, his question disturbed her, which was ridiculous since a person only reacted emotionally when their feelings were engaged. And hers weren't. Not even a little. "That's how I have to think of you," she insisted, "if I don't want to contaminate the results."

"And our outings? What have they been?"

She swallowed. Hard. "Opportunities to observe you in a natural setting."

"Got it."

He rolled her over in the grass and carefully worked an ant free from her hair, returning it to its designated path. "Why did you do that?" she whispered. "You could have simply crushed it."

Sadness dimmed his golden eyes. "I've learned to take care of fragile creatures. To protect them, particularly from myself."

"Oh. A protector. I like that." She gazed up at him uncertainly. "Are you mad at me for observing you?"

A shadow of his easy grin tilted his mouth. "Don't be ridiculous. We both agreed to a business relationship. I install a security system. You use me as a test subject.'' He flicked the tip of her nose. I'll tell you what. I was going to ask you out to dinner tonight, anyway. Why don't you bring along those questions so we keep this on a business footing. Maybe we can figure out what your last batch of testees objected to.''

''You'd be willing to do that?''

His smile faded. ''For you? Anything.''

CHAPTER SIX

CHECKING HER WATCH, Jane realized she only had five minutes to finish getting ready for Flynn. She didn't understand her nervousness. This was a simple experiment, no more, she assured herself for the twentieth time. She'd understand if this were an actual date. But it wasn't. In fact, the very last thing she wanted was another romantic relationship. Still, that didn't stop her from fingering the perfume bottle in her pocket, the one she'd created from her ninth formula. She frowned, catching her bottom lip between her teeth. She'd had twelve formulations to choose from. But had she gone with the next in line, LP-2? No, she'd gone straight for the cliché. LP-9, Love Potion number nine.

On the other hand, she'd done her best to ensure she didn't inadvertently taint the results. Despite knowing how much it exasperated Flynn, she'd slicked back her hair and fastened it in a knot at the nape of her neck and dressed in her plainest outfit. The simple gray dress would have done her grandmother proud—if she had a grandmother. Only a white Peter Pan collar and tiny pearl buttons from neck to hem relieved the ocean of gray that engulfed her.

A deep barking warned of Flynn's approach and a moment later the doorbell rang. Snatching up the atomizer of perfume, she dropped it into her purse along with her notebook and glasses. Shoving her feet into a pair of heels, she reached automatically for her lab coat, before catching herself. It was a telling moment, one she instinctively shied from, refusing to admit how important that one garment had become to her persona. Fortunately, she didn't have long to dwell on it. The doorbell rang again and the dog barked his way up the steps to help pressure her to greater speed.

Darting downstairs, she restrained Dipstick and pulled open the door. Of course, restraining a two-hundred-pound dog proved something of a challenge, particularly when he seemed determined to share his affections with most humans—with only a few notable exceptions. After gifting Jane with doggy kisses on every inch of exposed skin, he jumped up on Flynn and greeted him with a tongue to the cheek. Her nondate took the proffered affection with surprising equanimity.

As soon as the dog calmed, he shot Jane a look that made her want to go collect her lab coat again and button it all the way to her chin. "Ready?" he asked.

With a final, reluctant glance toward the steps leading to her bedroom, she nodded. "Sure. Let's go."

They left the house and followed the walkway to his rental car. "So where are we going?" she asked.

"I made reservations at a Greek restaurant overlooking the bay."

"Niko's?"

"That's the one. Hickory recommended it."

She couldn't remember ever having eaten there before. She definitely hadn't been with Mick, so she wouldn't have those memories to color her evening with Flynn. Not that she'd have permitted that to happen. She had better control of her emotions than to allow such a thing.

Niko's occupied one end of the shops lining the pier of Salmon Bay and offered a stunning view of the water and distant mountains. Jane particularly liked how they'd decorated the interior, or rather, the lack of decorations. The sheer simplicity of the restaurant made her breathe easier. Floor-to-ceiling windows took up three of the four sides of the two-story building. What walls there were had received a coating of fresh, crisp white paint. The golden oak floor blended nicely with the clear juniper they'd used for the trim work and ceiling beams. And each table had been spaced to afford an element of privacy.

The waitress escorted them upstairs, offering prime seats along the balcony railing. "A drink before you order?" she asked.

Flynn tilted his head to one side. "Sure, now that you mention it. How about some champagne?"

"Champagne?" Jane repeated. "Whatever for?"

He shrugged. "I saw your uncles drinking it. We can toast the success of your current experiment."

"Experiment?" The waitress jerked back, regarding Jane warily. "You're not that loony scientist, are you?"

"She's a scientist, though hardly loony," Flynn said with a smile. *Working his charm,* Jane thought in amusement. One flash of white teeth set in a ruggedly handsome face and the waitress instantly relaxed. "Don't worry—" he read her name tag "—Kelly. I'm today's lab rat."

"I wish you wouldn't call yourself that," Jane murmured. Needing to find something to occupy her hands, she snapped open her purse and dug through it for her notebook and glasses.

"You're already wearing them," he pointed out.

She lifted a hand to the bridge of her nose. "Oh. How silly."

"You're feeling self-conscious, aren't you?"

"Maybe a little."

He nodded toward her notebook. "I assume that has something to do with work?"

"You said we could review my survey." She glanced at

him hesitantly. "I have the questions jotted down in the notebook."

"You want to go over them? Decide which ones work and which don't?"

Was that irony? She couldn't be certain. She'd never been terribly good with subtlety or reading between the lines. "We agreed to stick to business, remember?" she informed him, just in case.

Flynn reached out and ran the tip of his index finger along the edge of her hand. "Then business it is."

Flame followed the simple caress, along with an utter unraveling of every muscle in her body. She'd never felt so...fluid. She stilled, afraid that if she moved so much as an inch, she'd slide under the table in a melted pool of feminine longing. What the hell was this? Flynn had touched her plenty of times before. And though each time had affected her, it had never been this dramatic.

Suddenly the room felt confined, like a tightly barred cage. As a test case, Flynn left a lot to be desired. He was opinionated, uncooperative and far too attractive. Somehow he managed to interfere with her thought processes, flustering her in ways no man ever had before. If she didn't regain control and fast, using Flynn as a test case would be a total waste. Her logic and reasoning could be called into question due to a personal bias and this particular experiment would have to be scrapped. She couldn't allow that to happen. Still... Her gaze ate him up. He was just so darned irresistible. In an effort to hide her reaction, Jane fixed her full attention on her notebook.

"You're hiding," Flynn murmured, just as the waitress returned with their champagne. "I wonder why?"

"You ready to order?" Kelly asked, flipping open her order pad.

Jane's nose remained buried in business. "I'm not choosy. I'll have today's special."

Flynn sighed. "For an appetizer we'll have the *tzatziki*."

Kelly offered a pleased smile. "You picked my favorite. Do you want a salad with that?"

"The *horiatiki*. We'll split a large." He pried the notebook from Jane's hand, forcing her to focus on the conversation. "Do you have any shellfish allergies?"

"No."

"Do you like shrimp?"

"Love it."

"Shrimp *mikrolimano* for Jane and I'll have the *exohicko*."

Kelly nodded. "Great choice. Our chef makes an outstanding sauce for the lamb. I'll have your appetizer up in a few minutes."

"No hurry," Jane assured her, holding out her hand for the notebook.

Flynn inclined his head. "None at all." He opened the booklet and flipped through the pages, lifting an eyebrow as he scanned her questions. "These are what you ask on your survey?"

"Yes." Her pen began an urgent tattoo. Realizing it betrayed her nervousness, she put it down. Instead, she played with her glasses, before dropping them with a groan. Yeah, that covered up her agitation much better. "The questions provide an informational baseline from which to proceed."

"Proceed? Proceed with *what?* Just what the hell are you cooking up in that lab? If you want my opinion, this information is none of your business."

She deliberately didn't answer his first slew of questions. "That information is necessary within the confines of my survey."

"Your survey, huh?" He gave her a pointed look. "The same one that scared off all your previous test subjects?"

"Yes, that one. If you'll recall, we were going to discuss that this evening. You were going to help me with my survey and how *not* to scare off the people I want to study."

"Oh, I remember. I'm the lab rat, you're the scientist." His gaze speared her. "I'd almost managed to forget our duly appointed roles this past week."

"That's at least the third time you've described yourself in those terms." A frown pulled her brows together. "Is that how you see yourself? As a lab rat?"

This time there was no mistaking his annoyance. "Aren't I?"

He straightened as he spoke, marking his presence with unmistakable male aggression. Here was a man unlike any she'd ever known, she realized uneasily. She sensed a power and authority that had been lacking in Mick, a strength equal to Hickory's but with a sensuous edge. He embodied the most potent of masculine traits, as well as the most annoying, and the sum total created a peculiar reaction, an imbalance she couldn't begin to understand.

"You're not a lab rat." She strove to sound brisk, but suspected the uneasy manner in which the words escaped gave her away.

He leaned close enough that without her glasses his features blurred, abating the hard edge in all but his voice. "Then stop treating me like one. I'm a man, in case you hadn't noticed."

"I noticed. Can't you tell how much I've noticed?" She snatched up her glasses and dumped them on top of her head. "You said this would be a business dinner, remember? You were going to tell me which question worked and which didn't. So, why are you so annoyed?"

"That was before I knew the nature of your business and

how intimate the subject matter," he shot right back. "I'm not going to sit here and discuss sexually provocative questions without knowing the reason. Now, would you care to explain what's going on?"

"I can't. It would taint the results."

"Either we do this my way or I walk." Flynn could see the word *walk* trembling on Jane's lips, knew that in another second she'd tell him to get lost, even though she'd kick herself afterward. Before she could, he fired off one final comment. "I'm sure you can get someone from town who's willing to cooperate with your survey."

Fumbling in her purse, she pulled out another set of glasses, apparently forgetting about the orange ones she'd stuck in her hair. She shoved the new ones on her uppity little nose and glared at him, her annoyance tough to take seriously when surrounded by oversize neon blue frames encrusted with iridescent sparkles. "You're not being fair."

"Tough. You want to keep this business? Fine. Explain to me how these questions relate to business."

"Excuse the interruption," Kelly said, setting a platter between them. "One *tzatziki,* two plates and some pita bread."

"That looks good." Jane seized on the opening with transparent relief. "What is it?"

"Yogurt with crushed garlic and grated cucumbers," Flynn explained. "Try it. It has a bit of a bite. But then, that's how I like most things in life."

Her mouth eased into a reluctant smile. "Somehow that doesn't surprise me."

"You still haven't answered my question," he prompted. "What's this study about?"

"Flynn, if I answered that question, I couldn't use you as a test subject. Do you want me to scrap my research to date simply to satisfy your curiosity?"

"No. That wouldn't be fair." He regarded her through narrowed eyes. "I'll tell you what. Will you explain it once you've finished with your experiment?"

"Absolutely."

"Fair enough. You want my opinion on these questions. Let's see what we have." Flynn leaned back in the chair and thrust his long legs out in front of him, thumbing through her notebook. "What sort of woman attracts you? Now, that's a legitimate question and easy enough to answer. All women attract me. You can keep that question. I can't see anyone objecting to it."

"Wait a minute. Time out." She studied him over the rim of her champagne flute. "Come on, Flynn. You don't expect me to buy your answer, do you?"

"Why not?" he asked pleasantly.

"Because every man I've ever met has a preference, whether he admits it or not. Some are attracted more to a woman who's short. Or tall. Or thin. Or voluptuous. Or young. Or blond. Or brunette."

"You're right. I'll take any of the above."

"You really don't care?"

"I don't care what she looks like. But I'll admit there are a few qualities that are essential."

"I thought so." She lifted an eyebrow. "Like what?"

"She needs to be intelligent. She should have a lively sense of curiosity and an even livelier sense of humor. It's also a good sign if she feels passionate about something."

"Passionate about something." She stared blankly. "I don't understand."

Now, why didn't that surprise him? Flynn slouched farther back in his chair and sipped his champagne. "I mean, that feeling passionate about something—anything—gives a person a zest for life. They're fuller, richer, more exciting to be around. You're passionate, for instance."

"I am?"

"Sure. You're passionate about your science."

"I…I hadn't thought about it that way."

"What about you? What attracts you to a man?"

To his surprise, she gave it serious consideration. Was she actually going to answer his questions? Amazing. "I'd have to say most of the qualities you've mentioned," she said at length. "Not that I've found anyone like that yet."

He couldn't resist probing. "What? No special scientist types in your sordid past?"

He wasn't surprised when she winced. "No. Not any longer."

"I gather that wasn't always the case?" For some reason, his question came out very gently. Encouraging. Downright sincere. Maybe those sparkle glasses had affected him more than he'd realized. Or maybe he simply knew what an asshole Barstow was and sympathized with what she must have gone through.

"No," she admitted. "It wasn't."

"And…?"

She retreated, drawing visibly inward. Wariness made her look less like the brisk scientist and more like the woman hiding beneath the lab coat. Even though she hadn't worn it to dinner, it cloaked her as surely as if she had. "And I learned to keep business separate from pleasure," she replied lightly.

"Even when you're attracted to business?"

"Yes. Even then." She plucked her notebook from his hands and looked up the next question. "We've established what attracts you in a woman. What qualities are off-putting? That's a safe-enough question for the survey, isn't it?"

"Absolutely. And I'll even answer it. I can't stand a woman who either can't make up her mind or who changes it more often than the weather. I prefer someone who knows what she wants and goes after it."

"Anything else?"

He hesitated and then opened a door, one he didn't open very often. "Just one more thing."

She put down her pen and really, truly looked at him. He hoped she finally saw the man instead of the test subject. "Do you want to tell me what it is?" she asked cautiously.

"I can't stand being manipulated or controlled. It..." Tension sliced deep crags into his face. "It used to happen a lot when I was a kid."

"Which made you feel powerless?"

"You got it. What about you?" he asked. "What sort of qualities in a man turn you off?"

"Dishonesty. I despise dishonest people."

Her reply had come so fast and with such an undercurrent of emotion, Flynn immediately thought of Barstow. It also confirmed what he already knew. She'd be furious when she discovered all he'd kept from her—and all her uncles had neglected to mention. The reasons wouldn't matter, only the fact that she'd been lied to. Again.

Hell. This was the precise sort of situation he'd sworn to avoid from now on. How many times did he have to repeat a mistake before he learned his lesson? He'd already screwed up more times than he could count, mainly due to poor choices. He'd sworn that would change. And it had...right up until three crazy old coots roped him into their conspiracy. Of course he had a choice.

He could tell Jane the truth.

Flynn swallowed more champagne and leaned forward. "Jane—"

"Next. How many dates before you sleep with a woman for the first time?"

What a thing to ask a man. He closed his eyes, unable to

confess his own particular sins in the face of such an outrageous question. A husky laugh escaped as he gave up trying to be noble. To hell with it. He'd just discuss Jane's survey and hope for the best. "I don't suppose you'd care to find out through personal experience?"

"No, thanks." Prim. Businesslike. But murmured in a voice as sultry as hell. A voice, moreover, that belonged in a bedroom, not conducting an interrogation in a public restaurant.

"No, huh?" He sighed. "A shame."

"Well?" She peered over the tops of her glittery frames. "How many dates does it take before you sleep with a woman? Keep or discard?"

"Honey, that's not a question most men are gonna be comfortable answering. You must know it depends on the woman and the circumstances."

"But on average?"

"Forget it, Jane." He shoved the *tzatziki* to one side. "Are you really going to keep that one on your survey? Is that a question you'd want to answer?"

"Six."

"Excuse me?"

"I wait precisely six dates before sleeping with a man."

"You're kidding." Flynn reached for his glass, almost tipping it over.

"Not at all," Jane insisted. "We kiss on the first date. No tongues. I allow that on the second. On the third date, some light petting. Heavy petting on the fourth. On the fifth date, anything goes except actual lovemaking. That comes on date number six."

He stared at her in open disbelief. All he could think about was Jane and Barstow, working their way up to date number six. Had they made it that far before the SOB had hurt her? Or had she realized he didn't have the qualities she needed in a mate before then? Hell, he hoped she'd seen through him by the third date. Check that. By the second. Just imagining the jerk unbuttoning Jane's ugly gray dress and putting his hands on her—

A choked sound from the far side of the table distracted him and Flynn caught the unmistakable gleam of laughter in her eyes. "You should see your face. You believed me, didn't you?"

Believed her? As methodical as she was? Hell, yes, he'd believed her. He shook his head, grinning. "You got me good, sweetheart. I'll give you that. Six dates before— Damn."

"As if. That's what you get for making assumptions about me," she scolded.

He held up his hands. "Okay. Fair enough. What are some of your other questions?"

"Nothing you'll want to answer." She checked her notebook. "How sexually experienced are you, the frequency of your sexual encounters, and how long it's been since the last one."

Dishes rattled ominously. For a moment, it looked like their salad would be decorating the floor. At the last instant, Kelly righted her tray. "*Horiatiki* for two," she announced, struggling to keep a straight face.

With more speed than grace, she dumped the salad plates in front of them. Crisp slices of cucumbers and peppers were accented with red tomatoes and white chunks of feta cheese. Jane diligently dug in to see if it tasted as good as it appeared. After several minutes, she lifted her head and peeked cautiously around.

"Just so you know, those *were* legitimate questions on the survey."

Flynn tore apart a crispy bread roll and popped a chunk into his mouth. "Do you really want to know how long it's been? Or are you more interested in how the encounter went?''

"No, of course not! You don't have to answer any of the questions.'' She cleared her throat. "Unless you want to.''

"To be honest, I'm a little touchy about some of these subjects.''

"Like your last sexual encounter?'' she dared to ask.

"Yeah. Like that one.''

"I gather it didn't end well?''

"Is that another of your survey questions?''

"No,'' she admitted. "I was making a stab at normal conversation.'' She peeked at him over her glasses. "How am I doing?''

Tension gave a rigid set of his shoulders and his fingers clenched his champagne flute. "Not bad, considering.''

"You mean, considering how lousy I am at this?''

He actually smiled. "Yeah. Considering that.''

Going for broke, she asked another. "So your last relationship ended badly. I take it that one was an exception?''

"I do my best to please. Some relationships are more successful than others.''

"I can sympathize with that.'' Slowly she removed her glasses. "Mick... Mick Barstow was my last relationship.'' She fought to open up to him, to be as frank as he'd been. "It didn't end well.''

"Mick's your scientist friend?''

"Yes.''

"Am I getting the fallout from that?''

"Probably.'' She moistened her lips. "It's not fair to color you with his paintbrush, I know.''

"But you're still hurting.''

"My pride is. The rest of me will survive.''

"Want to tell me what happened?''

She shrugged, drawing the atomic structure for hydrogen

in the tablecloth with the earpiece of her glasses. It was a distraction she employed whenever her emotions threatened to get out of control. For the first time, her technique failed. Hydrogen was too simple an element to successfully distract her. With Flynn, she suspected she'd have to sketch a far weightier element. One that had four or five orbitals instead of just a single ring.

"It's nothing new. I thought he'd fallen in love with me. Instead he'd fallen in love with my research. By the time I discovered my error, he'd convinced me to make him my partner and had attached his name to as much of my research as he could." She spared Flynn a quick look. "Nice little scam, huh?"

His expression closed over and he avoided her gaze. Didn't he believe her? Jane almost laughed at the irony. From the moment she'd first met Flynn Morgan, she'd doubted and questioned every word he'd uttered. If she'd thought about it, she'd have justified her reaction to him as natural skepticism, an appropriate trait in her line of research. But it didn't go over very well in their current setting. And even though she tried to convince herself that dinner was business-related, it certainly felt personal.

Too personal.

"What did you do once you found out what Mick wanted?" Flynn asked.

"I kicked him out."

"Had he contributed to any of your research?"

"Yes."

"How did you handle the division?"

At some point, the inquisition had done a one-eighty. Now she was answering the questions Flynn fired at her. "I returned his notes, kept my own. The parts that we worked on jointly will bear his name, as well as mine. The rest will have mine alone."

"Seems fair."

"I thought so. He didn't."

"Why are you telling me all this?"

"Because I wanted to," she admitted. And it was true. "Person to person, instead of scientist to lab rat."

He rewarded her with a grin that set off warning sirens. "I hope you don't regret it in the morning."

"I hope not, either."

But she suspected she would. Something was happening between them and it had little, if anything, to do with her experiment. If she didn't call a halt to it soon, she'd regret it—regret it far more than anything she'd experienced after Mick.

JANE STOOD IN THE LADIES' ROOM and stared at the atomizer she held. Okay. She didn't dare wait any longer to give this a try. She'd had an opportunity to judge Flynn's behavior quite a bit this evening, to observe how they'd interacted and how he treated her as a person and as a woman. Now she could see if that changed after she used the perfume.

She hesitated. Of course, she could always wait until the next time they were together and try it then. She didn't have to wear it tonight. She could use this opportunity to ask her questions and let it go at that.

"Oh, stop it, Jane," she muttered. "You know why you don't want to use the perfume." Flynn didn't like manipulative women. And if this wasn't manipulative, she didn't know what was.

"Excuse me? Did you say something?"

Jane looked up, not realizing someone had joined her. "Sorry. I'm just talking to myself."

"I...see."

She held up her perfume. "I was trying to decide whether or not to wear this."

"Pretty bottle. Whose scent is it?"

"It's my own." She sprayed it into the air.

The woman sniffed. "Oh, my. That's wonderful. You created this yourself? Are you serious?"

"Do you like it?"

"I *love* it. Why in the world would you hesitate using it?"

Jane thrust her glasses farther up on the bridge of her nose. "Because I don't want to unduly influence the man I'm with."

The woman stared. "You don't want to—"

"No." Jane frowned at the atomizer, tossing it lightly from hand to hand. "Wouldn't you rather have a man respond to you naturally, based on who you are as a person, instead of reacting to how you smell?"

"No. Anything that helps reel in your fish is fair game as far as I'm concerned." She eyed Jane's dress. "And you, hon, need all the help you can get. I suggest you give that stuff a squirt, unbutton your dress, pull your hair out of that bun and ditch the specs."

"I need my glasses to see."

"That's why they invented contact lenses."

"These are reading glasses."

"Try squinting." The woman caught Jane's atomizer midair and sprayed herself with it. "Thanks, sweetie. That really is a great scent. You ought to market it."

"Oh, dear. I'm not sure you should have—"

The woman held out the bottle and blasted Jane with it, too. "Now you can honestly say you aren't responsible for unduly influencing your man. I'll be happy to take the blame and you can tell him I said so."

The woman returned the bottle and sauntered out the door, hips swinging. Jane sighed. Well, that settled that. Apparently the second half of her experiment would continue on schedule. She turned and stared at herself in the mirror, her frown deepening. It wasn't that she disagreed with the woman's comments. But attracting a man wasn't her goal. She needed to judge Flynn's reaction to her with the only variable being her perfume. If she wore her hair down and unbuttoned her dress at this stage, it would taint the results.

Stop procrastinating, Jane! The deed was done. If Flynn felt she'd manipulated him, she'd deal with that later. Before she could find another excuse for postponing her experiment, she returned the atomizer to her purse. Too bad, she thought. Now she'd never know for certain whether Flynn would have been attracted to her without undue influence.

Snapping her purse closed, she hesitated. Whipping off her glasses, she dumped them into the purse, as well. Now she really was being ridiculous. It had to stop. It would be weeks before she had new test subjects. Flynn was her one-and-only chance to prove her uncles' support hadn't been misplaced. And after her experience with Mick, she was crazy to consider indulging in another romantic relationship. Spinning away from the mirror, she reentered the restaurant.

Time to get to work.

CHAPTER SEVEN

"HOW WAS THE SHRIMP?" Flynn asked.

Jane offered a gut-twisting smile. "Incredible," she enthused. "If I'd known Niko's meals were so good, I'd have tried this place ages ago."

"You've never been before?" Now, why didn't that surprise him? "Do your keepers lock you in that lab twenty-four hours a day?"

"No. I set my own hours." She evaded his gaze, which told him all he needed to know. "I just like to work."

"Yeah, right. What you mean is, you don't function well in the real world, so you avoid it whenever possible. Work comes first, right?"

She cleared her throat. "Speaking of which... Are you ready to finish the survey?"

Aw, hell. He should have seen that coming. Whenever she got flustered, she retreated into that damn notebook. He stabbed a final bit of lamb wrapped in filo pastry. "Sure. Why not?"

"There's just a few more questions."

The lenses magnified her dark green eyes, softening them, making them incredibly vulnerable. He didn't think he'd ever known a woman with eyes quite that shade. They were unusual, just as she was unusual. Her head bent as she studied her notebook, revealing the pale length of her neck. A tiny mole resided just behind her ear. God, it was sweet. He hadn't noticed it before, but it served to emphasize the graceful curve of her neck.

For the first time, he appreciated the fact that she wore her hair up instead of hiding that tempting little freckle. How would she respond if he kissed his way from mole to shoulder? Would she react like a woman or revert to scientist-mode?

"Here we are." She scribbled a quick notation. "What do you consider to be a successful date?"

"I don't see why anyone would object to that question. Now, you answer me a question."

"But—"

"Hey, it's only fair." He waited until he had her full attention and asked the question that had been driving him crazy for the past half hour. "What do you have on under that dress? Silk or cotton?"

Her deliciously wide mouth dropped open. "I beg your pardon?"

"Do you only dress like a nun on the outside? Or does it go right through to the skin?"

Her mouth closed, forming a very unkissable straight line. "This is your way of getting back at me for asking those questions, isn't it?"

He sighed. "I guess that means you also won't tell me whether you're a panty-hose woman or the lacy-garter sort."

"You're right. I won't."

Kelly appeared at his elbow, her face carefully expressionless. "Would you care for anything else?" she asked blandly as she removed their dinner plates. "Coffee? Tea? Dessert? A fire hose?"

"Coffee," Flynn requested.

Jane folded her arms across her chest. "Tea."

He snorted. "That figures."

Silence reigned until Kelly returned with their drinks. Jane busied herself steeping her tea. He busied himself blistering his tongue on his coffee. Apparently satisfied with the viscosity of her tea, she next fussed over adding an impressive amount of sugar to her cup before squirting everything in sight with lemon.

"Sorry," she murmured.

He sighed, swiping the juice from his mouth and chin. "Forget it. I deserve it for being so rude."

She bit down on her lip, a lip he'd gotten damn possessive over. "You weren't rude."

"Sure I was. And you were right." He gave her a direct look. "I suspect I was getting back at you for some of those questions you asked. A little quid pro quo. I apologize."

She took a quick drink of tea, the cup clattering against the saucer. "To be honest, I've realized something."

"What's that?"

"Mixing business with pleasure doesn't work. And it's a mistake to try."

"You know something? You're right." He finished off his coffee and stood. "Ready to go?"

She didn't argue. "All set." He yanked his wallet from his back pocket and removed several bills, dropping them to the table. She gestured toward the money. "I'm supposed to pay for the evening."

"Not when you're with me."

Flynn didn't say a single word the entire way to the car. Once there, he opened the door for her—ever the gentleman—and waited while she slid into her seat. Was it her imagination, or did he sniff her? She clutched her purse between her fingers and wished with all her heart that she hadn't been squirted with the perfume. Maybe the evening would have ended differently if she'd just stuck to business, as she'd planned.

"I'm sorry tonight didn't go well," she said the minute he climbed into the car.

"Forget it."

"I..." She made a futile gesture. "I'm not much of a people person."

"Yeah. I noticed."

"I'm far more successful in the lab."

"I'll have to take your word for it."

"I'm serious, Flynn."

"I'm well aware that you're serious."

They were fast approaching her house and she didn't want the evening to end until she'd had an opportunity to make amends—or at least, amend things the best she knew how. "Right now, my research is everything. Maybe you think it shouldn't be, but that doesn't change the fact that it is. And..." Was it her imagination or did the small bottle of perfume nestled within her purse weigh more heavily than normal against her thighs? "And those questions, as explicit as they were, are necessary for my research."

"It's not the questions I objected to."

"It was trying to keep the evening on a business footing, right?" A strand of hair came loose from the knot at her nape and she tried to slick it back into place. It sprang stubbornly against her temple, curling uncontrollably. "We should have gone for social."

"Honey, can you even tell the difference between the two?"

She responded to his irritation with a little of her own. "I'm not that oblivious."

"Keep telling yourself that. Hell, you can't even conduct a conversation without reverting to science-speak."

"Science-speak? Oh! How sophomoric. I should have known trying to keep tonight strictly business wouldn't work. That's why I don't like mixing the two."

"You don't get it, do you?"

"Get what?"

His hands tightened on the wheel. "You were right earlier. You should have put business aside for just one damn night." He shot her an infuriated look. "But I suspect you wouldn't know how."

They turned into the driveway and she swallowed. How odd. Her throat felt tight and she fought the unexpected rush of tears. Why? It wasn't as if Flynn had told her anything new. It was just... Coming from him it hurt more than it should have. He switched off the engine and climbed from the car. This time she didn't wait for him to open her door, but jumped out and hastened around the hood to his side.

Explanations scalded her tongue, but none of them seemed appropriate. Flynn didn't say anything, either. He planted a hand under her elbow and practically marched her down the walkway toward the house. They reached the bottom of the porch steps and Jane slowed, unwilling to allow the evening to end on such a sour note.

Turning, she broke into speech. "I really am sorry."

He gave an easy shrug. "Forget it."

She twisted her hands together. "You don't understand and I'd like to explain."

"Okay." He folded his arms across an impossibly broad chest, drawing his shirt tight enough to reveal the delicious definition of muscles. "Give it your best shot."

Jane looked hastily away. "I don't often get the chance to experiment on someone."

"I suspect you take the opportunity on a regular basis. Isn't that part of the problem?"

She bowed her head. "Yes," she whispered. "People around here aren't too happy about that."

Flynn released his breath in a gusty sigh. Aw, hell. Why'd she have to go and show him that pale white—incredibly vulnerable—expanse of neck? "Maybe if you treated them like people instead of lab rats, they'd be more friendly."

"That's what Milton the bartender said."

His gaze softened. "But you didn't listen, did you?"

She shook her head, knocking her glasses askew. "No."

"Because your experiments are more important than people's feelings." He didn't phrase it as a question.

It struck him as criminal that a woman so brilliant, a woman gifted with such potential, couldn't comprehend the most basic facts of human nature. It was a damn shame, especially since she hid quite a few fine qualities beneath the starchiness of her lab coat.

"I don't mean to hurt people," she confessed.

"Don't you understand, Jane?" He cupped her chin and tilted her face, forcing her to look at him. "You don't *see* them as people. That's your whole problem. All you see is how they fit into your current project."

"What am I supposed to do?" Frustration edged her voice. "There are occasions when I need test subjects."

He couldn't help smiling. "And the town of Salmon Bay is chock-full of them, is that it?"

"Something like that," she muttered.

"What about friends? Or don't they matter to you?"

She pulled free of his grasp. "My work fulfills me. It provides everything I need."

"Does it?"

"Yes!"

He caught hold of her again, drawing her close, inhaling her delicious scent. "So you don't need friends. But what about a lover, Jane? Or don't you need that, either?"

She was so close he felt her slight tremor. His last question had hit and hit hard. He heard the desperate give and take of her breath, the hitch that warned of emotions on the brink. With that one question, he'd vanquished the scientist and revealed the woman—a woman as appealing as any he'd ever held.

Gently, he plucked her glasses from the tip of her nose, followed by the pair perched on top of her head. He tossed them both to the grass. They bounced into the garden, winking at him from beneath a hydrangea bush. Her arms slowly dropped to her sides and her purse slipped from her shoulder. It thudded on one of the decorative—and unfortunately, jagged—rocks lining the walkway. There was a faint tinkling of glass.

"Oops," he murmured.

"I think I broke my perfume."

Sure enough, the most enticing of scents drifted upward and enclosed them in a cloud of sweetness. "It's unusual. Your perfume, I mean. I was going to say something earlier." His mouth twisted. "For some reason, I got distracted."

"Thank you. I've had unusual success with this particular scent."

He fought to think, a near impossibility given the circumstances. "Success?"

Her hands fluttered in the darkness, finding the front of his shirt and smoothing the crisp cotton. "Success with the perfume formulation."

"You...?" Her soft touch threatened to drive him insane. "You created it?"

"It's what I do. Didn't I mention that?"

"Lab work. Experiments. Rats. Weird questions. Damn weird questions. That's all you mentioned."

"Oh." She moistened her lips and he followed the movement with hungry eyes. "Well, I create perfumes. Very special perfumes."

There was a question he needed to pose, a logical progression to their conversation. But he was damned if he could come up with what he should be asking. All he could think about was taking that mouth with his and discovering if it tasted as delicious as it looked. He lowered his head, giving her ample time to pull away. Then he surrendered to the need that had been steadily growing from the first moment he'd seen her.

He kissed her, taking a bone-deep pleasure in tasting the most luscious mouth he'd ever sealed with his. He'd half expected her to cut the kiss off mid-liplock. Instead, she opened to him, her tongue slipping home with delightful aggression. If he thought her smile and laughter wreaked havoc, it was nothing compared to the rich flavor of her. Lemony tea mingled with champagne, her breath warm and delicious and ripe for plundering.

Desire slammed through him. He molded her closer, binding them together, struggling to take it slowly, to give her a simple if thorough kiss before going on his way. He caught her lower lip between his teeth and tugged. Just one simple kiss and he'd leave. One more.

Okay, maybe two.

"Flynn?"

"Don't talk. Kiss."

"I have to ask you something."

"Later."

"No, really." She pulled back ever so slightly, a tiny frown puckering her brow. The streetlights radiated across the planes of her face. The soft glow emphasized the high cheekbones and ripe, full mouth, and turned her eyes to ebony. "I have to know. Why are you kissing me?"

"*What?*"

"Kissing me. Why are you doing it?"

Desire cooled. "Why the hell do you think?"

Her hands curled into his shirt and clung. "I don't know.

I swear I don't. Is it... Is it irresistible? Is it because you can't help yourself?''

"More questions, Jane?''

She bowed her head, exposing the nape of her neck again. "Yes," she whispered.

He couldn't stand it a moment longer. Thrusting his hands deep into her hair, he scattered the clips holding it in place. To his amazement, tight curls corkscrewed around her face and down her back. Her hair was thick and long, far more so than he'd have guessed. Loose, it enhanced the delicacy of her features. A breeze caught in the ringlets, whipping them in a wild disorder contrary to her nature. Or at least, contrary to the nature she chose to reveal.

"Well, well," he breathed. "Would you look at this."

She lifted a self-conscious hand to her hair. "It's curly."

"Incredible." He filled his hands to overflowing. "Why the hell do you slick it back when you could have..." He allowed her curls to filter through his fingers, a disordered tumble of sheer femininity.

She made a small sound of disgust. "It gets in my way when I work. It could compromise my experiments or cause an accident." She poked his chest with her index finger. "I once knew a woman who melted her hair because she didn't take proper precautions. It never did grow back right. It took the curl right out." Her brow wrinkled. "Or did it put the curl in? I never could get that story straight."

He groaned in exasperation. "Fine. Tie it up when you're working. But leave it down when you're not in the lab." He nuzzled the silken curls. "You don't need to be a scientist all the time, do you?"

"You don't understand—"

He scooped her close and she broke off, her breath coming in tiny, urgent gasps. He took it as a good sign. "There's something between us, isn't there?'' he demanded. ''Do you still wonder why I kissed you?''

''I had to be sure.''

''Feeling insecure?''

''It's just that you're... And I'm...'' Her hand released his shirt long enough to flutter through the air. ''Oh, hell, Flynn. I needed to make sure you wanted to kiss me. That you weren't doing it just because that's how you always end your dates.'' Her brows lowered. ''Even the bad ones.''

''Honey, I've been wanting to try out your lips since we first met.''

He tucked her close once more, taking her mouth in another gentle kiss. But at the first touch, the desire he'd felt earlier shot out of control. With a groan, he cupped her neatly rounded backside and lifted her against him. And then he stroked into her mouth, deep and slow and thorough. This was crazy. Insane. They stood on the sidewalk in front of her house, and all he could think about was unbuttoning her dress and finally putting to rest the most important question of the evening....

Cotton or silk, panty hose or garters.

She squirmed, her breasts flattening against his chest. ''I shouldn't be feeling like this.''

''That makes two of us.''

Her arms formed a stranglehold around his neck. ''No, I mean, I *really* shouldn't be feeling like this. It's okay for you. Expected, perhaps. But I'm supposed to keep an analytical distance.''

He chuckled. ''Give it up, sweetheart. You can't be a scientist all the time. Every once in a while you have to let the woman out of the lab.''

She eased back. Confusion haunted her expression, underscoring some private, internal debate. He could guess what it concerned. Barstow and this damn experiment of hers. No doubt she had a rule against mixing pleasure with lab rats.

She swept her lips with her tongue. Her eyes widened and she jerked her gaze upward to fasten on his mouth. In that instant he knew he had her. "I can taste you," she murmured in surprised delight.

"And?"

"Nice. Very nice."

He hooked a finger in the front of her dress and gave a little tug. "Then come closer, honey, and stop being such a stranger."

Jane resisted, but the top button slipped free, exposing the hollow of her throat. Just that innocent bit of pale skin nearly unmanned him. He swore beneath his breath. How was that possible? He'd made love to more women than he could count. Hell, he'd turned down more women than he could count. But what he'd felt about those others bore no comparison to what he felt for Jane.

He gave another experimental tug at her dress, a more determined one, and she slammed full-tilt into him. Her enthusiasm caught him by surprise. He tripped over the same rock that had broken her perfume and stumbled onto the lawn. His heel hit the dew-slicked grass and he went down as if he'd been poleaxed.

"Flynn!" She tumbled into his arms, her elbow finding his gut with distressing accuracy.

His breath escaped in a pained grunt. "Right here."

"Oh, no. Flynn? Are you all right?" She wriggled around a bit, which didn't help him regain his breath any. "Did I hurt you?"

"Not yet, but I figure it's only a matter of time."

"I'm sorry. Sometimes I can be a bit of a klutz—"

Laughter rumbled through him and he cushioned her more firmly against his chest, buried beneath gray cotton and blond-streaked curls. "How is this your fault, when I'm the one who tried to rip your buttons off?"

"I hadn't quite thought of it in that way." She wriggled around some more and his laugh turned to a groan. "You are hurt!"

"Yeah, honey. It hurts bad."

"Oh, dear." She leveled herself upward, straining more of her buttons.

Unable to resist, he plucked one more free. A hint of lace appeared in the deepening vee of her neckline. Using his knees, he gently eased her legs apart so she straddled him. Gray cotton billowed protectively around them. Hell, maybe he'd find out what she wore under her dress, after all. *Then* he'd give her a simple good-night kiss and go on his way.

"If you'd just let me get up, I could—"

He managed another realistic grimace. "Don't leave me."

"I won't. Where do you hurt?"

His groan turned to laughter and back to a groan again. "Jane, honey, as tempted as I am by that line, I'd be a total heel if I took this any further. Right now, I'm just a bit of a heel. Give me any more cause and I'm afraid I'll be forced to go into full-blown heeldom."

"Excuse me?"

"Now, I know Mick did a number on you. But even you can't ride a man who's spreadeagled in the grass, with your buttons half-undone—my fault, I confess—and your dress hiked to your thighs, and be naive enough to ask where it hurts."

Jane was smart, he'd give her that. It didn't take more than five short seconds for comprehension to dawn in those forest-dark eyes of hers. Any other woman would have either hit him where it would live long in his memory of least-favorite moments. Or she'd offer a sultry, knowing look and take that hurt to new and delightful heights. He braced himself, half expecting Jane to inflict the least pleasurable of the two options. Instead, she proved that he'd filled his arms with a woman far different from any who'd gone before.

She glanced carefully around and then reached for the next button binding her dress together. One by one the buttons loosened until she'd popped open every last one of them.

Lace. Hell. And silk. And... No! He couldn't believe his innocent little scientist was a garter woman. Hot damn.

"There. Does that make the hurt better?"

"Not even close."

He hooked a finger in the front of her bra and pulled her down so her gray granny sack tented protectively around them and her taut wriggling body covered every inch of him. Then he plundered. Over and over until he was certain he'd gotten it right. He slipped his hands beneath their improvised tent. Starting at the top, he worked his way down. Well, for crying out loud. Who'd have thought such a crisp little lab coat could hide all these lush curves? To hell with stopping with one polite kiss. This called for serious investigation.

He levered upward, dragging her along. She murmured a mild complaint, but he forced himself to ignore it. "Wrap yourself around me," he ordered.

She stared blankly for a moment, then caught on. She was quick, despite the handicap of being a scientist. And speed was a definite asset when it came to their current situation. Showing delightful dexterity, she locked her arms and legs around him and hung on. He staggered upward, tripped on her purse and almost crashed to the ground again. Snagging the strap, he made it to the porch steps before foundering.

"You stopped kissing me," she accused him.

"Yeah, that happens when I need to breathe."

"Inside. We need to get inside."

He fought his way up the steps, one by one. "No, we need to get naked."

They sprawled across the porch. Somehow she'd lost most of her dress along the way and one shoe. For a prissy scientist, she sure as hell knew her way around passion. He grabbed the front doorknob, thanking every lucky star he possessed—which weren't too damn plentiful—that she'd left it unlocked again. He shoved it open. Then, using every ounce of remaining strength, he hitched the strap of her purse over one shoulder, hitched his half-naked date over the other, caught a hunk of gray cotton between his teeth and dragged all his possessions over the threshold.

He collapsed in the foyer, breathing hard. Looking over his shoulder, he saw her shoe lying drunkenly in the middle of the doormat. Screw it. He kicked the door closed and addressed himself to more important matters. Like ripping off her bra. Putting thought to action, he sprang her tightly caged breasts from their prison, filling his hands with them. They expressed their gratitude by pearling before his eyes.

"Beautiful," he murmured.

They were every bit as tempting as the pale skin at her nape and the hollow of her throat. But not quite as tempting as that mouth, or the dark green eyes that had grown slumbrous with passion. She lay beneath him, her limbs flung outward, her mouth a glistening temptation, her breasts shimmering ever so slightly. He could take her right here in the foyer and she wouldn't lift a finger to stop him. She was as unlocked and open to invasion as her house.

He shook his head. The foyer was too painful and he wanted it to be good. Or at least comfortable. Hell, he'd settle for any surface that didn't have splinters.

"Cushions," he explained concisely, heaving himself to his knees. "We need cushions."

"In the living room."

He almost thought he'd have to drag her down the hallway the same way he'd dragged her in here. But she surprised him. Showing an amazing amount of energy, she ripped his shirt open, spewing buttons in every direction. They pinged off the wall, off the door, off the floor and off his nose.

"Sorry."

"Don't mention it."

"We were working on cushions?" he prompted.

She sat up, raining kisses across his belly, up the center of his chest to his chin. "Follow me."

"You're still sitting on the floor and if I get down that low again, I won't be mobile any time soon."

"Oh. Right."

She scrambled upward, her breasts swaying beneath the effort. For some reason her feet found it confusing to have one shoe on and one off. She flung out her arms, pinwheeling—a sight that would live long in his memory. Then she toppled over backward, landing hard on her backside. Flynn fought to suppress his laughter. It wasn't too difficult, considering the painful ache gathering in his groin. Looked like he'd have to take charge if they were ever going to get down to pleasure.

"Which way?" he asked.

She pointed. Okay, he could do this. After all, his life depended on it. He grabbed her arm and heaved, pulling her upward again. Planting his shoulder in her belly, he lifted. Her pert little bottom wriggled close to his face. He gave it a friendly pat. Nice. Very nice. He gave it another friendlier pat. It wriggled even more. If he didn't find those cushions soon, they'd end up on the floor again.

Heading in the general direction she'd indicated, he found the living room. Good. No splinters, after all. There were cushions. Lots and lots of cushions. He dropped her to the couch and she bounced right off, fortunately taking a number of cushions with her. Thrusting curls from her face, she fixed him with a decidedly grumpy expression.

"Look where I am again," she complained.

He looked, and that one glance stole his reply clean away. She sat perched on the cushions, her hair in a tousled mass of ringlets that drifted well below her shoulders. They even covered her breasts, all but the blush-pink tips that poked impudently through the curls. Her hands were folded in her lap, covering the scrap of silk that passed as panties. Tinted stockings inched up impossibly long legs, taunting him with trim ankles, slender calves and dimpled knees. The taunting ended at the palest, prettiest, most kissable thighs he'd ever seen on a woman.

Dragging his ripped shirt off his shoulders, he yanked open his belt, unzipped his trousers, kicked off his shoes and stripped down to skin. All the while, Jane sat there like a properly trained scientist, wide-eyed with well-placed curiosity, her lush mouth parted just enough for him to see her clever little tongue.

"Your turn," he announced.

"Yes, please."

He'd do this in an orderly fashion, he decided as he joined her on the cushions. That should appeal to the scientist in her. He'd start at the top and work his way down. He filled his hands with curls and her mouth with his tongue. It was a great way to start. She moaned, cupping his raspy jaw in her palms. Tipping back her head, she offered him greater access and he seriously thought he'd lose control right then and there. But he couldn't stop. Loving her mouth consumed him. He wanted it to be right for her. Perfect. He wanted her to know that she was more than just a scientist.

She was a woman.

Finally he tore his mouth from hers. "That was my first stop. Time for this bus to move on to stop number two."

Her brow crinkled in delightful confusion. "What's stop number two?"

"I'll show you."

He worked downward. Methodical. Orderly. Desperate. Her breasts beckoned, pouting at the length of time he'd spent on her mouth. It seemed appropriate to make up for his lapse in manners. He plumped, he suckled, he scraped the taut buds with his teeth.

"That's bus stop number two," he thought to mention.

"Please, Flynn, I can't take any more. Go to three. Hurry!"

"Bossy little thing, aren't you?" He wandered from her breasts to her belly. "Bet people jump when you use that tone of voice, don't they?"

"I'm begging you. Please!"

"Tell you what. I'm a generous guy. Why don't we get these panties and garter belt off and I'll see if stop number three doesn't show up."

"Yes," she sobbed. "Off, off, off."

He released her garter. Hooking his thumbs in the waistband of her panties, he dragged the scrap of silk downward, taking her stockings along with it. She lay beneath him, as open and eager as any woman he'd ever known. For someone so uptight, she sure let down nicely.

"Anyone getting off at stop number three?"

"I am! Flynn, please. I need to get off!"

"Yes, ma'am. Just let me get the doors open and off you go."

He parted her thighs, slipping a finger into the fragrant

center of her. She was hot and moist. Dipping inward again, he circled the pearl at the apex with his thumb. The simple touch left her shrieking.

He grinned. "That good?"

"Better. Oh, Flynn. You've got to do something."

Who was he to argue? He applied himself with greater diligence. Her shriek had turned to a groan and she shook her head back and forth. "No. No, no, no. Not that. I need more. I need—"

"Tell me, sweetheart. What do you need?"

"Park the damn bus!"

"What...now? But we haven't even gotten to the fourth stop yet."

"Titanium. Forty-seven point eighty-eight. Vanadium. Fifty point nine four one five. Chromium. Fifty-one point nine thirty-eight. Manganese—"

"What the *hell* are you doing, woman?"

"Listing," she burst out. "Listing the transition metals."

That was a new one, even for him. "I'm making love to you and you're listing transition metals? Have you lost your mind?"

"No!" She groaned. "No, but I'm going to explode if I don't distract myself. I can't stand any more. I—"

"Oh. Well, if that's all. I can take care of it."

His thumb found the slick nubbin again and he flicked it once, twice. On the third stroke she shrieked, louder this time, coming apart in his arms. The tremors seemed to last forever, ripping through her, tearing her to pieces. He held her until the final spasm had died.

"Now it's my turn. We're going to get back on that bus and start over. Only this time we're taking the express." He reached behind him, fumbling for his trousers. Yanking his wallet from his pocket, he flipped open his billfold and...

Nothing. Shit!

Wild-eyed, he grabbed Jane's shoulders. "Condoms," he shouted.

She smiled drowsily. "Hmm?"

"I. Need. *Condoms!*"

"Okay." She waved a hand in the general direction of the foyer.

"What?" He looked over his shoulder. "The hallway table?"

"No."

"That chest thing with the doors?"

"Nope."

"*What? Where?*"

"The drugstore."

He forced air in and out of his lungs. No. She couldn't be serious. Okay, he had one last hope. "Are you on the Pill?"

"Can't. Makes me sick."

He threw back his head and let out a roar he suspected echoed through every corner of Salmon Bay. If he were a betting man, he'd be willing to lay odds that Paulie was laughing himself silly right this very minute.

CHAPTER EIGHT

"I'LL BE DAMNED," Hickory murmured. "Right there on the lawn."

Rube blinked in astonishment. "Oh, my. That's not like our Jane, is it?"

Dipstick thrust between them, peering out the window. He voiced his own opinion with a low, drawn-out whine.

"Not even a little. She's acting totally out of character."

"She did it, didn't she?" Rube released a yelp of delight. Reaching into his pocket, he pulled out a fistful of sour balls and tossed them into the air. Dipstick scrambled after the unexpected treat. "Yahoo! She actually did it. Yes, she did. Her perfume works."

"Can't be sure," Dogg rumbled.

Hickory slammed his cane against the floor. "What else could it be? It's certainly encouraging."

"Encouraging. Yes."

"But not conclusive proof. Is that what you're saying?" Hickory pulled the drapes closed, affording the lovers some privacy. Though considering they were grappling around in the front yard in full view of anyone strolling by, his consideration was undoubtedly wasted.

"Maybe. Maybe not."

Hickory sighed. "Thanks for your clarification."

Rube slipped past and stuck his head through the narrow gap in the curtains. "My, oh, my," he breathed.

Hickory hooked his cane in Rube's belt and towed him

away from the window. "Still... Even if the night's events aren't a result of her potion, there are some side benefits for Jane. I guess we could call it a bonus." He smiled at the thought. "We didn't take that into consideration when we purchased Mr. Morgan. Did we?"

"No bonuses tonight."

"Dammit all, Dogg!" Hickory glared. "Your predictions can be so pessimistic. Are you telling me they're not going to—"

"Yes. They're not."

"Hell."

"No?" Rube pouted, cautiously unhooking Hickory's cane. "Why not? They looked so eager. Yes, they did. Very eager. Want me to check?"

"No, I don't want you to check." Hickory reacquired his wayward brother before he reached the curtains and propelled him toward the couch. "Dogg doesn't know for sure that nothing will occur. He's just making a prediction based on random elements combined with assumptions of probable behavior."

"I'm right."

In a practiced move, Hickory tossed the cane toward a freestanding mahogany coatrack. The gold ball on the handle caught neatly on a hook and swung wildly back and forth like a giant pendulum before clattering to the floor. He sighed. "Dammit. What could go wrong? What random elements have I overlooked?"

"No protection."

"Oh, please." Hickory threw himself into his chair, dismissing his brother's comment with a sweep of his hand. "A man of Flynn's experience comes to a party without his gift wrapped? I find that difficult to believe."

"Better for Jane if they wait."

"More dangerous, you mean," Hickory shot back. Dipstick approached with the cane and deposited it at his feet. "It allows their relationship to progress instead of remaining a meaningless fling, doesn't it?"

"Yes."

"So what do we do now? If he's reacting to her perfume, then what's happening makes perfect sense. But what if it's not her scent? What if there's something more between them?"

Dogg shrugged.

Rube sucked on his sour ball, his anxious gaze drifting toward the closed curtains.

Hickory sat silently, contemplating the atomic reaction decorating the tip of his cane. Then in another swift movement he sent it spinning toward the coatrack again. This time it caught the hook. He chuckled. "I know how we can find out for certain. Come with me."

"Where are we going?"

"To the lab. We're going to determine whether it's the potion or natural combustion. I've been giving this problem with her perfumes a great deal of thought and I believe she's missing a secondary reactant. Maybe tonight she found it."

"Another reactant." Champagne hissed as Rube poured the sparkling wine into three crystal flutes. One by one, he dropped in three sour balls. "My goodness. Now, that's an interesting idea."

Hickory's eyes narrowed. "If there is one, I suggest we find it before someone else does."

Dogg nodded, issuing a dour prediction. "Mick."

Hickory nodded. "Yes, Mick. Come on. Let's get to the lab." He led the way while his brothers and Dipstick followed. The instant they stepped outside, the dog abandoned them to snuffle in the bushes. To Hickory's disgust, he found the lab unlocked. "What the hell are we paying Morgan for, anyway?"

"To catch Barstow. Can't catch him if he doesn't try and steal something," Dogg offered. "Can't steal anything if things are locked up."

"More importantly, where does she keep the perfumes and who has the key?" Rube demanded. He prowled around the lab and poked chubby fingers through neatly organized shelves. "Does she even lock up her samples?"

"Yes, she locks them up, and I have the key," Hickory announced. He put down his glass of champagne and crossed to one of the temperature-controlled cabinets. Pulling a slender billfold from his back pocket, he flipped it open and swiftly selected one of the implements it contained. Then he neatly picked the lock.

Rube released his breath in a long sigh. "Hickory, my dear brother, you never fail to surprise. When did you learn to pick locks?"

"Just because we're related doesn't mean you know everything about me." Hickory abandoned the cabinet and crossed to a nearby computer station. Sitting at Jane's desk, he typed rapidly. "And let's not forget that we won't be sharing my lock-picking skills with Jane."

"Can't do it much longer," Dogg reminded him. "Not once Morgan installs the security system."

Hickory shrugged off the comment. "I'll make sure he gives us the necessary codes. Now, let's see…" He scanned the latest entry. "According to the notes on her computer—"

Rube's mouth dropped open. "You've raided her computer?"

"I'm raiding her computer as we speak. Why do you think I'm sitting here? Because I was suddenly overcome with the uncontrollable urge to play Freecell?"

Rube frowned. "But to raid Jane's computer—" He tsked in displeasure.

"If she didn't want anyone reading her notes, she'd encode them." Hickory shut down the computer and returned to the cabinet. Running a finger along the glass vials, he plucked one free. "According to her notes, she was testing LP-9 tonight. And according to *my* notes, LP-9 corresponds to an active pheromone sample."

"But... But that's supposed to be a blind study," Rube protested.

"It is blind." Hickory smiled blandly. "For her. Next I'll take a small sample and we'll put together one of her perfumes."

"Number nine. Out of sequence."

"Yes, Dogg. I found that intriguing, too, especially considering her numerical sequence fixation. Two always follows one and three always follows two. She doesn't like doing things out of order." Hickory paused in his preparations. "Our fault, I suppose."

"But she used number nine."

Hickory nodded. "I suspect it means she's attracted to Morgan."

Rube poured more champagne and then slipped an extra sour ball into his flute. "Oh! I get it. LP-9...love potion number nine. Isn't that sweet?" He waved the magnum of champagne at Hickory. "Is it ready?"

"Just finishing now." Hickory sniffed the perfume. "I do believe this is a new blend. It's quite extraordinary."

"Too bad we don't have anyone to test it on."

"I have that all taken care of," Hickory assured him.

"We have a test case?" Rube blinked in surprise. "Really? Who?"

A rattle of metal buckets sounded from the front of the lab. Hickory returned the vial to the cabinet and picked up the atomizer he'd prepared. "I believe our subject has just arrived," he announced with a complacent smile.

Rube's eyes widened. "Mrs. Motts? You're going to tes
it on—"

"The cleaning lady," Dogg confirmed.

"Don't mind us, Mrs. Motts," Hickory called out.

The cleaning woman paused in the doorway and gave hin
a no-nonsense look. "I never do, unlike most in this town."

"Really?" He leaned against the workbench nearest he
and slowly placed the atomizer on it. He adjusted it ever so
slightly, turning the glass spray bottle so it glinted beneatl
the overhead lights, catching her attention. "Scientists don'
worry you?"

"Nope." Her gaze fastened on the bottle. "I mind m
own business and thank you to mind yours."

"Quite." He nudged the atomizer in her direction an
waited. It didn't take long.

Her expression turned wistful and she took a telling ste
closer. "Is that Miss Jane's latest perfume?"

"Why, yes." He sniffed the air. "It has a most unusua
fragrance."

"She does make up some yummy ones." The cleanin
woman hesitated. "I confess, I have a true weakness fo
female geegaws like perfume and such. Do you...do yo
think she'd mind my giving it a little try?"

"No, Mrs. Motts," he said as innocently as he coul
manage—which probably wasn't too innocent. "I'm su
she'd be delighted to have you sample it."

She wiped her hands on one of her rags, shifting fror
foot to foot, but not coming any closer. "Miss Jane's alway
been good to me. I wouldn't want to do anything to upse
her."

"Ah, yes. In that case, we'll keep this our little secret."

"Well, now. If you're sure it won't do any harm."

"Didn't say that," Dogg muttered.

Ignoring him, Mrs. Motts reached for the atomizer an

generously spritzed herself with the scent. "Oooh-eee. Don't that stink pretty?"

Hickory took a deep breath. "Why, yes. As a matter of fact, it does." Helping himself to more champagne, he eyed her over the rim of his crystal flute. "And now let's see if that's all it does."

"So what now?" Rube whispered as Mrs. Motts propped open the door to the lab and dumped a pile of cleaning rags on a nearby worktable.

"Now we wait." Hickory made himself comfortable in Jane's computer chair. "And we observe."

Rube topped off their glasses, then reached into his pocket for more sour balls. Candy wrappers floated around his feet. "One or two?"

"None."

"One it is." The odor of tart lemons filled the air.

Hickory sighed. "Someday I'm going to be able to enjoy a glass of champagne without lemon sour balls ruining the flavor."

"Oh, no. It's nowhere near as good." Rube took a long swallow and sighed with pleasure. "You should know by now that sour balls go with everything."

Dogg grunted.

"See? Dogg likes them."

"Don't be ridiculous. I'd know that grunt anywhere. Dogg hates them."

"No, no—"

"Incoming," Dogg warned.

An instant later Dipstick thrust his nose into the lab. Spying company, he erupted through the door and barked a happy greeting.

"Oh, no you don't, you mangy mutt." Mrs. Motts fended him off with her broom. "You're not going to make a mess of my floors like those other times. I'll take my mop to your furry hide. See if I don't.''

Dipstick responded with an immediate tongue-washing, managing to do a thorough job despite her threats, which were completely spoiled by an almost girlish shriek of laughter. Spying Rube, the animal gave the cleaning woman a final lick before galumphing across the floor toward his candy-sharing friend. Skidding to a halt, Dipstick tried to paw his two hundred pounds into Rube's pocket. When that didn't work, he knocked over Dogg's champagne flute and lapped up the wine before happily crunching on the sour balls. Then he thanked the three with wet doggie kisses.

"That animal is a menace," Mrs. Motts announced, the minute she'd recovered. She snatched up the perfume and doused herself with it again, pausing long enough to scowl, as though daring them to criticize her liberal use of the atomizer. "And he licked off all the good stuff, too.''

"Saturate away, my dear," Hickory said dryly. "I'm sure there're a few molecules of air around here you haven't managed to contaminate.''

"You scientists sure talk funny.'' She planted her hands on her ample hips. "I ask you, between you and that drool-infested mutt, how's a body supposed to get any work done? Candy wrappers. Piles of hair. Muddy paw prints. You're all a pain in my backside.''

Hickory encouraged her with a wave of his hand. "Just do your usual splendid job, Mrs. Motts.''

She lifted an eyebrow at that. "Splendid, huh?''

Hickory blinked. "Did I say splendid?''

"Heard you," Dogg confirmed. "Thought it. Said it. Splendid.''

"How intriguing.''

"Well, I think she does a stupendous job," Rube hastened to say. "Positively stupendous. Paradisiacal. Prodigious. Downright ineffable."

"You boys swearing over there?" Mrs. Motts demanded. "I don't abide foul language. You cut it out or I'll have words with Miss Jane."

"I'm sorry to say he swallowed a thesaurus." Hickory pounded Rube on the back. "Never fear. We'll have it coughed up in no time."

Mrs. Motts shook her broom in their direction. "Don't you three have somewhere to be?"

"Why, yes," Hickory replied, eyeing her with bright curiosity. "Right here."

"I'm set upon, I am," she grumbled. "Three delinquents, that's what you are. Standing around getting in my way. Dragging in a mutt the size of a horse. Drinking. Swearing. Staring funny at a poor old helpless woman."

Rube released his breath in an excited sigh. "I am staring."

Hickory glanced at Dogg. "How peculiar. Do you feel it?"

"No."

"Well, I do." Hickory tossed his cane in Dogg's direction. "I believe I'll see where this leads."

"Me first." Rube fluffed his blush-pink tufts of hair, offering Mrs. Motts his biggest, happiest smile. "Care for a lemon sour ball?" he offered generously.

The cleaning woman groaned. "You boys aren't going to let me get my work done, are you?"

"Probably not," Rube confessed shyly. "Do you mind?"

"Miss Jane won't be pleased."

He put a finger to his lips. "We won't tell her."

"She likes the place clean so her experiments don't get contaminated. Leastwise, that's what she told me."

He ignored that, instead tilting his head to one side and

humming a little ditty. Unable to resist, he began to sway, his feet pitter-pattering in a brisk two-step. "Would you like to dance?"

Mrs. Motts folded her arms across her ample bosom. "You better be joking, Junior."

"Junior," Rube repeated, blushing to the tips of his ears. "No one ever called me that before." He batted his eyes at her. "I'd really like to dance with you. I can hum some more, if you think it would help."

"Oh, for crying out—" She jammed her mop into a bucket of soapy water, suds slopping over the side. "You know, I didn't believe folks in town when they said you three were crazy. I'm beginning to rethink that position."

"Oh, we're not crazy. Just a wee bit eccentric." He flung his arms wide to show her a "wee bit."

"Got it." She tossed aside her mop and spun toward the door, only to find Hickory standing there. "You want to dance, too, Mr. Ponytail?"

"But, of course." He plucked his cane from Dogg's hand and twirled it. "And I'm a much better dancer than my brother."

"That may be, but I don't dance with men who have hair longer than mine."

"Hah!" Rube laughed triumphantly. "That means I win."

Dogg stepped in. "Nobody wins. Time to go."

"But—"

Grasping Rube and Hickory by the arms, Dogg propelled them out of the lab and into the fresh air. "Breathe," he instructed.

"Well, my goodness." Rube blinked in confusion. "I offered that lady my sour balls. What in the world possessed me?"

Hickory frowned, digging the tip of his cane into the grass. "Did what I think just happened actually happen?"

"Yes." Dogg sighed. "The perfume works or you're drunk. I vote for drunk."

FLYNN AWAKENED to a pounding at his hotel room door. Stumbling out of bed, he snatched up a pair of jeans and pulled them on. Yanking open the door, he glared at Mick Barstow. "This is becoming a bad habit."

"I want to know what the hell's going on," Barstow announced, shoving his way into the room.

"Yeah? That makes two of us. What the hell do you want?"

"I thought you were here to install a security system. But you're helping with her experiments, aren't you?" Mick demanded. "That's why Jane's crazy uncles bought you at an auction. So she could try her love potion on you. And it worked, didn't it? That was what last night was all about. Am I right?"

"I'm getting tired of asking, so this time I suggest you give me a straight answer. What the *hell* are you talking about?"

"Jane's perfume experiments. The one she tried on you last night."

"I'm not part of any perfume experiment."

"Bull! I saw you. Both of you."

"Saw us?" Flynn's eyes narrowed. "Where?"

Mick sputtered. "You were practically humping Jane right on her front lawn."

"Wrong thing to say." Flynn uncoiled faster than a desert rattler. Snatching Mick from the chair, he half marched, half dragged him toward the door. "Thanks for stopping by. Don't bother visiting again."

Mick's brown eyes widened. "You don't know, do you.

You don't know about her experiments or the potion she used on you last night.'' He crowed with laughter. "Those old geezers are good, I'll give them that. She's run out of people to experiment on in Salmon Bay so they imported you. Very clever."

Flynn tightened his hold on Mick's collar, choking off the bastard's words, along with his breath. Once he'd turned a pleasant shade of purplish-red, Flynn eased his grip a trifle. "Talk fast. What experiment and what potions? I thought she created perfumes."

"I'll tell you, I'll tell you. They're perfumes, all right. *Pheromone*-based perfumes."

Pheromones. Flynn tried to recall what he'd read about the subject, but his brain still wasn't firing on all cylinders. He glared at Mick and gave the weasel a little shake. "Explain," he demanded curtly.

"Let me come back in first."

Reluctantly, Flynn stepped aside. "Make it fast. I've decided I don't like you much. And people I don't like don't stay upright too long."

"The feeling's mutual," Mick muttered, taking a seat. "But I plan to use Tucker instead of my fists."

"Yeah, I'm real scared now." Flynn propped his hip on the dresser and glared impatiently. "Cut the bull, will you? You can start by explaining about Jane and her pheromones."

"Fine. Science 101 in two syllables or less."

"You're right. You're gonna be using two syllables or less." Flynn folded his hands, dying to give them a thorough workout. "Because that's all you'll be able to manage without any teeth. Now, you want to trade insults until I really lose my temper, or you want to start talking?"

Mick swallowed. "I'll get to the point."

"Good choice."

"Right. Pheromones." He smoothed the corners of his mustache. "Basically, pheromones are chemicals found in most animals and insects that cause the organism to respond to a member of its species in a specific manner."

"One animal makes another animal do something, is that it?"

"Yes, by chemically affecting various behaviors."

"Be more specific."

"Let's see... There's food gathering. Defense. Creating and maintaining a society." He shrugged. "Ants, for instance, use them to put down trails or recognize others from their nest. In beehives, the queen releases a pheromone that suppresses the reproductive abilities in other females. Certain mammals use them as territorial markers to warn off the competition." He paused significantly. "Most interesting of all is that they're used to affect sexual behavior, to signal the readiness to mate."

Flynn's eyes narrowed. "What's this got to do with me?"

"Jane is using what she believes are human pheromones in her perfume. Specifically, female pheromones."

"And their purpose?"

"To cause behavioral changes in the opposite sex. To initiate mating behavior." Mick cleared his throat. "To be precise... They, ah, are supposed to make you horny."

Flynn gritted his teeth. "Jane used these pheromones on me last night?"

"Considering what you were doing on her lawn, I'd say that was a good bet." An excited glitter appeared in Mick's eyes. "Did she do it? Did her formula work?"

"How the hell should I know?" He shot Barstow an aggrieved look. "Isn't there a law against that sort of thing?"

Mick shook his head. "Animal pheromones are used all the time. Pig pheromones are particularly popular with certain perfume manufacturers. But they don't work. At least, not on humans.''

''Why not?''

''Pheromones are species-specific.'' Mick grinned. ''I could tell you which perfumes to avoid if you don't want to get up close and personal with a hog.''

''Cut the crap, Barstow. What about Jane?''

His smile faded. ''We were working together on her pheromone experiments until.... Until suddenly we weren't.''

''Until she threw you out, you mean.''

Mick's eyes narrowed. ''Is that what she told you?''

''You calling her a liar?''

''Not to your face,'' he said wisely.

''So you were working with her and...what?''

''It's a controversial field since there's quite a bit of debate over whether these pheromones even exist.''

''But Jane thinks she's discovered something.''

''Right. Her discovery came rather conveniently on the heels of our breakup. She's on the methodical side, so she wants to be sure of her accuracy. Instead of patenting the stuff, or turning it over to a research facility, she's doing the formulation herself. In other words, she'd trying to create a perfume she can market all on her own. You're the guinea pig she's using to determine whether she's actually got something worth licensing.''

''Lab rat.''

''What?''

''Forget it. What's your interest in this, Barstow?''

''I told you. When we broke up, I accidently left one of my files behind. I need it and I'll pay you to retrieve it.''

''You can't just ask her to give it to you?'' Flynn asked skeptically. ''You have to pay someone to steal it?''

''Jane's not feeling terribly generous toward me right now. This is her way of getting even over our breakup. She knows I can't complete my own research without those notes and she's deliberately withholding them.'' He stood up. ''Come on, Morgan. I'm not asking you to do anything you haven't done before. This time it'll be for a good cause. Plus, you'll be getting a little of your own back at her for conducting pheromone experiments on you without warning you what she was up to.''

Flynn hesitated. ''Did she really use pheromone perfume on me?''

''No question.''

Damn. ''And this file… I can read it before turning it over?''

''Every word.''

Flynn thought fast. ''How much is it worth?'' Barstow mentioned a figure that left him whistling. ''You really must be desperate.''

Mick shrugged. ''Can you get the file?''

Flynn let several seconds tick by. ''I'm not sure. I'll let you know.''

''Don't wait too long. I need it soon or it won't be worth anything to me.''

''Like I said… I'll let you know.'' He jerked his head toward the door. Barstow took the hint. The second he'd left, Flynn kicked the door closed, swearing furiously. Time to have a long talk with the uncles.

Then he'd have an even longer talk with Jane.

JANE SLIPPED DOWNSTAIRS, feeling as peculiar this morning as she had last night. Perhaps it had something to do with the fact that she hadn't dressed and still wore her nightgown. She hesitated in the doorway to the living room, struggling to recall the last time she'd wandered through her house undressed. Not that she was actually undressed, she hastened to remind herself. She just wasn't dressed.

Never. The answer was definitely never.

She couldn't remember a single time she'd come downstairs without throwing on clothes first. Not even as a child on Christmas morning. Dipstick lumbered to his feet and approached, his massive head tilting to one side. He stuck his snout toward her and tested the air, then sneezed violently. Heck, even he sensed a strangeness about her.

Something odd had occurred last night. Something that had never happened before. Her eyes widened in alarm. Oh, no! What if the perfume had the opposite effect of its design? What if it stirred a reaction in the wearer instead of the one inhaling it? Or... She began to pace. What if when she'd been squirted by the woman in the rest room, she'd been contaminated in some way?

"That's impossible," she whispered. "Female pheromones only act on males. And male pheromones only act on females."

Dipstick whined, shivering from head to tail and sending wisps of white, brown and black hair spinning into the air.

She fought to remain calm, to employ logic. "If the perfume worked, Flynn's reaction—assuming it was in direct response to the pheromones in the potion—made perfect sense. He was reacting to a chemical stimulus...a...a chemical phone call. He answered and I—"

Jane groaned, covering her face with her hands. "And I have no excuse for remaining on the line. None at all."

She pattered toward the living room again and surveyed the damage from their joint enthusiasm the previous evening. Cushions from the couch were upended. The throw rug had more humps in it than a herd of Bactrian camels. Her brow wrinkled. Did camels form herds? She'd have to remember to look it up and find out. Moving briskly around the room, she adjusted the rug, making sure she centered it properly, and rearranged the cushions on the couch.

There. All neat and tidy.

Then she stared at her sterile little room and for the first time saw it through a stranger's eyes. Through Flynn's eyes. It was perfect. Too perfect. Pristine and artificial and downright virginal. Lifting her nightgown to her knees, she raced around the living room, tugging at the rug until it sat askew, snatching up the couch cushions and tossing them into the air. Dipstick circled her, barking hysterically. On the wall were two Frank Lloyd Wright prints and a black-and-white photo of Einstein. She knocked all three out of alignment.

Next she ran for the front door and threw it open. Mr. Keenan stood by her mailbox, holding one of her shoes. She blushed, remembering why it had been left on her doorstep. He gawked as she bolted past, Dipstick hot on her heels. "What in tarnation…?"

Ignoring him, she sank to the ground at the edge of her garden, not caring that grass and dirt stained her nightgown. She snatched free handfuls of flowers as fast and furious as she could manage. A familiar-looking flash of neon blue glitter caught her eye, winking at her from beneath a hydrangea bush. Squinting, she realized that her glasses had somehow found a way into the flower bed. Oh, good heavens. It must have happened when Flynn had taken her apart the previous night. Her mouth firmed. Tough. They could stay there, permanent reminders to her lapse in judgment.

She plucked more flowers. Rose thorns dragged painful scratches across her palms, but she didn't care. She turned her attention to the pansies, ripped them free without inflicting any damage to herself. They simply bobbed their poor severed heads in abject misery, making her feel a bit guilty. Next, she tackled the poppies, the bright orange clashing with the red roses and purple pansies. Once she'd filled the skirt of her nightgown, she hoisted it high and stomped back toward the house.

Pausing beside Mr. Keenan, she glared at him. "Don't look at me like that!"

"Miss Jane, I have to tell you, everyone in town's worried about you. You haven't been yourself lately." He hesitated, then blurted, "We're thinking of letting you experiment on us, if it'll make you feel better."

Tears pricked her eyes. "Thank you, Mr. Keenan. But I don't think it'll help."

Returning inside, she closed the door. Then she shook the flowers free of her nightgown and dumped them onto the gate-leg table. Not wasting any time, she shoved them willy-nilly into her Simpson vase. Water. Flowers needed water. She marched into the kitchen and turned on the tap. For the first time in all the years she'd owned the vase, she filled it to the brim. Returning to the living room, she fully extended the table—another first—and placed the vase dead center.

"Hell's bells, I can't even do that right," she announced in disgust. Seizing the vase, she moved it away from the middle. It still didn't look right, but she didn't have the energy to figure out why. At least it wasn't square anymore.

Finished, she looked around her less-than-perfect room. And then she did the unthinkable. She burst into tears. Sinking to the floor, she wrapped her arms around her dog. "I made an absolute ass of myself last night," she whispered, burying her face in his ruff. "What's wrong with me? My perfume works. I should be thrilled. I should be shrieking for joy. Why aren't I happy?"

Because if the perfume had worked, then Flynn had been responding to an uncontrollable urge rather than an honest attraction to her as a woman. He wanted her because he found her perfume irresistible, not her.

Her tears fell faster. For a logical woman, she could be a total idiot. She'd known Flynn was a dangerous man the minute she'd opened the door to him. If she'd believed in gut instincts, maybe she'd have paid attention to them and sent him on his way.

But no. Instead she'd chosen to play games, to secretly involve him in her experiments. Worse, she hadn't warned him what she was up to. Once he found out, he'd be furious. And then... Her breath came in a teary hiccup. And then, on top of all that, she'd gone and done the impossible.

She'd fallen head over heels in lust with him in one short week.

It was ridiculous. Unbelievable. And yet, it had happened, and she'd never been more miserable in her life. Her feelings were impossible. They wouldn't lead anywhere, other than down a pain-filled road. Even if they grew to something more than lust, Flynn Morgan wasn't a man who believed in permanence despite his desire for marriage and children. He certainly wasn't the type who'd settle in Salmon Bay. The sooner she realized that and overcame her bout of temporary insanity, the better. The decision made her cry all the harder.

With a grumbling sigh, Dipstick sank down beside her. Nuzzling her ear, he covered her with hair and sympathy.

CHAPTER NINE

"WHAT THE *HELL* IS GOING ON?"

"Good afternoon, Mr. Morgan. We've been expecting you." Hickory leaned back in his chair and gestured toward the sofa. "Have a seat."

"You're not getting me comfortable." Flynn folded his arms across his chest and glared. "I'm pissed and staying that way."

Hickory's pale blue eyes brightened with amusement. "Would you care to tell me what's gotten you so...ah... pissed?"

"Knows about the perfumes," Dogg murmured.

"How?" Hickory asked.

"Barstow."

"Ah. I see."

Rube paused, a lemon sour ball halfway to his mouth. "That was very bad of him to tell."

Flynn scrutinized his "buyers," a jaded cynicism slipping over him. It was a familiar feeling, one that had taken hold at a time most tots were learning not to wet their beds. "I gather you didn't just buy me to install your security system?"

"Yes, we did." Hickory's contradiction surprised him. "Our arrangements haven't changed. The perfumes she's working on are secondary to that."

"Oh, please. Cut the crap, would you? You bought a lab

at for her experiments. Catching Barstow is an added bonus.''

"I'm sure you find this situation difficult to understand." Hickory cupped his hand over the top of his cane and regarded Flynn intently. "Please try and look at it from our perspective. Jane is a brilliant woman, but she's rather oblivious to the ways of the world. She needs your help."

Flynn couldn't argue with that. He'd never met a woman more in need of help than Jane Dearly. But it wasn't the sort of help these three had in mind. She needed to explore the human side of her nature. The emotions were there somewhere, locked beneath a crisp white lab coat, protective glasses and a painfully tight hairstyle. He'd seen them in that delicious smile she occasionally flashed, heard them when she'd laughed. Loosened them when he'd yanked the clips out of the most beautiful explosion of blond-streaked curls he'd ever seen. And finally freed the full depth and scope of her emotions when he'd stripped her bare and gathered her beneath him.

Yeah, Jane needed a man, all right. Too bad he wasn't that man. Someone else would have to coax the passion free again, someone who wasn't all wrong for her.

"Hell! There are alternatives to dragging me into this, you know." Flynn paced across the room. "Have you any idea what almost—what *could* happen if her pheromone experiments are a success?"

Hickory suppressed a smile. "Yes, Mr. Morgan. We do."

That stopped him. "You do, huh? Mind if I make a suggestion?"

"Go right ahead."

"If you want her more worldly, then move to a bigger city where she'll meet more people. Lock up the lab every once in a while and go on vacation. Send her out into the big, bad world. Whatever. But don't bring the big, bad world and dump it in her bed. That's just nuts.''

There was a long silence and it took Flynn only a moment to understand why. He swore. ''You bought me in order to keep her here, didn't you? You don't want to move or lock up the lab or send her out into the world. You're afraid if you do, she'll find someplace she likes better than Salmon Bay and leave. Now, that's low, even for you three.''

Anger darkened Hickory's face. ''You know nothing!'' In an explosion of movement, he hurled his cane at a nearby coatrack. It caught the hook and whirled violently in a circle before flying off and clattering against the wall.

''You're going to break your little cane doing that,'' Flynn mocked.

Hickory gripped the arms of his chair, fighting for control. Slowly the tension eased from his body, though a bleakness settled deep into his face, making him look infinitely old and weary. ''Listen to me, Mr. Morgan, and listen well. Jane is not some sad, neglected child. Don't treat her as though she were the one shoved out of a fast-moving car, with Lost Springs Ranch left to pick up the broken pieces. She's a beloved member of our family. She's a chemist, raised by us and trained by us. Everything she needs for her research can be found right here, assuming you're successful in protecting that research. There's no reason for her to go elsewhere.''

Hickory's words about Flynn's background stung, hitting too close to home. But he ignored them. Hell, he was used to the taunts by now. But Jane... He focused his full attention on defending her rights. ''So, everything she needs for her research is here? That's great, if she were nothing more than a chemist. What about the woman? What about those needs?''

The three sat stubbornly silent.

Flynn's eyes narrowed as he cut right to the heart of the matter. "You don't want to let her go, no matter what's best for Jane."

"We're best for her," Dogg rumbled.

"She's ours and we're keeping her." Hickory focused on the wall behind Flynn. "We…we love her."

"She's all we have. If she leaves…" Rube's cherub face crumpled. "We'll be all alone."

Aw, hell. Flynn rubbed his hand along his jaw. If the little guy started bawling, he was out of here. "Let's talk about her research," he suggested.

Hickory seized the change of subject with obvious relief. "I don't know why you're so concerned about that. She's simply developing perfumes."

"Yeah, she mentioned that last night. What she forgot to add was that they were pheromone-based perfumes and that she was using me to gauge their effectiveness. Is that the real reason you bought me?"

"That wasn't our primary intention. We weren't even certain she'd test them on you."

"But you suspected. In fact, knowing Jane, you could pretty much bet money on it, right?"

"It was logical to assume she'd use you as a test subject." Hickory dismissed the concern with a wave of his hand. "So she's having you participate in some of her experiments. Why are you making such a fuss about it?"

"Because you lied to me. You said I was supposed to rescue her. You didn't say anything about experiments."

"Oh, it's nothing life-threatening or dangerous," Rube hastened to assure him. "She wants to spray you."

"Spray me." That was a new twist.

"Or spray herself. Not quite sure which way she'll do it."

"Yeah? Well, I can tell you which it is and I can also tell you what happened as a result."

Dogg nodded. "Know. Saw. Conclusions uncertain."

They saw? Hell. How could they avoid it? That was his fault. He and Jane had practically made love right there on the front lawn. "Well, my conclusions aren't in the least uncertain," Flynn bit out. "My guess is you paid five grand to get your niece rescued, and then to get her laid. That way she wouldn't have to go looking for action elsewhere and leave Salmon Bay."

"Ten. Paid ten thousand."

"What Dogg means is that it's a bit more involved than that," Hickory said, cutting in. "Yes, we did pay ten thousand for you. No, it wasn't to get Jane laid—a quaint if rather crude expression. She's testing perfumes. Granted, they are pheromone-based. But there's nothing dangerous about what she plans. She simply wants a man's reaction to them."

"Uh-huh. Pull the other one."

"I'm quite serious."

"You want me to be her personal test subject? That's the extent of it?"

Dogg snorted. "Sniff her. Seduce her. Scam Barstow. *That's* it."

Enough was enough. Flynn didn't care why these three lunatics had purchased him. He wasn't playing along. "Pay attention, gentlemen. You may have bought me, but I'm not for sale. Not for what you have in mind. If Jane wants a lab rat, she can look elsewhere. I'm not interested." Yeah, right. Look at how disinterested he'd been last night. Even without her perfume, he'd been dying to give that mouth of hers another trial run. "I'm not donating my body to science. Are we clear on that point?"

The wizard—Hickory—regarded him with a complacent

smile, one that made Flynn distinctly uneasy. "Oh, we understand your position, Mr. Morgan."

"Glad we have that cleared up." He crossed to the bow window and stared at Jane's house. The two residences sat side by side, sharing an enormous lot in the back. The lab, a large single-story concrete building—functional if not as aesthetically appealing as the houses—squatted between the two property lines. Had Jane's parents occupied the one house while the uncles joined forces to purchase the huge century-old home they currently inhabited? It must have made for a cozy arrangement. How had Laura's husband dealt with the strangeness?

As Flynn watched, Mick Barstow hastened between the two houses from the general direction of the lab. Son of a bitch! Looked like the bastard had decided to take matters into his own hands. Dogg joined Flynn at the window and shook his huge, shaggy head.

"Trouble."

"Why's he trouble?" Flynn asked, interested in hearing another opinion.

"Wants Jane's research."

He already knew that much. "Does he also want Jane?"

"No. Just the research." Flynn could feel Dogg's eyes on him. "It's you she wants."

"Jane needs me," he corrected him. "That's all."

Liar! She'd wanted him physically last night, though she might be having second thoughts in the cold light of day. Or she might change her mind once she found out about his deal with the uncles. But last night, she'd been as desperate for him as he'd been for her. His brows drew together. Were those pheromones a two-way street, driving the female into a frenzy of lust as well as the male? He'd have to remember to ask her.

"Stay for the next two weeks," Hickory said. "Finish

installing the security system and deal with Barstow. If you're also willing to continue with Jane's experiments, we'll make a sizable contribution to your bank account, as well as increasing our donation to the ranch."

Flynn didn't give a damn about the money for himself. But how could he pass it up for the ranch? He swore beneath his breath. He didn't like being backed into a corner. He hadn't as a kid and he sure as hell didn't as an adult. Right now, his back was to the wall. "I'll stay the two weeks, as promised. And I'll handle Barstow. As for the experiments... I need to talk to Jane first."

Rube rubbed his hands together, his chubby face wreathed in smiles. "Now we're getting somewhere."

Before Flynn could comment further, Dipstick erupted into the room, heading straight for Rube. "Greedy dog," the cherub muttered, unwrapping a sour ball and tossing it toward the animal. With one snap of his massive jaws, Dipstick gobbled up the treat and thanked the man with a thorough face-washing.

Jane followed the Saint Bernard into the room, picking up Hickory's cane almost absentmindedly and hanging it on the coatrack. To Flynn's disappointment, she wore her hair tightly bound once more. And she'd donned a crisp white lab coat and decorated the top of her head with another pair of glasses. These were red-white-and-blue with star-shaped frames. The scientist had returned with a vengeance, despite the whimsy her frames provided, Flynn realized, vaguely disappointed. She'd wrapped her work-persona around herself like a security blanket and it would take some serious effort to get her unwrapped again.

"Uncle Rube," she scolded gently. "I've warned you about giving Dipstick sweets."

"Just one," Rube muttered. "Little one. Tiny one. Hardly one at all."

She ruffled his tuft of hair and dropped a kiss on his forehead. "They're all the same size and you know it."

"Oh, no, they're not. I measured them. Each one's a teeny-tiny bit different. Microscopic. But it's there."

"What can we do for you, my dear?" Hickory interrupted.

"She wants Morgan."

A hint of red crept into Jane's cheeks at Dogg's announcement, the color intensifying when she saw Flynn standing at her uncle's side. She recovered swiftly, which was more than he could say for himself. Lust punched him, as strong and overwhelming as the previous night. He shook his head in an attempt to clear it. Damn it all! How long did those pheromones last, anyway? He couldn't remember a time he'd been so thoroughly aroused without being in a position to ease it as he wanted—repeatedly and at great length.

"I'd like to speak to Mr. Morgan about security measures for the lab." Her gaze swept the trio of uncles. "That *is* why he's here. Right?"

Hickory smiled. "Why, no, my dear," he replied gently. "We bought him as a birthday present for you. Isn't that correct, Mr. Morgan?"

Sheer self-preservation kept Flynn silent.

Aside from the wash of color that returned to Jane's cheeks, she handled the comment with amazing serenity. "Why, thank you, Uncle Hickory. What a lovely gift. Quite thoughtful. Unfortunately, this particular present isn't quite my size and color, so I'm afraid I'll have to return it."

Flynn chuckled, pleased to see the fleetest of smiles cross Jane's mouth, as well. "Did you want to speak to me?" he asked.

"If you wouldn't mind." She had trouble looking at him. No doubt her memories of their encounter last night were as vivid as his own. She chose to glance at her uncles, instead. He doubted she missed Hickory's smug satisfaction, Rube's gleeful anticipation or Dogg's hopeful expression.

Flynn sighed. Apparently subtlety wasn't their strong suit. "Why don't we take it outside," he suggested.

"Good idea." She snapped her fingers for Dipstick and then gave her uncles a final warning look. "I'll talk to you three later."

The minute they were outside, the dog took off running, finding interesting scents to investigate under a nearby bush. Flynn walked in the general direction of the lab, waiting patiently for Jane to find the words that would salvage her pride. Words like... *I don't know what happened last night. It was just one of those things. I never do that on a first date.* Or his personal favorite... *You took advantage of me during a weak moment.*

"Thank you for last night."

He was so surprised by such sheer frankness, he could only stare.

"And I mean all of it, too," she persevered with only a hint of nervousness. "Every last bit. In fact, I especially appreciate how it ended."

"How it ended?" *He* sure as hell didn't appreciate the ending. Nor did he appreciate the frustrating aftereffects, aftereffects that still lingered. "You liked that part?"

"Not *that*. Not...not the very end when we didn't have— And we had to—" She closed her eyes and groaned. "I really stink at this, don't I?"

"I hadn't noticed," he lied.

"I meant I appreciated your kissing me good-night when you were so annoyed. It was very generous of you. Not many would have." She shot him a quick look from beneath her lashes. "If anything, I took advantage of you. You were a perfect gentleman."

"That's a first. I don't think anyone's ever accused me of that before."

"You made the evening special. Very special."

"I aim to please."

"I...I just hope I didn't hurt you when I tackled you."

"Everything's in full working order." Painful working order. Which reminded him. He turned her to face him, tipping her chin upward so she couldn't shy away from his question. "Why did you do it, Jane?"

Alarm turned her eyes to a vivid green. "Do what?"

"Wear the perfume. Didn't you think I'd respond to you without it?"

"Oh, God." She started to reach for the glasses stuck in her hair, but he stopped her.

"Don't. Don't hide behind those. You don't need them. Just explain it to me."

She moistened her lips and he fought to keep his hands off her, to keep from exploring that mouth all over again. To keep from tumbling her to the sweet, cool grass and finishing what they'd started the night before. "You know about the perfume?" she questioned cautiously.

"That it's pheromone-based? Yes. That I was a test subject last night? Yes, again."

She clasped her hands together. Not that it helped. He could still see the betraying tremor. "When did you find out?"

"This morning."

"So last night—"

His mouth twisted. "Was a true test. I didn't know about anything other than the survey, so your results weren't compromised."

She nodded, though he didn't see the relief he'd have expected from a dedicated scientist. "Did my uncles tell you about the pheromones?"

"Not until I confronted them just now. I heard what you were up to from another source."

Her comprehension was instantaneous. "Mick."

"Mick," he confirmed. "Now for the million-dollar question. Why, Jane? Why did you use me like that? Have you any idea how that feels?"

"I almost didn't go through with that part of the experiment. Isn't that funny? But then, the decision was taken out of my hands. And once it was..." She shrugged, her shoulders slumping. "I went along with it."

"Taken out of your hands?" His eyes narrowed. "How?"

"Does it matter?"

He'd been in enough nasty situations to know it did. "Yes."

She gazed at him, as though assessing his truthfulness. Apparently satisfied with what she saw, she took a deep breath. "I was in the ladies' room trying to decide whether or not to test the perfume on you when a woman helped herself to a sample squirt. Without my permission, I might add."

"I wonder if her night turned out as interesting as ours."

"She doesn't deserve the sort of night we had," Jane retorted, her undisguised annoyance amusing him. "I hope her date dropped her at the curb and took off."

"Unfortunately, that would negate the results of your sample, wouldn't it?"

"I hadn't thought of that," she muttered.

"What happened after she tried the perfume?"

"She turned the bottle on me."

"Why?"

Jane set her jaw, fumbling once again for her glasses. This time, he let her hide behind them. "She said I needed all the help I could get if I wanted to attract a man. Since I wouldn't take my hair down or unbutton my dress, she doused me with perfume.''

"Aw, hell.''

Ever so gently he eased her into his arms. She didn't resist. She slipped her hands around his waist and nestled her cheek against his chest. "Don't be upset,'' she ordered his top button. "I wasn't. She just confirmed what everyone has been saying about me all these years.''

"That you're more scientist than woman? You're not being a scientist now, are you?''

She shook her head, a tiny ringlet escaping the prison of her hair clip.

"And you sure as hell weren't being one last night.''

A gurgle of laughter slipped free. "If I'm not careful, I'm going to ruin my reputation.''

"Maybe a little ruining is just what you need.''

She pulled free of his arms, the vulnerability he'd glimpsed earlier more fully expressed this time. "We need to discuss the security features you've installed in the lab. I found Mick in there again.''

"None of the systems are activated yet. Until they are, locking the door would probably be a good idea.''

"I did. This time I made sure of it.'' She gazed at the whitewashed block building with a frown. "Mick still got in.''

"Who all has keys?''

She sighed. "Oh, everybody. Me. The uncles. Mrs. Motts, the cleaning lady. Mick used to, but I took the key back.''

"And changed the locks?''

"No,'' she admitted. "He returned the key. Why would I—'' She winced. "Forget I asked that.''

"Done.''

She gave him a direct look. "He wants something, doesn't he? That's why he keeps coming back.''

"I think that's a safe bet."

She started to wrap her arms around her waist, then jammed them into her coat pockets instead. Both actions were telling. "I need you, Flynn."

"You need a security expert, is that it? Just a security expert?"

She didn't pretend to misunderstand. "I haven't changed that much in the past twenty-four hours. My experiments are important to me. My career is vital. I can't afford to jeopardize either one." Her tone held an edge of urgency, the vulnerability he'd seen earlier threading through her voice and catching him off guard. He was used to people who played games. But Jane Dearly wasn't a game player. "I suspect if I don't let you finish installing a security system—including for my lab—that's precisely what will happen."

"Tell you what. I'll make a deal with you."

She stared at him, the lenses of her reading glasses magnifying her eyes. If she'd bothered to look in the mirror, she'd have realized they made her appear utterly defenseless, instead of like a serious scientist.

"A deal," she repeated. "Okay, I'm listening."

"So far you haven't been willing to let us fool with the lab." He cocked an eyebrow. "I gather that's changed?"

"Yes."

"Then let me take you to this place I know not far from here. Paulie and I installed the owner's security system. You can check it out and see if it isn't what you want." Maybe he'd even manage to keep his hands off her while he showed her around.

The ringlet shivered against her temple. "And my experiments? What about those?"

He folded his arms across his chest. "I'm not sure. What do you suggest?"

"I still need a human guinea pig for some of my perfume experiments." A look of pure mischief crossed her face. "For some reason, people around here aren't too keen on helping out."

"Gee. I can't understand that."

She rewarded him with a quick grin. "Considering they've been the subjects of various experiments since I was five, I guess I've tried their patience a bit."

"For the sake of argument, let's say I agree to continue as your official lab rat." He held up his hand before she could leap to any assumptions. "I said, for the sake of argument. I haven't made any promises yet."

"Go on," she prompted impatiently.

"How do you know my reaction will be a result of the perfume as opposed to my normal reaction to you as a person?"

Her mouth curved into a wry smile. "I think we'll know if you're responding to one of the perfumes rather than to me. But just in case, it's a double-blind study."

"Double-blind?"

"It's common practice." She shoved the glasses on top of her head, knocking loose another curl. "See, the potions are all numbered. Some contain the pheromone solution and others are plain perfumes. I don't even know which are which."

"Seriously? How did you pull that off?"

"Hickory helped. I filled each bottle and marked it with a secret code that I recorded in my computer. My notes identify which codes match the plain perfumes versus the ones with the pheromone-based solutions. But the labels on the bottles are just an unrelated sequence of letters and numbers. In other words, Hickory can't tell the difference just by looking at the bottle or at the label."

"He doesn't know your code or whether a particular bottle contains a working pheromone perfume, is that it?"

"Not unless he deliberately looks it up in my computer. That makes it a blind study. Next, he switched my labels with his, mixing the sequence in the process, and placed his own secret code on each vial. I don't know his code, any more than he knows mine."

"And since you don't know his code, that makes it a double-blind."

"Exactly. After the study is completed, he'll match his codes with mine and I'll check the computer to see which studies correspond to the pheromone solutions. If something peculiar occurs with an active sample, I can test it some more." She slanted him a teasing glance. "For all I know, last night's perfume might have been just that. Perfume."

"Wait a minute. You mean—"

"You got it." She grinned. "It might not have been pheromones that prompted our little lust-fest, but sheer, unadulterated lust."

CHAPTER TEN

"DO YOU WANT TO START right in on the next experiment or look over the lab and explain what you installed at this other place?" Jane asked.

She glanced at Flynn expectantly, surprised to discover he still hadn't recovered from her observation about last night. If anything, he looked downright furious. A tiny frown formed between her brows. Did he find her so unattractive that he couldn't imagine feeling lust for her unless it was perfume-induced?

She assumed her most professional demeanor, the one that caused people in town to give her a wide berth. "Are you coming, Flynn?"

"Wait a minute." He caught hold of her arm. "Was last night a result of the perfume or not?"

"I have no idea. I won't until we conclude the experiments."

"Look it up."

"Excuse me?"

"Check your computer and find out."

She pulled loose from his hold and planted her hands on her hips, glaring in exasperation. "I already explained this to you. It's a double-blind study. I can't just 'look it up.'"

"Then give Hickory your codes and have him check."

"You know I can't do that, either."

"Why not?"

"Isn't it obvious? It would compromise my experiment."

Her annoyance faded, replaced by concern. "What's going on, Flynn? I thought you were willing to help with this project. Have you changed your mind?"

"It's a responsibility issue."

"Responsibility," she repeated. What in the world...? Comprehension dawned, along with a resurgence of her earlier annoyance. "In other words, if it's plain, old-fashioned lust, it's not your fault?"

"The other way around, sweetheart. If my reaction to you is a result of your pheromone perfumes, then it's out of my hands. But if it's lust..." A muscle moved in his jaw. "Then our actions are my responsibility."

"I hate to burst your little guilt-bubble, but it doesn't work that way." She yanked open the door to the lab complex and marched into the foyer. "Let's discuss this in my office."

"What do you mean it doesn't work that way?"

"I mean that if you were an ant or a bee or a moth—" She broke off. "Particularly a silkworm moth. There have been fascinating studies done on them. Did you know a female silkworm moth can signal her mate from a distance of up to—"

"The point, if you don't mind?" he interrupted impatiently.

"Oh, sorry." She offered a sheepish grin. "I get carried away sometimes."

"Gee. I hadn't noticed."

She didn't believe him for one little minute. Maybe it had something to do with the sarcasm running rampant through his tone. "My point is, if you were a different species, you'd be physically incapable of resisting a pheromone directive. But humans are a bit more complicated than that. We're multilayered and therefore have the capacity to filter a pheromone prompt through the behavior modifications that society imposes.''

"In other words, society puts the brakes on the urge to screw our brains out.''

"Crude, but basically correct.'' She dropped into the seat behind her desk. "I guess I'm warning you that pheromones don't let you off the hook. You're still responsible for your own behavior. The perfumes might enhance a natural attraction but they're not going to send you into a frenzy of lust.''

"Excuse me for pointing this out,'' he bit out with a renewed sarcasm that made her wince. "But what do you call our antics on the front lawn last night?''

Heat rose in her cheeks belying her role as a cool, logical scientist. "Our reaction did get a little out of hand,'' she conceded.

"Our?'' He leaned back in his chair and regarded her with a watchful gaze. "Are you telling me that this pheromone works on both of us?''

It was the same question she'd asked herself this morning and she was forced to give him the same embarrassing answer. "Pheromones affect only the opposite sex of the same species.''

"And you're using female pheromones in your perfumes, right?''

She gritted her teeth. "Yes.''

"I *see*.''

She didn't want to think about what he saw. She suspected she knew. "Shall we get busy with the parameters for the next round of experim—''

"One more question.''

It was a wonder her molars didn't crack in half. "Fine. What?''

"How long do these pheromones last?''

"I can store them in my lab for up to—"

He waved her silent. "No. That's not what I'm asking. I mean... Once you put on the perfume, how long do the effects last?"

"Oh." She adjusted her glasses. "That's an interesting question. To be honest, it depends."

He stared at her in disbelief. "Are you saying you don't know?"

"Not exactly. You see, it depends on their purpose." She ticked off on her fingers. "In order for pheromones to be effective, they have to be species-specific, so the message is communicated only to those whose behavior it's intended to influence. It has to be concentrated, so a little goes a long way. And depending on how it's dispersed—air or water— it'll be either volatile or stable. Volatile for an aerosol dispersion and stable for—"

He groaned. "Honey, you're really cute when you go into professor-mode. It gets me downright excited. But what I'm asking is... *How the hell long is that perfume going to drive me crazy?*"

"Are you..." She could scarcely believe it. "Are you still experiencing residual side effects?"

"I'm hard as a rock. Is that residual enough for you?"

She blinked. That couldn't be. "That can't be."

"Want to check?" He started to stand.

"No, no!" She ripped off her glasses and threw them onto the desk. "I'll take your word for it."

He subsided in his seat and managed a mocking grin. "Maybe it's because you've been talking dirty to me. Or maybe it's those damn glasses. Or the way you keep fiddling with the top button of your lab coat. Or maybe you just smell good enough to eat."

"But I showered."

"I'm sure there's a point to that comment," he stated

impatiently. "Right now it escapes me. You want to try again?"

"I washed off last night's perfume. You're—" She cleared her throat and fumbled for her glasses, slipping them on the tip of her nose again. "You're not under any pheromonal influences. At least, none that I'm aware of."

He exploded from his chair. Before she could do much more than emit a tiny shriek, he plucked her out from behind her desk and spread her across the wide wooden surface. Papers scattered in all directions.

"No pheromones?" he demanded, covering her body with his.

"What are you doing?"

"Answer the question." He wrapped his arms around her. "Do you have a pheromone perfume on?"

She squirmed. "No!"

"Great. Then here comes experiment number two."

Her glasses were the first to go. She heard them bounce on the rug somewhere to her left. As though unable to resist, Flynn thrust his hand into her hair, loosening the curls. Ringlets floated free in a silken halo across her blotter. Next, he sent the clip flying after her glasses. She closed her eyes and waited breathlessly for him to strip her naked and have his wicked way with her. When nothing happened, she peeked at him from beneath her lashes. He regarded her with open amusement, a sexy grin spread across his equally sexy mouth.

"You have a curly hair fixation, don't you?" she asked, desperate to break the nerve-racking tension.

"Only your curly hair."

"Oh." She cleared her throat. "I don't mean to complain, but there's a pen stabbing me in the back."

He rolled her slightly to one side and yanked the ballpoint

free. "Any more complaints, observations or comments before we get down to business?"

"Just one." She tried to read his expression, but without her glasses and with his face so close to hers, his features were a pleasant, if enigmatic blur. "Why are you doing this?"

"Don't you know?"

She shook her head. "Is it because you're still angry about the perfume?"

"Do I look angry? Feel angry?"

"You look and feel…" Oh, dear. He *was* hard as a rock. How…impressive. "Lusty."

"Good call."

"Then, if it's not too naive a question, what are we doing on my desk?"

"I'm making a comparison."

"Between last night and now?"

"You really are one smart woman. Now, shut up and get to work."

A gurgle of laughter escaped. "Work?"

"Yeah. Work."

She couldn't resist running a finger along his jawline. His eyes darkened, the gold burnished with a hunger that made her want to pick up where they'd left off last time. "Kissing you is work?"

"Hard work. Now, get busy so we have another basis for comparison."

Her laughter died. This morning she'd awoken with the knowledge that she'd fallen in lust with this man. Even though she'd been distressed by that fact, she'd been able to deal with it because it was a temporary, if inconvenient sexual reaction. Understandable, given her background and experience. She might not like it. Still, she was realistic enough to accept that reason didn't always play a part in sexual attraction, no matter how much she might want it otherwise.

But somehow those feelings had undergone a radical change. They'd grown, become something deeper and more substantial. She didn't understand it. Not even a little. It didn't make the least sense, especially given the brevity of their association. Nevertheless, she was forced to concede the truth.

When Flynn left, she'd be devastated.

He rested above her, waiting for her to make the next move. A slight smile tilted his mouth, and he regarded her with a mixture of passion and amusement. "Having second thoughts?" he asked, reading her with frightening ease.

"Yes."

She shouldn't be doing this, shouldn't be feeling like this. Scientists were supposed to keep their emotions separate from their work, maintain a barrier between the two so their experiments didn't become tainted by the subjective.

Slowly, she reached up and pushed a strand of dark, wavy hair from Flynn's brow. It was already too late. She was as tainted as they came. And right now she didn't give a damn.

"It was the perfume," she said, trying to convince him. Trying to convince herself. "What happened last night was a chemical reaction. A response to an irresistible pheromonal influence."

"Prove it. Put your mouth where your money is."

"You want proof? Okay." She lifted upward and brushed her lips against his. Softly. Lightly. No more than a whisper of a touch. She tried for a careless smile. "See? Nothing."

"Again."

Damn. She lifted upward once more. Her mouth closed on his this time, lingering, sliding along the full width in a gentle exploration. She half expected him to assume control, to become the aggressor. Heck, she hoped he would, taking the decision out of her hands. But he didn't and she relaxed back against the desk. What further proof did he need than that? If he'd lusted after her because he'd found her irresistible as a person, he'd have responded by now. His resistance simply proved the success of her perfumes.

Disappointment ate deep into her heart.

"Have I proved my point?" she asked, shoving at his shoulders.

"Again."

He wanted more? Fine. She'd give it to him. She laced her fingers together at the back of his neck and tugged him downward. Slanting her head to one side, she took his mouth in hungry demand, urging his lips apart and sliding her tongue home. He tasted incredible. She drove into him over and over, biting at his lip, soothing it, then biting once more.

Desire shot through her, hot and demanding, filling the air with a far different scent than her perfumes. Still he didn't touch her, forcing her to remain the aggressor. Parting her thighs, she wriggled beneath him, her dress slipping to her waist. He surged into the open cradle she'd bared and she locked him in place with her legs, wrapping him in warmth.

He was as hard as he'd claimed, the length of him pressing aggressively through the rough denim of his jeans and the thin silk of her underpants. She eased her hands between them, filling her palms with the impressive bulge running the length of his zipper. Ever so gently she squeezed. His breath exploded in a rush, giving lie to his detachment.

"Again?" she dared to tease.

"You're cheating."

"I'm just doing what you asked."

"Are you claiming a clinical detachment? That's pretty damned nervy."

"I'm a scientist." She trotted out the lie for his inspection. "I'm always clinically detached."

"You're clinically full of it, lady."

Laughter rumbled through her. "That, too."

His gold eyes took on a tender light and he twined a ringlet around his index finger, watching in seeming fascination as it wrapped tightly around him. "You're wishing we were close to a bed so we could finish this, aren't you?" he asked.

"Actually, I'm wondering if you remembered to pick up some condoms."

"Back right pocket."

Temptation beckoned and she fought to control it, with only limited success. "There was a point to this experiment, if I recall. And I'm pretty certain making love on my desk wasn't it."

"You're right. We were comparing the lust we felt last night under the influence of your perfume with what we're experiencing right now. So do me a favor and compare this."

He carefully untangled himself from her hair and reached between them, replacing her hands with his. His fingers were cool against scalding heat as he stroked a burning path down the center of her underpants. His fingertip traced the elastic edge, stroking along the inside of her thigh. Occasionally, he wandered off course, encroaching past the silk barrier into the moist, heated center of her. If his touch had sent her crazy last night, it drove her straight over the edge today. She bucked beneath him, muffling her shriek in his shirt.

"I seem to remember that scream. So that's still the same. You might want to make a note of that." He cocked an eyebrow. "No?"

"No!"

"You sure? I'm positive I can find that pen you were lying on top of. And I'm pretty sure you have paper around here somewhere."

"Please, Flynn. I can't take any more."

"Yup. That's the same as last time, too. In fact, I think you've got it word-for-word. You sure we shouldn't be taking notes as we go along?"

She wasn't quite certain what she said at that point, but whatever it was had him tugging her panties to one side and reacquainting himself with the various dips and valleys he bared.

"Oh, yeah. This is definitely familiar. Only one difference I've noticed so far." He circled, then swooped in for a landing down her center runway. "You're squirming a whole lot more. Why do you think that is?"

"Flynn!"

"Whatever's the matter, honey?" He blinked in mock innocence. "Is there something wrong?"

"We can't do this," she babbled desperately, spreading her legs as wide as they'd go. "Not here. What if Paulie walked in and—"

"He'd get an eyeful."

"Yes." She groaned. "That's precisely my point. And…"

"But we have to repeat last night's experiment. Isn't that what we agreed? Remember this?" He flicked her with his thumb. "One."

Her voice hitched repeatedly like a broken record stuck in a groove.

"You were saying?"

"I was saying—" Her breath came in desperate pants. "I was saying that if you stop, I'll kill you."

"Oh, I wasn't planning to stop. Don't you worry about that. After all, we want to keep the parameters of this experiment as close to last time as possible.'' He flicked again. "Two.''

She shuddered, fighting for breath. "Three! Please, please. One. Two. Three. Do three *now*.''

"You mean this three?'' Flick.

A roaring filled her ears and she let out a scream that threatened to crack glass, tumbling over the top, just as she had the previous evening. Her bottom lifted toward his clever hand, every muscle in her body constricting. Spasms racked her as sobs ripped through her chest.

She didn't know how long it took before she calmed enough to take note of her surroundings. When she did, she closed her eyes, fighting tears. She'd really made a mess of things this time. And on her desk, no less. How would she get any work done in here ever again? Every time she looked at her desktop, she'd remember what had happened.

"Any questions?'' he teased.

"No!'' She fought for control. "No, you've proved your point.''

"Sheer lust, right? Not perfumes?''

"Sheer lust,'' she confirmed. "No perfumes.''

A rough satisfaction eased his expression, blunting the passion that rode him so hard. He gathered her close and kissed her again. Where before it had been a desperate joining of lips and tongue and teeth, this time the caress contained a gentler, more tender quality, as if he truly cared. As if it wasn't just a desperate urge to mate with the nearest convenient female.

Her brows drew together in confusion. Maybe Flynn was right. Maybe last night had nothing to do with her pheromone perfumes. Maybe what they'd experienced was simple, old-fashioned lust. She didn't know whether to be delighted that she inspired such passion in a man or upset that her perfume had most likely failed.

Fighting for control, Flynn gave her a final kiss. "Soon. We're going to have to find a bed real soon." His mouth traced a path to her ear and she shivered as the warmth of his breath gusted along her neck. He drew in a deep breath.

And then he froze.

"What am I smelling?"

"Smelling?"

He reared back. "Perfume. I can smell your perfume."

"That's impossible. I'm not wearing any."

"The hell you aren't."

He ripped free of her arms and Jane levered herself upward. She glanced downward and groaned. She lay sprawled across the desk, her dress hiked to her waist, her legs spread wide. Her panties all in a twist. She slid off with more haste than grace and yanked her dress downward.

What had she done? What had she been thinking? She shot Flynn a quick, nervous glance. And what must he think of her?

"I'm telling you the truth, Flynn." She attempted to smooth away the creases in her lab coat but the wrinkles stubbornly remained. "I was squirted with perfume last night, an unfortunate accident, you must admit."

"I'm not admitting anything, right now."

She gave him a direct look. "It happened. Then the...incident...between us occurred. I took a long, hot shower afterward, soaping myself well. Any lingering traces of perfume would have been removed in the shower. And even if they hadn't been, the ingredients are only active for a limited amount of time. I'm sure we're well past—"

"I. Smell. Perfume!"

She folded her arms across her chest and scowled. Now he'd gone and made her cranky. *"I'm. Not. Wearing. Any!"* Unfortunately, she found it a trifle difficult to be impressively indignant with tousled ringlets bouncing in her eyes, around her cheeks and down her back. Not to mention that disastrous state of her dress. No doubt she looked like a wayward Shirley Temple.

"Come here." He reached for her arm and yanked her close again. "Yup. It's there." He lifted her arm to her nose. "Sniff!"

She sniffed. Uh-oh. Her eyes widening. Son of a— "I...I don't understand it. This can't be. I swear, I washed it all off."

"Well, somehow it got back on you. Now, think. You didn't put any on, right? So you must have picked it up from another source."

And then it clicked. "My purse." To her distress, tears filled her eyes and she blinked rapidly in an effort to clear them. "Flynn, I'm so sorry. I never even thought of that. The perfume bottle broke in my purse, remember? When it dropped on the rock outside the house?"

"And you cleaned it up this morning, is that it?"

"After..." She cleared her throat. "After I showered. And after I had breakfast this morning. And...and right before I came over to talk to my uncles. Then we came in here and..." She glanced at the desk and quickly away, squirming in embarrassment. "I think you know the rest."

"So our little experiment on your desk—"

"Wasn't a valid test. It could have been a result of the perfume again."

He swore, long and virulently. "That's just great."

"Look, you're upset. With just cause, I admit."

Flynn flashed her a smoldering glare that had the words evaporating on her tongue. "You have no idea."

"I seriously didn't realize I was—"

"Contaminated? That doesn't change what's happening here. I'm in a state of perpetual pain thanks to your damn experiment."

"Then the sooner we finish the testing process, the better for all concerned," she said attempting to soothe him. "Why don't we both sit down, calm down and take care of the last of the paperwork. I'll stay well away from you the whole time."

She didn't think she'd ever heard the word he said spoken aloud. He added a few more for good measure. "And that's what you can do with your paperwork," he concluded.

"Please, Flynn. I just have a few final questions to ask." She winced at his expression. "They're nothing like the ones from the other night."

"No."

Oh, dear. This didn't look good. If she didn't get him to agree, the past day and a half would have all been for nothing. "I understand why you're upset."

"You just don't give a damn."

"That's not true." She shoved her hands into the pockets of her coat and faced him down. "Do you really think I enjoy being taken apart? On my own desk, no less? Nothing like this has ever happened before."

"Not even with Mick?"

She fought to control her devastation. "What happened with Mick was extremely unpleasant." Her gaze clung to his. "What happened between us was incredible."

"Aw, hell," he muttered. For a moment, she didn't think her honesty would make a difference to him. Then he sighed. "Okay, fine. What are your questions?"

"Forget it, Flynn," she said, reaching a decision. She'd put him through enough. "No more questions. We're through."

"No, we're not." He paced the length of her office. "If we were through, I'd be on my way back to San Francisco and you'd be back in your lab."

"Flynn—"

But he hadn't finished. "You'd be in your lab, playing with your secret potions and solutions and compounds, trying to create chemically what you refuse to find naturally. And why?"

"Please, Flynn," she whispered. "Don't."

"Because you're scared." He turned to face her. "Aren't you, Jane?"

CHAPTER ELEVEN

FLYNN'S WORDS HIT HARDER than he'd intended. Jane stared at him, her eyes huge and distressed. She bit down on her lower lip, a lip still swollen from his kisses. He longed to soothe her mouth, ease the hurt with a gentle sweep of his tongue. But he knew where that would lead.

To a world of hurt.

Her chin quivered ever so slightly, but she stuck it in the air, anyway. "You're right," she confessed. "I am afraid."

"Mick sure did a number on you, didn't he." It wasn't a question.

"Yes, he did a number on me. But I can't blame him for the person I've become." She shoved back her chair and stood, as well. "Come on. I'd like to show you something."

She led the way out of the office and pulled open a heavy glass door that led into her lab—the only part of the complex he hadn't explored. Removing a pair of safety glasses from a container, she handed them to Flynn. "Always put these on whenever you come in here."

He did as she instructed, surprised at how tidy she kept the place. For some reason he'd expected to see beakers of peculiar-colored substances bubbling away over Bunsen burners with coils of copper tubing running to strange machines with complex gauges. Sure, there were a few odd-looking devices, but they looked more like parts of a computer than the stuff of Frankenstein movies.

"Welcome to my home," she stated quietly.

Her comment bothered him. A lot. "It's a lab, sweetheart, not a home."

"It's home to me," she explained. Something in the way he said it had him studying her with a watchful eye. "I've spent a lifetime in here. I've probably spent more hours in this one building than anywhere else, even my house."

"Now, there's a scary thought."

"Want to hear a scarier one?"

"Can I handle it?"

"I don't know." She fixed him with deep green eyes, forest eyes, eyes that were at once sweetly naive and painfully shrewd. "I've only shared this place with four other people. Five, including you."

It was a telling admission and one that worried him. Her uncles had made a bad mistake keeping their niece imprisoned in this tiny town, and Jane was paying the price for it. It was like discovering Sleeping Beauty wandering alone through her castle, unaware that life existed beyond the wall of thickets that separated her from the outside world. Someone needed to rescue her.

The thought stopped him cold and he rubbed a hand across the back of his neck. Aw, hell. Surely he wasn't seeing himself in the role of Prince Charming? That would be too damn funny. He couldn't think of anyone less equipped to play the part of hero than Flynn Morgan. The mere idea would send Paulie into a fit of hysterical laughter. Then his partner would slug him for stumbling across another damsel in distress and he'd be back where he started just a few short weeks ago.

"I'm one of the people you've shared your lab with," he prompted. "I assume your uncles make four. Who's number five?"

"Mick."

He'd figured as much. Still, the thought annoyed him. Mick didn't deserve a place in Jane's castle.

She wandered past a workbench, running a hand over the stone surface. Nicks and stains marred the surface. Above the bench were shelves, neatly filled with glassware. Above others were ventilation hoods. And beneath the various workstations were locked cabinets. There were a half-dozen sinks placed at various distances along the benches, each with three different handles. The hot and cold water were obvious. He didn't have a clue about the third.

"It's for deionized water," she explained, noticing his interest.

"Is this where you invent your perfumes?"

"Not in this part of the complex. That's done in the organic chemistry lab. We also do purification work there, identification and synthesis of various compounds." She shot him a teasing look. "That's where I keep the high explosives."

"Yuck it up, sweetheart. But your bill just doubled."

She grinned. "Oops."

"So what's this room used for?"

"It's our analytical lab. There's nothing too hazardous in here other than some solvents and acids. And I keep those secured."

"That's a relief." He eyed some of the more impressive equipment. "What do you analyze?"

"Anything. Everything. Basically, I have every piece of equipment necessary to analyze the composition of my perfumes. I can even analyze the air, people's physiological reaction to the various solutions, not to mention—"

"Jane."

She sighed. "I'm rambling, aren't I?"

"It's not that I object to learning more about your work,

Under other circumstances you could talk to your heart's content. But that isn't why you brought me in here, is it?"

"No."

"I didn't think so. If it wasn't to show me your lab or to discuss security measures, then why?"

She turned and faced him. He'd never seen her look so vulnerable. He wanted to warn her, explain how dangerous it was to open herself to a man like him. Such frankness could only lead to one place. And it wasn't a place he wanted to take her or have her go.

"You told me about your experiences at Lost Springs." She shrugged self-consciously. "Or some of them. I imagine there's a lot you've left unsaid."

"Count on it."

"Trust doesn't come easily to you, does it?"

"Not even a little."

She nodded in perfect understanding. "It doesn't to me, either. But I suspect it's for a different reason than it is for you."

"Mick?"

"He was a contributing factor, but he wasn't the main cause."

He released his breath in a slow sigh. "If it wasn't him, then it had to be that trio of lunatics who raised you."

"If you mean my uncles, then yes."

"I'll bet they had some crazy notions about parenting, didn't they?"

He half expected her to leap to their defense. But she didn't. She simply shrugged. "They raised me the best they knew how. I was loved, Flynn. That made up for a lot."

For a verbal slap, it was a gentle one. He suspected he'd gotten off easy. "What you mean is, it was more than I had. More than I'd allow, if truth be told." He turned a skeptical gaze on her. "But you can't tell me they taught you not to trust."

"Not exactly," she conceded. "The number one rule my uncles drummed into me was to question and analyze all the various elements in my world. Don't ever assume. Don't take anything for granted. Doubt everything until you've had a chance to weigh the evidence for yourself."

"It doesn't sound like you did a very good job questioning and analyzing Mick."

The jab hit home. She winced, but didn't back away from the comment. "Yes, well... As a result of that particular incident, I've become more careful. Probably more reserved, too. It also brought home my uncles' rule in a rather painful object lesson. Ever since then I've questioned everything."

He began to understand. "That doesn't mean—"

"Everything." She gestured toward the equipment surrounding them. "Do you know I can take a sample of your kiss and analyze its specific molecular structure?"

His eyebrows shot up. "Sort of takes the fun out of it, don't you think?"

"See that machine over there next to the hood?"

"The one that looks like a computer with a smokestack?"

"Yes. That one. It's a gas chromatograph mass spectrometer. GCMS. I can analyze the precise mixture of molecules with that baby. And that one, there?" She pointed. "By my computer? It's a UV-vis. It'll measure the visible color of a solution. Want to identify a compound? I can do it. Need an explosion-proof refrigerator? Got that, too."

He shot her a wary look. "Do I *need* an explosion-proof fridge?" Hanging around her, he just might.

She shook her head in exasperation. "Don't you understand? Whenever I'm puzzling through a problem I try and break it down into its particular components and figure out the solution. It's how I was trained."

"And that's good, right?"

A smile flirted with her mouth, a smile of such rich promise, he almost dumped her on top of one of her worktables to finish what they'd begun in her office. "It's supposed to be, but I'm not totally convinced. I've recently discovered there's something I've overlooked."

"And what's that?"

Her eyes had taken on a faraway expression. "I'm beginning to suspect there are some things in this world that can't be analyzed in a lab."

"You're only finding that out now? Sort of late in the day, isn't it?"

She shrugged. "I guess I've been asleep all these years."

"And now it's time to wake up?" Prince Charming to the rescue.

"Past time, don't you think?"

He pulled back and gave her a once-over. "Now that I look at you, I guess you are getting a bit long in the tooth."

Her laugh had a rough quality to it. "What can I say? I'm a slow learner." Her amusement faded. "Which leaves me in a bit of a quandary."

This was leading somewhere, but he was damned if he could figure out where. "What's your quandary?"

"I don't trust anything I can't analyze. It's not…safe. And yet, if I'm to see and enjoy what's beyond my lab, I'll have to take certain things on faith."

Hell, he knew the hazards of that sort of attitude. "I'm not sure what I'm about to tell you will make you feel any better."

She shrugged. "It can't make it any worse."

"Yes, it can." He moved in on her, plunging his hands into her hair. Damn, she felt good. Soft and sweet and utterly feminine, despite her attempt to disguise that fact. "You might not trust anything outside of your lab. But I've taken it a step further. I don't trust anything, period." He nodded toward her equipment. "Whether it's in here or out in the big, bad world, it's all suspect as far as I'm concerned."

She lowered her head to the curve of his shoulder. "We make quite a pair, don't we? Suspicious. Distrustful. I don't believe in anything I can't analyze in my lab and you don't believe in anything at all."

He needed the reminder. "This is a bad idea, Jane."

"What is?"

"Us. Touching."

"Ah." She closed her eyes as though rejecting his words. "You're right, of course."

"We should end this now. Before you get hurt again."

He could feel her smile through his shirt. "What about you? Or don't you get hurt?"

"I don't have a heart to risk."

"Lost it long ago, did you?"

"It was carved right out of me as a child."

She looked up at him. He'd never known compassion was colored green. But he learned it in that moment, witnessing the emotion in the darkening depths of her eyes. If it had been any other woman, he'd have found a few pithy words to wipe it away. But looking down at Jane, he couldn't bring himself to say anything that might hurt her. She meant well. She just didn't understand what sort of man he was. With any luck at all, she'd never find out.

She lifted a finger to his face, tracing the lines bracketing his mouth. "I guess we'd better come to an agreement."

Uh-oh. "What sort of agreement?" he asked warily.

Her fingers wandered lower, finding the vee of his shirt. "Since neither of us is very good at trusting—"

"I think it's safe to say we stink at trust." Her touch was driving him insane and he briefly considered asking her to stop. She traced the vee again, this time in the other direction, and he shook his head. Screw it. Let her play. He didn't need his sanity.

Her finger drifted lower still, plucking at his shirt buttons. "And since we're both determined to keep our relationship casual, than maybe we could—"

He knew where this was heading and he needed to stop her before she got there. "Try for nonexistent, instead of casual? Good idea."

She stilled. "Nonexistent?"

"Sure. You know…" Man, he hated being honorable. It was fast becoming a royal pain in the ass. "No touching. No kissing." No desktop bus stops. "We don't want to compromise your experiment, right?"

She struggled to summon a smile. "Just what I was about to suggest. We keep our relationship safe. We keep it strictly business." To his disappointment, her hand dropped from his chest and she peered up at him, searching his expression. "Right?"

"Are you hoping I'll talk you out of it?"

"Yes."

He released his breath in a long sigh. "I'm not going to. It wouldn't be…appropriate."

"Got it." She straightened her wrinkled lab coat. Or tried to. Not that it did much good, he noticed in amused disgust. He'd done a thorough job of creasing it for her. "You analyze our security needs and I'll conduct my experiments."

"And we'll both avoid your desk?"

Her laugh sounded almost natural. "And the front lawn, my porch steps, the foyer, my living room—"

He caught the tiny catch in her voice, saw the gleam of tears and something inside broke. "And your lab," he muttered.

Her nose wrinkled. It made her look like a bewildered

rabbit. A helpless, infinitely kissable, little rabbit. "My lab? Why should we avoid my lab?"

"To make sure we don't ever do this again."

He plowed his hands in her hair again and tipped her face to his. His mouth found hers with unerring accuracy. With one kiss, he plunged straight into lust. It felt as though he'd slammed down the accelerator on a car capable of hitting a hundred in under three seconds. The bottom dropped out of his world and he fell in a long, endless tumble. He scoured her mouth, his kisses harder than they should have been, more desperate, starving. He was a man who'd gone too long without true sustenance. And now that he'd found it, he wasn't about to give it up.

Their embrace would soon get out of hand, but he didn't give a damn. She felt like fire in his arms, burning him, filling him with a desperation to complete what should have been completed long ago. He'd been a fool to turn Jane down when the path of least resistance led to the one place he most wanted to be...her bed.

He plucked at the buttons of her lab coat. "What do you say, sweetheart? Here and now. We can initiate your lab and really make it feel like home."

She clung to him, her face desperate with desire. "We're not supposed to do this," she gasped.

The reminder cut. "Then stop me." As a plea, it came off halfhearted at best.

"Don't you think I've tried?" She lowered her head to his chest and sucked air into her lungs. "You know I can't."

"Why?"

"Because. You said..." Her hand fluttered helplessly through the air, filling in where words failed her. "And I agreed."

"Will it screw up your experiment, if we...indulge?" He fought the image of Paulie's fist hooking toward his cheek.

This wasn't the same as that other time, Flynn tried to tell himself. It was different with Jane. "Just a little?"

"Yes. No. I'm not sure." She moistened her lips. "I'm wearing the perfume. Maybe that's why—"

"Fine. Blame this on the perfume if it makes you feel better. If it won't mess up your results, then shut up and kiss me."

"What happens if it gets out of control?"

"Then we make love until neither one of us can move." His laugh held a rough edge. "You can blame our lapse on the pheromones. I'll blame it on resorting to the lowest common masculine denominator."

She stared at him in shock. "Is that what you really believe? That it's nothing more than lust? That you're..." She thrust wayward ringlets from her eyes. "That you're lowering yourself?"

Aw, hell. Now he felt like a total heel. "No. No, I don't mean it like that. But—" Someone needed to stop them before they took this any further. Looked like he'd be the one, after all. He took a deep breath. And then another. Dredging up every ounce of self-control he possessed, he nudged his voice from desperate to reasonable. "But how many times do I have to tell you, honey? I'm trouble. More trouble than you can handle."

It was the truth. He'd worked so hard to change, fighting to grow from the man he'd once been to a man that didn't make him heartsick every time he looked in a mirror. And all it took was a pair of pretty green eyes, a sexy mouth perfectly shaped for kissing and the most incredible body ever hidden beneath a lab coat, and all his good intentions evaporated. Since he couldn't seem to stay in control of the situation, maybe he could encourage her to do it for them both.

If their relationship went any further, he'd end up hurting

her when he left, which meant he had to convince her to hold him at a safe distance. Only one problem. She needed to test perfumes that had the delightful effect of making mincemeat of his good intentions. Now, how the hell was he supposed to keep his hands off her when she specialized in sex perfumes?

"Jane, we have a choice to make."

She regarded him warily. "What choice?"

"We can continue with what we started last night or we can fulfill our original agreement. It's your choice. I'll finish installing your security system, show you what we can do for your lab. And you can continue testing your perfumes. But if we end up in bed together, our work relationship ends."

"You don't think we can deal with both?"

He didn't pull his punches. "You know full well that sleeping with me will ruin the experiment. As for me... I can't work around you. I lose focus and make mistakes. Your uncles are paying me a lot of money and I won't screw them over just because I can't keep my hands off you. So which is more important to you? A few nights of pleasure, or your experiments?"

She did just as he'd hoped. She withdrew, masking her vulnerability beneath the facade of a cool, remote scientist, a look she'd no doubt patented at age five, as well. "That's it? One or the other?"

He was protecting her, he tried to convince himself, not hurting her. "Those are your choices."

Slowly, she pulled free of his arms. "I think we were right earlier. We'll keep our relationship strictly business."

He'd never doubted what her answer would be, so why did it hurt? He'd never been hurt by a woman before. Hell, he'd never gotten close enough to allow a woman to hurt him. "You got it."

He turned his back on her before he did something incredibly stupid. Like kiss her again. This was for the best, he reminded himself. It would keep them both out of trouble in the long run, whether she knew it yet, or not.

So, why did it feel so wrong?

"WELL?" MICK DEMANDED. "Have you reached a decision? Are you going to help me?"

Flynn lounged back in his chair, hiding his annoyance at Barstow's latest intrusion beneath a bored expression. "Yes. I'm going to help."

"Excellent." He grinned in triumph. "And what have you discovered so far?"

"Nothing."

"What do you mean, 'nothing'?"

"You're a smart man, Mick. I'm sure you know what it means." Seeing that his careless words had only exacerbated the situation, Flynn sighed. "I mean that I haven't had the opportunity to go through her computer. She didn't want any help with her security system until just recently. It took me a while to convince her she needed my services. It'll take a while longer before I can find what you're looking for."

"You don't understand. I need those notes!"

"And you'll get them. Until then, stay off her property."

"Why should I? Last time I was here, you threw me out. You said you weren't going to help me. Now you are?" Barstow's eyes narrowed suspiciously. "What changed your mind?"

Flynn tilted his chair onto two legs. "I had time to consider your request, okay? I'll look into it. But I'm no thief."

"Anymore."

The legs hit the floor with a bang and Flynn unwound his frame from the comfort of his chair, annoyed at having to make the effort when he was so bone-weary. "You don't want to start something with me, Mick. You truly don't."

"Oh, yeah?"

Cocky little bastard. Flynn approached. "Want me to explain why not?"

Apparently, Mick's bravery only went so far. He backed away from Flynn, talking fast. "I know things about you, things that can cause you some serious damage. I'll use them if I have to. The truth has a way of coming out, you know."

"You're right. It does."

He didn't take the hint. "I need those notes and I need them soon."

"Stay away from Jane Dearly."

Mick stilled, only his eyelids moving as he blinked rapidly. "You *can't* be attracted to her," he finally said, amazement clear in his voice. "She's not even close to your sort."

"And what, exactly, is my sort?"

"Not Jane. She's a nice girl."

Anger roiled through Flynn, knotting in his gut. "Get out of here, Mick. If you're really as smart as all those fancy college degrees claim, you'll stay away from me for a while. And if you want to avoid serious hurt, you'll stay away from Jane, too."

Mick must have sensed he'd pushed his luck as far as it could be pushed. With surprising dignity, he paced to the door and yanked it open. Then he looked over his shoulder at Flynn. "Time's running out for me, Morgan. I'm boxed in a corner with only one way to turn. And that way is those notes. Either you get them or I will. If I have to do it, it won't be pretty and it won't be with the sort of finesse you're capable of. But it will get done."

Flynn thought fast. "You'll have them. But not until the

night before I leave. I'll get them for you then. It's safer that way.''

"You better, Morgan. Fail me and I promise...you *will* regret it.''

That said, he left, leaving Flynn wondering what the hell was in those notes.

CHAPTER TWELVE

"I DON'T WANT TO LEAVE THE LAB. I'm working, in case it escaped your notice."

"Oh, I noticed. I've noticed that you've been holed up in here for the past four days. You promised to look at a security setup for your lab. Instead, every time I've come in here you've drenched yourself in perfume, planted your hands on those curvy little hips of yours and dared me to act like a randy teenager."

She pulled her nose out of her computer screen long enough to glare at him. "I notice you haven't reacted!"

"Maybe because I don't take well to threats."

"Threats?"

"What else would you call it?"

"I'd call it an experiment."

"Bull. It doesn't matter what I do. I can't win, can I?"

Wariness winked behind her rainbow-colored glasses. "What do you mean?"

He ran his hand through his hair and grimaced. The past few days had been the most difficult he'd endured in a long time. Hell, he'd even welcome Paulie with open arms right about now. He could use a good dose of realism, which just went to show how truly desperate he felt. "I mean that if I kiss the hell out of you, I'm in trouble. And if I don't kiss the hell out of you, I'm in even more trouble."

"All I want is a little honesty. If the perfume causes a reaction, tell me. Is that too much to expect?"

"From a guy like me?" She winced at his sarcasm. "Absolutely."

She closed her eyes and sighed, exhaustion settling across her features. "This isn't working, Flynn."

Enough was enough. "You're right. It's not. And I know just what to do about it." He caught her hand in his and began towing her from the lab. "Come on. We're leaving."

"I can't, Flynn. I'm right in the middle of—"

"You're always right in the middle of something." He turned a warning glare on her. "Dig in your heels and I swear I'll toss you over my shoulder."

"You wouldn't."

"Try me." Once outside the lab, he pointed to a coatrack he'd installed beside the glass door. "See that? It's for you."

She stared in bewilderment. "Okay. Thank you." She cleared her throat, shrugging in bewilderment. "What does it do? Where do I input codes?"

"Codes?" He groaned. "It doesn't take *codes*. I told you. It's a rack. You hang things on it. You know. A *rack?*"

"Oh. I thought it was another of your electronic doohickeys."

"No. It serves a much more practical purpose. Now, pay attention." He plucked her glasses off the tip of her nose. "Glasses." He folded the earpieces and dropped them in the pocket of her lab coat. "Glasses in pocket."

"Oh, for—"

But he wasn't through yet. Not even close. He rummaged in her hair, quelling her struggles with ease. "Clip. Clip in pocket."

"You really are obsessed with my hair, aren't you," she complained, shoving at his hands.

"Yes. And now I'll show you what else I'm obsessed with." Before she could do more than squeak in alarm, he tackled the buttons of her lab coat. "Lab coat. Remove lab coat."

"Stop it, Flynn. This isn't funny anymore."

"You got that right." It wasn't in the least funny. The minute he'd stripped her of her security blanket, she'd gone into a flat-out panic. "Lab coat on hook."

"I *need* that."

He stopped her when she reached for it. "No, you don't. Not when you're outside the lab. You don't need to tie your hair up, either. Or wear your glasses."

"I do if I'm going to read something."

"How many pairs do you have in the house?"

Her mouth opened, then closed again. "Okay. Fine. But what if I'm conducting an experiment outside of the lab?"

"Here's a shocking suggestion. Why don't you do it in your everyday clothes?" He didn't wait for a response. "Get your purse. We're leaving."

"I have an extra pair of glasses in my purse, you know."

"I don't doubt it for a minute. So long as you don't have a lab coat in there, I think we're safe."

"You certainly have a fixation about that particular garment," she grumbled. But at least she did what he asked.

"That's because I know what it represents. You use that damn coat to hold people at a distance. To announce, 'I'm different.'"

"I most certainly do not," she instantly objected.

"Sure you do. You spend half your life putting up barriers to keep people at a safe distance."

To his surprise, she didn't continue to deny the assertion. "How would you know?" she asked instead.

He dropped an arm around her waist and swept her toward the door. "I know because I do it, too," he informed her calmly. "But I'm not quite as obvious."

That made her sputter a bit, just long enough for him to

get her out of the building. He felt her gaze as they walked across the backyard, curiosity coming off her in waves. "So what do you use to keep people at a distance?"

"You tell me."

Her response came with painful promptness. "You treat everything like it's a joke or as if you don't care. You don't take anything seriously." She threw a glance over her shoulder. "Like my lab coat."

"That's where you're wrong, honey. I take that coat very seriously. That's why we're leaving it on the hook."

"Why? Where are we going?"

"Out."

She returned to the subject of deepest concern, like Dipstick worrying a bone. "I have more lab coats in the house, you know. And lots more glasses."

"Yeah." His mouth compressed. "That's why we're going out. Go inside and get your purse. I'll wait here. Fair warning, take longer than five minutes and I'm coming in after you."

"We'll see about that." She stomped toward the house, curls bouncing along her spine, muttering her displeasure all the way.

As soon as she disappeared from sight, Flynn turned to where Paulie hovered in the bushes. "You're as bad as her crazy uncles. Come on out of there."

"Hey, loitering in the bushes is sheer self-preservation," he claimed. "Last time you two were together on a lawn, I understand some very eye-opening events took place. I wouldn't want to walk up on anything untoward."

"If anything untoward *were* taking place, I'd trust you'd keep your eyes closed and make yourself scarce." Flynn dismissed the discussion with an impatient shake of his head. "Update me, Paulie. How close are we to finishing up? I'm ready to pack it in."

"Almost done. There are a few last connections." He grimaced. "Then there's her lab."

"Damn. I can't get her to agree on a system for in there." Flynn's jaw firmed. "Enough is enough. I want you to take care of it today. I don't care what Her Highness says, you know what I want installed. Get it put together as quickly as possible and do your best to hide the alterations. I'll keep her busy for most of the day. That should give you time to get the preliminary work done."

"What about Barstow?"

"I'd almost managed to forget about him." Flynn sighed. "He's after a file on Jane's computer. See if Hickory can print it off and I'll take a look."

"And then?"

"And then, we give the man what he wants." Flynn glanced toward Jane's house. "He's paying enough for it."

Paulie shook his head. "Your scamming's going to get you in serious trouble, boy."

"I was born in serious trouble." Cynicism colored his voice. "This will just get me in a little more."

"What happens when Lady Jane finds out what you've done?"

Flynn clenched his hands at his sides. "Then she'll be only too happy to see the last of us. The wisest course, wouldn't you agree?"

"Normally? Yes. But this woman's different."

"You don't have to tell me that."

"I like her."

It was a major confession and one Flynn had never heard from his partner before. "Forget it, Paulie. The lady's out of our league. She's a hurt waiting to happen and I'm not gonna be the one to inflict it."

As though his comment had summoned her, Jane appeared in the kitchen doorway, purse in hand and a pair of glasses defiantly perched on the tip of her nose. Paulie lowered his voice, offering a final parting shot. "It's not all business with her, no matter what she says."

"Yeah? Well, it's all business with me."

Then he gave lie to his words by striding across the lawn and snatching Jane into his arms with such determination, it knocked off her glasses. The kiss he gave her was long and thorough and left him in a painful state of arousal. It was a state he'd unfortunately become all too familiar with.

"Why did you do that?" she demanded. "I thought we had an agreement."

Flynn captured her chin in his palm and gently turned her face to his. Wary green eyes gazed up at him. So serious. So vulnerable. So incredibly beautiful. "You told me to say something when your perfume was working. Well, mark this down as a red-letter day in your notebook, sweetheart. It's working. At least, something's working."

"You're just saying that."

"I believe in your perfumes, Jane," he insisted quietly. "More than that, I believe in you."

Tears filled her eyes. "Thank you."

"You're welcome." He bent and picked up her glasses, handing them over with a wry grin. "I see you've come prepared."

"Yes." She fumbled as she put her glasses in her purse, and he found her momentary awkwardness endearing. "You never said. Where are we going?"

"To a former client's house. His name's Vince Martelli and I want to show you his setup."

"Oh, right. I remember you mentioning him."

They accomplished the drive in a comfortable silence. Clouds scuttled in from the west and closed down over the Cascades, hiding the mountains from view and bringing with it a misty rain. Fortunately, it let up by the time he pulled into the driveway of a huge mansion. "This is it. Paulie and I installed the security system for this place about three years ago."

"You came all the way up from San Francisco to do one house?"

"Vince's primary residence is there." He slanted her an amused glance. "This is just his getaway cottage."

She shook her head in amazement. "Some cottage."

"Vince liked the work we did on the first place so much, he insisted we come out and do this one." He shut off the engine. "I called him when I first arrived and asked if I could take you through. He's out of town but gave me the codes to get in."

"He obviously trusts you."

"I'm a trustworthy man, these days." He needed to keep reminding himself of that—especially around Jane. Maybe it would help him keep his hands off her. "I've worked hard to earn my reputation in this business."

She smiled, tempting him to kiss her again. "I don't doubt that for a minute." She opened the car door. "Come on. Show me what you're planning to do to my poor lab."

"Jane, listen." He caught her arm before she could leave the car. "Once I'm done with the lab, my contract with your uncles will be fulfilled. I'll be returning to San Francisco."

She strove for an I-don't-give-a-damn attitude. It killed him to see how miserably she failed. He swore beneath his breath. He was going to strangle her uncles for putting him in this position. They'd claimed they'd researched him. But they couldn't have done a very good job of it. Otherwise they wouldn't have let him within a million miles of their precious niece. In fact, the only thing keeping her safe right now was his ragged sense of honor. The cynical side of his nature questioned how long that would last, how long it would take him to put honor aside and revert to his baser personality.

Not long, if he didn't stop kissing a certain curly-haired, green-eyed, sweet-smelling chemist.

Without a word, she climbed from the car and started up the sidewalk ahead of him, every movement a blatant invitation. Her curls blew around her head, whispering silken pleas for him to gather them up and twine them in his fingers. Her cute little backside swaying seductively from side to side added another, far louder call. *Take. Me. Swish. Take. Me. Swish.* Hell, even her dress taunted him, fluttering in a teasing dance around her trim calves.

"Stop doing that," he ordered.

She spun around, staring in bewilderment. "What? What am I doing?"

He started to answer, then gave it up. He couldn't think of a single thing to say that wouldn't make him sound like a raving lunatic. His eyes narrowed suspiciously. "Are you wearing perfume?"

"I thought we already established that, remember? When you kissed me not an hour ago?"

"Did you put more on?"

"Finding me irresistible again?" she asked sweetly.

Aw, hell. "Forget I asked. I already know the answer." He pushed by, grabbing a surreptitious sniff. Yup. She was wearing it, all right. He paused on the porch and tapped a series of numbers into a keypad mounted by the front door. "Ready for the lecture on security equipment?"

"I look forward to it."

Over the next hour, Flynn went over every inch of the house with Jane, deliberately driving her crazy with an endless stream of technical details. He wanted to be certain Paulie had plenty of time to get his work done. She took it well, he'd give her that. Her eyes only glazed over twice.

"Are we almost through?" she finally asked.

"Just about. There's only one more room."

"No, please. I've had enough, Flynn. You've convinced me. I know exactly what I want for my lab."

"What?"

"Nothing. Not one blessed thing. It's too much hassle. And video cameras watching me all the time?" She shook her head, shuddering. "Forget it."

He shot her a curious look. "You've mentioned that before. It's not so bad, honest. At least let me show you Martelli's office. He has a lot of expensive high-tech computer equipment in there, so it's the most secure room in the house. It has a lockdown feature that might work for you, if you want to keep things simple."

She caved. "Okay. One more." Her jaw poked out. "But only one."

The office was in a beautifully renovated basement, and he gave Jane a few minutes to admire the setup before continuing his lecture. "This might work best since it doesn't take a lot of effort on your part. Once you leave, you push a button. That sets the alarm. If someone breaks in, the door locks behind the intruder. The minute he tries to leave, the whole place shuts down—electricity, phones, everything. Then the system sends an automated call to the police."

"What if I want to return to the lab after I've set the alarm?"

"If it's late and you want to lock yourself in or if it's for a quick visit and you don't want to turn off the alarm, just leave the alarm set and walk in. To get back out, all you have to do is punch in your code before you open the door to leave. Forget that minor detail and all hell breaks loose."

"Got it." She looked around a final time and nodded. "Okay. This will do. It doesn't sound too complicated."

"Then let's go." She preceded him up the steps and

reached for the knob a second before he realized what she intended. "*Jane, don't!* I haven't punched in the code."

She twisted the knob at the same instant she looked over her shoulder at him, wrinkling her brow in confusion. "What...?" The lights winked out and the soft hum of equipment purred into silence. She cleared her throat. "I guess I shouldn't have done that, huh?"

Only one reply came to mind. "No shit, Sherlock."

"THE COPS SHOULD BE HERE before too much longer."

"Can't you call them and explain it's a false alarm?"

"The phones are down, remember?" Flynn's voice came to Jane from across the room. For some reason he'd insisted on putting as much distance between them as possible. "I'd call on my cell phone, but I left it in the car."

She sighed. "I'm not sure I like this particular system, after all."

"It's set up this way to trap the burglar inside until the police can arrive."

"You might have warned me before we went up the steps," she mentioned. She slid cautiously to the floor with her back against the wall, her arms wrapped around her bent legs. "If you had, we wouldn't be in this predicament."

"I'd just finished explaining how it worked. I said you had to punch in the number before you accessed the door. What more did you need?"

She shivered at the anger in his voice. "Still... You might have warned me a little sooner. And a little louder."

Silence.

"Flynn?"

"What?"

"I figured it out."

"What did you figure out?"

"Why you said what you did in my lab the other day."

"Right. I'm glad you figured it out." He sighed. "Whatever the hell that means."

"I mean all that stuff you spouted about not being willing to work on the security system or help with my experiments if we slept together. You said it so I'd choose business over pleasure and back off. You were protecting me, weren't you? It was really very sweet. Honorable, even. But after I thought about it for a while, I realized it was all a put-on."

"It wasn't a put-on. I was being serious."

She rested her cheek on her knees, hearing the lie in his voice. "Don't," she pleaded. "Not here. Not now. Not when it's just the two of us."

Silence.

"I can smell you," he whispered.

"I'm sorry."

"You smell good."

"Flynn?"

"What?"

"How'd you get that bruise by your mouth?"

He remained quiet so long, she didn't think he'd answer. Finally, he said, "Paulie socked me."

"Why?"

"It's a long story and I'd rather not go into it. Suffice to say I did something he didn't like, he pegged me for it and I deserved the pegging. Now answer me a question."

"Okay."

"What's that thing on top of Hickory's cane?"

"The gold handle? It's a chemical reaction."

"I'd pretty much figured out that part. What sort of reaction?"

"The criscrossing lines are a deuterium nucleus colliding with a tritium nucleus. They then fuse, which is the solid center part. When that happens a neutron and a helium nucleus are released and burn instantaneously——not to mention explosively. Those are the parts at the top that form the handle.''

"Uh-huh. Translation?''

"It's a model for a fusion reaction. Hickory was part of some hush-hush project years ago and each of the scientists involved received a similar model. Hickory chose to stick his on top of a cane.''

"A fusion reaction. As in...blowing-things-up fusion?''

"It can be, I suppose. Actually, I like to think of it as sunshine.''

"Come again?''

"The sun. It's a giant fusion reactor, the byproduct of which is heat and light. So I guess you could say Hickory carries life around on the end of his cane since without the sun we wouldn't be here.''

"And these are the people that raised you?''

She grinned. "Yeah. Mind-boggling, isn't it?''

"It boggles mine.''

Silence.

"So how did you get into the security business, anyway?'' she asked, desperate for something to say.

"Dumb luck. It seemed like a growing field. It meant I could start my own business and—'' He sighed. "And that's all a load of crap. You want the truth?''

"Yes.''

"You're not going to like it.''

"Then I won't like it. But at least I'll know it's the truth.''

"Okay, honey. I hope you're sitting down.''

She clutched her hands in her lap. This was going to be bad, she just knew it. "I'm sitting.''

"I said it was dumb luck, but I lied.'' His voice had dropped so low she could scarcely hear it. For the first time ever, an oddly vulnerable note crept into his voice. "It was dumb, all right. But far from lucky. I became an expert on security systems while learning how to circumvent them."

"Circumvent? You mean..."

He didn't pull any punches. "I mean I was a thief. I got caught. And I went to jail."

"Oh, Flynn. I'm so sorry."

"Don't be. It was a life lesson I desperately needed. I wasn't in for long, mainly because one of the companies I hit wanted to hire me to foolproof their system. And I chanced upon a liberal judge. After that, I went straight, worked off my debt and started my own company."

"That's what you meant about working hard to earn your reputation, isn't it? So now you're one of the good guys?"

"No." His voice grew rougher still. "No matter how hard we try and convince ourselves otherwise, I'm no good for you, Jane. I wish to God I was. But I'm not."

"You could be," she whispered. "If you wanted."

Silence.

"Jane?"

"Yes?"

"I'd like to sit with you."

"I thought you wanted us to sit apart. Far apart."

"I've changed my mind. It's not going to be pretty once the cops arrive, especially if they run my name. It might take a while to get hold of Vince and have him vouch for us."

Oh, Flynn! "Yes, please. I'd like to have you sit with me."

She could hear him creeping cautiously across the room. "Your perfume might as well be a homing beacon."

He settled down next to her and drew her into his arms. She looked up at him, not that she could see anything in the dark. "I really am sorry about setting off the alarm."

"Don't be."

"Since we seem to be in a confessional mood, I have one of my own to make," she admitted.

"Tell me."

"You know when I said I don't experiment on people in Salmon Bay anymore?"

"I remember."

"There's a reason."

"Which is?"

She leaned into him, needing his warmth. "When I was sixteen I developed a truth spray."

There was dead silence for a full minute. Then Flynn began to chuckle, the sound dark and rich and filling the room with gentle tenderness. "I wish I'd been here to see it."

"No, you don't." She closed her eyes, shivering at the memory. "There were three divorces, two arrests and a change of paternity on at least one birth certificate. Not to mention various and assorted other tragedies like broken friendships and a few wrecked partnerships."

"What happened after that?"

"I tucked my truth spray away and swore off using the town as my personal testing ground."

"That must have been a tough situation to deal with." His sympathy settled around her, wrapping her as securely as his arms.

"It didn't help my social life, that's for sure."

He hesitated. "I have a confession to make, too."

"Another one?"

"Yeah. Another one."

"Let me guess. You're glad I locked us down here?"

His laughter stirred the curls at her temple. "I wouldn't go that far."

"Then what's your confession?"

"I've never sat in the dark with a woman before." He

eased her onto his lap and she snuggled close. "I've never just held a woman. Not like this."

"But... You've been with so many. Surely—"

"All those others..." He shrugged. "We'd have sex and then one or the other of us would leave. Sometimes we'd sleep. But we never *held* each other. That would have been too personal. Too...trusting."

"I'm the first?"

"Yeah. I just wanted you to know that."

Her head dropped to his shoulder and she shut her eyes against the unexpected rush of tears. "Thank you," she whispered.

"Anytime."

"Flynn?" She traced the back of his hand, feeling the power and strength of his grasp, remembering that power and strength stroking across her body. The care. The tenderness. The protective self-sacrifice. He'd told her the truth. She should tell him, too. "It's...it's the perfume."

"What?"

"The perfume's affecting you. That's why you're attracted. It's not me."

His chuckle slipped through her, soft and intimate and deliciously warm. "Honey, I've been attracted to you since we first met. There hasn't been a minute we've been in each other's company—or out of it, for that matter—that I haven't wanted to hold you like this. All that can't be from perfume, pheromones or not." He nuzzled her ear. "It's you, Jane."

His words condemned her and the tears spilled free. She turned her head so he wouldn't feel them. It hurt. Hurt worse than anything she'd ever felt. He didn't know the truth and she couldn't tell him the rest—tell him how she'd ruined her experiment, all because of feelings he refused to acknowledge. Not now. Not when the truth would send him away and she'd never see him again. So much for her precious honesty.

This time when the silence fell, it remained unbroken.

CHAPTER THIRTEEN

"COME ON, JANE. You need to get out of the lab for a while."

"Not now."

"Think of poor Dipstick. He needs the exercise."

"Dipstick has free rein of the yard. He can run around all he wants."

"That's not the same as walking down by the water. Think of how much he'll enjoy that. Think how much you'll enjoy it."

She dragged her gaze from her microscope. "You're not gonna let me work, are you?"

"Nope."

"You'll keep interrupting until I give up, won't you?"

"Count on it."

She sighed. "All right, fine. Let's go."

"Great."

Leaving the lab, she hung up her coat on the peg outside the brand-new security door Flynn had insisted on installing. Next she slipped her glasses into the pocket. The clip from her hair followed and her mouth curled to one side. Flynn had certainly trained her well. Stepping outside, she slowed. "Oh, good grief. Have you lost your mind, Flynn Morgan? We can't go for a walk. It's going to rain."

"Nah. We have plenty of time." He caught her hand in his. "Come on."

"I'm not dressed for a walk. And I'm not dressed for rain, either."

"Now, Jane. You can't let Dipstick down at this late date." He whistled for the dog, who immediately came charging across the lawn. "I thought we'd walk along the sound."

"Do you know how far that is?" she grumbled. "You really are tempting fate."

He shrugged. "I seem to do that a lot." It wasn't until they were as far from home as they could get that she discovered the real reason he'd insisted on the walk. "I'm leaving tomorrow," he announced abruptly, his hand tightening around hers.

Was he afraid she'd bolt? Surely he realized she had more gumption than that. She swallowed. Hard. "I suspected as much, considering tomorrow it'll be two weeks since you arrived."

"There's something we need to discuss before I go."

Uh-oh. "What's that?"

"Mick."

"Forget it, Flynn," she said flatly. "That's not a subject open for discussion."

"You must know he's after something in your lab."

She shrugged. "My pheromone formulas, I assume."

"Why would he want them?"

"Because he can sell or patent them."

He took a minute to digest that. "Why haven't you already patented them? Wouldn't that afford you some protection against anything Mick might do?"

"Sure, if I were ready to go to patent. But I'm not."

"Why?" he asked again.

She sighed, realizing he wouldn't drop the subject until she answered. "It's sort of like cooking. You have a basic dish you're creating and you test any number of ingredients in differing amounts to discover which offers the most effective recipe overall.''

"So you have to do tests to discover which recipe works?"

"Pretty much. When it comes to my formulas, there's a huge range of combinations and components involved. I need to file a patent that covers all the applicable formulations. That's the only way to get the broadest patent coverage possible. Otherwise, my competitors could simply change one small thing and get a competing patent.''

Flynn swore beneath his breath. "Nothing's easy, is it? So even if Mick doesn't steal the formulas outright, he can change the recipe slightly and file his own patent.''

"Which is why I have to test these formulas before I file. Patent infringement occurs a lot in this field.'' Her mouth thinned. "It's *not* going to happen to me.''

"Okay. That makes sense. But what if Mick somehow gets his hands on your research? Can he get the jump on you? Could he just file as many combinations as possible and hang you up in court attempting to prove they're your discoveries?''

"Mick wouldn't do that.''

"Yeah, honey. I think he would.''

"You shouldn't make blanket statements about people you don't know.''

He looked away. "I know people, Jane. I know how truly rotten they can be. When it comes to greed or money or ego—especially ego—there's no act too low or despicable.''

She sighed. "You always see the worst in people. I really need to work on that with you.''

A drop of rain slapped his cheek. "It's too late for me. Let's worry about you, instead.''

"It's never too late to change.''

"Now, there's something I will agree with you about. But

first the person has to want to change.'' He eyed her speculatively. ''You've already said he attached his name to as many of your projects as he could. Do you really think he's above stealing them if he has the opportunity?''

''I guess not.''

''Considering your past association, you might have trouble convincing a judge that he doesn't deserve part ownership in your pheromone perfumes. Especially if he were able to compromise your computer files.''

''Point taken. I'll put your security suggestions into effect as soon as possible.''

''There's more—''

''Well, I don't want to hear it.'' The rain began in earnest and Jane indicated a dirt path leading up a hill through the woods. ''If we go over the ridge instead of around it, we can cut a lot of time off the walk back.''

Dipstick took charge at that point. Leading the way, he snuffled through the brush, chasing imaginary rabbits. Jane used the excuse of the steepness of the hill to keep from talking. Once they reached the summit, Flynn started back in on her.

''Something clued you in to what sort of man Barstow was. What happened?''

''I don't want to talk about it.''

''Come on, Jane. Tell me.''

''What did you do to earn that bruise?'' she countered. The rain came down in cold, hard sheets, soaking her dress and dripping from her hair. She had to practically shout to be heard over the pounding downpour. ''It was a woman, wasn't it?''

''We're talking about Mick.''

''Now we're talking about you.''

''Jane—''

''This conversation is over.'' She shoved a branch out of

her path and hastened down the hill before he could argue the situation. "If you want to review security measures before you leave to make sure Mick can't break in again, fine. But I'm not discussing my past mistakes and that's final."

"Slow down, honey. This path is getting a bit steep."

She waved him off. "If I slow down, you're going to argue with me some more."

"No, if you don't slow down, you're going to—"

Her foot caught on a root and shot out from under her. She landed on soft, damp earth. It cushioned her backside very nicely. Unfortunately, soft, damp earth on a steep downward slope in the pouring rain didn't hold up well. She slid as though someone had glued rollers to her butt.

Dipstick thought she'd discovered a fantastic new game. He charged along beside her, barking his encouragement. The one time she skidded to a halt, he jumped on top of her, sending her on her merry way again. She vaguely thought she heard Flynn crashing through the bushes behind her, but she couldn't be certain over the noise of her shrieking. At the bottom of the hill, her heels caught a root stretched across her path. With all the grace of the world's worst gymnast, she shot into the air, did a full midair somersault and landed flat on her back.

Jane lay there, stunned, the air knocked clean out of her, rainwater running up her nose. A minute later, Flynn belly flopped down beside her. He looked like a mountain of mud with two gold eyes—two angry gold eyes.

"Ouch," he commented.

"Am I dead?"

"If you're not, I can take care of it for you."

"*What* did I do wrong? I'm the one who fell. And it's all your fault."

"I told you to slow down."

Tears joined the raindrops streaming down her face. "You asked me about Mick."

"I want you to realize what he's capable of. I want you to think long and hard about how far he'd go to get his hands on your perfumes."

"I already know that!"

He levered himself up on one elbow. He took one look at her face and swore. "You look like hell."

"I feel like hell." She sniffed. "And my butt hurts."

"Do you think you can sit up?"

"No."

"Are you injured?"

"Yes."

He leaned over her, gently touching her arms and legs. "Where, honey? Aside from some scrapes and bruises, I don't see anything too bad."

"I already told you. My butt hurts."

"I'd offer to kiss it and make it better—"

"Don't you dare! I was just kidding. You don't have to kiss anything."

"Tell me what Mick did to you or I just might." He settled her on his lap. "Truth time, honey. What happened?"

Oh, what the hell. He'd told her about his past. It seemed only fair to return the favor. "Mick filmed us, okay?" She closed her eyes and dug her nose into the pile of wet, musty leaves plastered to Flynn's shirt. "We were working on male pheromones at the time. He secretly filmed us making love during a pheromone test."

Slowly, Flynn lifted her face to his and a deadly light appeared in his eyes. "He what?"

"He was recording our progress with the experiments on videotape, which I knew about. What I didn't discover until much later was how he planned to try out a new pheromone experiment on me, the results of which he proceeded to immortalize on tape. The aborted results, I might add."

"Aborted because you discovered the camera?"

"Yes."

"Where's the tape now?"

"I have it. That's why he won't pull anything, Flynn. If he does, I have the tape as evidence as to who worked on what. And none of my female pheromone research belongs to Mick. If he tries to claim anything that doesn't belong to him, I hire a lawyer."

THEY STRUGGLED HOME THROUGH the pouring rain. Jane's dress clung to her, catching between her legs with every step she took and rubbing the tender skin of her thighs. By the time they trudged into her front yard, she was about as miserable as she could ever remember being.

"Do you think we could go inside and shower?" Flynn asked.

She turned on him. "You are not stepping one foot into my house unless you hose down."

He regarded her with surprising equanimity. "Fine. Where's the hose?"

She pointed to a hook on the side of the house. "Wash off from top to bottom."

"No problem."

He turned on the spigot and held the nozzle over his head, standing stoically beneath the gush of chilly water. Mud, leaves and sticks poured off him. She didn't think she'd ever seen him quite so...scruffy. A tiny giggle escaped and he shot her a sharp glance. She quickly pinched her lips together. It didn't help. She tried to cover her mouth, but her laughter still leaked through the cracks.

She was in serious trouble. She knew it even before she saw the warning blaze of gold or heard the growl rumble through his chest. Common sense urged her to run for the house as fast as her sopping dress would allow. Before she could act on that momentary spark of brilliance, he turned the hose on her, full blast.

"Yuck it up now, blondie."

"Flynn!" she shrieked, covering her face. "Turn it off. It's freezing."

"You think? Hell, yes, it's freezing. But did I complain? No! I stood here and took it like a man. Turn around. Your backside is a lot dirtier than your front."

She spun around, screaming even louder as the stream of water shot straight up her dress. "That's enough! That's enough!"

"Oh, no, it's not."

He wrapped an arm around her waist and hauled her against him. Water poured down over the top of them both. He helped the mud along, his hands and on occasion the hose, dipping in and out of the various openings of her dress. Finally, she stood, clinging to him, shivering uncontrollably. But at least he'd washed away most of the debris she'd picked up on her downhill slide.

"Shower," she said, teeth chattering so hard she could barely speak. "Hot."

He turned off the hose and coiled it with more speed than skill. "You better have two bathrooms available or I'm coming in with you."

"Have two." She lifted her dripping skirts and pelted onto the porch. Pushing open the front door, she hesitated. "Unzip me," she told Flynn.

"You're kidding. Out here?" He slid her zipper down the length of her spine. "That's almost as daring as making love on the front lawn."

"No one can see. The rain drove everyone indoors." With a final nervous glance over her shoulder, she shrugged.

The dress dropped in a sodden heap on the wooden planking. She scurried inside, peeking at Flynn from around the door. "Are you coming?"

"Aw, hell," he muttered.

He yanked off his shoes and ripped his shirt over his head. Then he unzipped his trousers and stripped to his boxers. Just as he stepped over the threshold, Dipstick came charging up the steps and plowed past them. Barking furiously at having been left out of the fun with the hose, he shook his head.

"Dipstick, no!" Jane shouted.

Dipstick listened as well as every other soaking wet dog. Working from his head downward, he shook himself from snout to tail, sending muddy water, leaves and twigs flying in all directions. He gave his back leg a second shake as punctuation.

Flynn sighed. "Do you have a spare tub where Dipstick and I can get cleaned up?"

"Top of the steps, turn right. There's a full bath at the end of the hall." He started toward the stairs and Jane caught his arm. "Flynn?"

She didn't know what she wanted to say, but oddly enough he understood. "You're welcome." He flashed her his most endearing grin. "You get warmed up in the shower while I take care of Dipstick."

Trudging up the stairs behind man and dog, Jane realized the truth. How odd to discover you'd fallen in love with someone because he'd offered to wash the dog so she could have the first shower. She walked into the bathroom and closed the door. She never knew how long she stood in the middle of the tile floor, tears streaming down her cheeks. When she finally awoke to her surroundings, she turned the shower on full force and stepped beneath the hot spray.

What she felt for Flynn wouldn't work, she tried to tell

herself as she shampooed the last of the day's events from her hair. Nothing could possibly come of their relationship. She'd gone from lust to love, whereas Flynn had gone from...perfume-induced lust to more perfume-induced lust. She applied a soapy washcloth to every nook and cranny she possessed. He didn't believe in love. Heck, he'd flat-out told her he didn't believe in anything at all. Her tears came harder and she dropped the washcloth to the floor of the shower stall. And tomorrow... Tomorrow he'd turn in his final report on her security needs and leave.

Sliding down the tiled wall, she crouched, curled in a tight ball. Beneath the sound-deadening drum of the water, she sobbed.

"Aw, hell," came a familiar-sounding voice. Arms lifted her, held her, comforted her. "Shh. Don't cry. You're killing me, sweetheart. Please don't cry."

Jane covered her face, unable to look at him. "What are you doing here?" she hiccuped the question.

"You took so long I got worried."

He reached past her and turned off the spray. Gathering her closer, he carried her out of the stall. She noticed then that he was deliciously, deliriously naked. "I'm sorry I worried you."

Snagging a couple of towels off a nearby rack, he dropped one on top of her curls and used the other to rub them both dry. "Why were you crying?" Her lips trembled and she pressed them into a firm line, struggling to find a reasonable excuse. He tipped up her chin and kissed her before she could. "Don't do that," he murmured.

"Do what?"

"Don't scrunch your mouth up like that. You might unplump it."

A gurgle of laughter escaped past her tears. "Unplump?"

"Yeah. Unplump." He traced her bottom lip with his

index finger. "Do you know your smile was the first thing I noticed about you? I spent most of our dinner date trying to prick your sense of humor so you'd show it to me."

"It's my bruises."

"What?"

"I was crying because of my bruises."

"Not because I'm leaving tomorrow?"

"Maybe that, too," she confessed. "Stupid, huh?"

"I didn't mean for you to cry. Or for you to miss me when I left."

Tears filled her eyes again. "I know," she whispered. "It's not your fault."

"I shouldn't have kept kissing you."

She leaned forward and captured his mouth with hers. "Like that?"

"Yeah. And like this..."

He tipped her back, protecting her from the chilly tile with a towel. He kissed her, dipping in and out in smooth, leisurely strokes. She sighed in sheer pleasure and he quickened the pace ever so slightly.

"I could do this all day. I could do you all day."

"And I'd let you." *All day.* They didn't have another "all day." All they had was tonight. "Make love to me, Flynn."

He pillowed his cheek against her breasts, fighting a private war. "I can't do that. I can't make the hurt any worse. I did that once. I won't let it happen again."

"Tell me what happened. Get it into the open so we can deal with it."

He sat up. Reaching behind him, he dragged more towels off her rack. Swathing them both from head to toe, he carried her into the hallway. "Which way?"

"Directly across." He nudged her bedroom door open

with his hip. Carefully placing her on the bed, he backed off, distancing himself. "Flynn?"

He paced to her dresser, picking up one of the dozen Josh Simpson globes decorating the surface. He stared into the colorful ball, much as she did when puzzling through a problem. "Her name's Kim Jones. And I ruined her husband's life."

She didn't try and negate his statement. She didn't say, "Oh, no. I'm sure you're exaggerating." Or, "Don't be so hard on yourself." Or any of the other platitudes people often felt obligated to spout. Instead she asked, "How did you do that?"

He shrugged. "I installed a security system in her home."

"How did that ruin her *husband's* life?"

Flynn's mouth twisted. "I believe the ruination part occurred when my security cameras caught her husband in bed with another woman. Her best friend, as a matter of fact."

Oh, no. "Didn't he deserve to get caught?"

"Nope."

She closed her eyes for a brief instant. If she hadn't heard the pain in that single word, she'd have thought he didn't care. But he cared. "I don't understand. Why didn't he deserve to get caught?"

"Because it was a setup and I fell for it hook, line and sinker. The con artist got conned." He returned the globe to its stand and sat on the edge of the bed, facing her. "Kim approached our firm because she suspected her husband of having an affair—or so she said. I decided to rescue Kim from the bastard."

"Very gallant," she approved.

"It would have been, if it had been true." His mouth tugged to one side. "I set up a few extra cameras to record his activities while she was at work."

"So what's the catch?"

"Kim had arranged for her best friend to set her husband up, get him in a compromising position on film so she'd be in a better bargaining position in divorce court. Since his firm takes a dim view of extramarital affairs, she was in a very strong position. My reward for helping her scam her poor beleaguered husband was a punch in the mouth."

"Courtesy of Paulie?"

"The very same."

"I see." And she did. "Kim's husband was your ant."

He stared in bewilderment. "Huh?"

"The ant you pulled out of my hair. You said you'd recently learned to protect fragile creatures, particularly from yourself. I thought you were talking about a woman. But it was Mr. Jones you inadvertently hurt."

"You're right. He was my ant. One of many." He left the bed and put some distance between them again. But he continued to face her, to meet her gaze with absolute frankness. "I'm good at hurting people. Most of the time it's not deliberate, but that doesn't change the end result."

"Why are you telling me all this now?"

"Because you deserve to know the truth. You deserve to know why I'm leaving tomorrow. I've hurt enough people in my life. You're not going to be one of them."

Jane caught her lower lip between her teeth. "I have a confession to make."

He looked like a man prepared for the worst. "Go on."

She yanked open the drawer to her bedside table. Condoms overflowed. "The only way you can hurt me is by walking away before we empty this drawer."

Flynn swore. "Honey, there's not a man on this planet who can work through all those in one night."

"I guess that means you won't be able to work through the ones I put in all the other drawers, either?"

"Other drawers?"

She crouched on the bed, shedding towels. "I don't think there's a single drawer in this entire house that isn't stuffed full of foil packets. All colors, all types." She emerged breathlessly from the last towel, revealed in all her glory. "I wasn't taking any chances, you see. I wanted to be prepared no matter where we ended up."

"I'm leaving tomorrow, Jane. I can't stay."

"Then when you leave, we'll both have a smile on our face." She demonstrated.

His mouth settled in a grim line. "That looks like a pretty wobbly smile to me."

"I can fix it, honest. All you have to do is drop that towel and we'll both have happy faces."

He choked on a laugh. "You want this towel off, you have to come over and get it."

She wasn't likely to receive a better invitation. But she'd make him pay for giving her such a hard time. Rising from the pile of towels strewn around her, she dropped onto all fours in the center of the mattress and negotiated a leisurely path toward the bottom of the bed. Reaching the bedpost, she grabbed hold of the wooden post and wrapped her legs around it as though it were a fireman's pole.

"Did I ever tell you I was an excellent climber?" Muscles straining, she demonstrated, working her way up the bedpost.

Flynn's towel did a lovely imitation of a well-pitched tent. "Come down," he demanded.

"Condom first."

Foil wrappers practically exploded from the drawer as he fumbled to nab one. The towel he'd insisted she remove went flying. Satisfied, Jane slid downward. He caught her when she was halfway to the mattress. His chest scraped along her back as he gathered her in his arms from behind.

"Keep your legs around the post." He filled his hands

with her buttocks and slowly allowed her to slide down, impaling her. "Now ride me, sweetheart."

She gripped the post, unable to move a muscle. "I can't ride. I'm—" Her eyes squeezed shut and she dissolved in his arms. Came apart. Flew apart. "Flynn!" she sobbed. "Flynn, I missed the bus."

He chuckled close to her ear. "There'll be another one along soon." He unwrapped her from the bedpost and maneuvered them to the bed. "Real soon."

Jane followed him down, inhaling a perfume sweeter than anything she could create in her lab. Flynn. She drew him deep into her lungs, filling every sense with his essence. And he returned the favor. He inhaled her, tasted her, drank her in. She wrapped herself around him instead of the bedpost. Kissing. Lapping. Nipping every inch of exposed skin she could reach.

He groaned in her ear, filling her, expanding within her. Pressing. Pushing. Surging.

She rocked. Bounced. Rocked again. And finally stilled.

Something was wrong, she belatedly realized. Terribly wrong. And then she looked at him. Looked long and hard. His expression was determined...and distant. He was a man who knew what she wanted and was intent on giving it to her. But he wasn't *with* her.

"*We'd have sex and then one or the other of us would leave,*" he'd said to her in Martelli's basement. "*Sometimes we'd sleep. But we never held each other. That would have been too personal. Too...trusting.*"

She couldn't let him do that to himself again, to allow the past to eat any further into his soul. The time had come to let go. To let go of the past. To let go of fear. To let go of his distrust.

"Flynn," she whispered. He didn't hear, so she gathered his face in her hands. "Flynn. Look at me."

He looked. And he saw. "Don't." He swallowed harshly. "Don't do this."

But she couldn't *not* do it. "I'm Jane Dearly. And I love you."

"Jane, please." He choked. "I can't."

"I don't want to have sex with you, Flynn. I want to make love to you."

His chest heaved against hers and his beautiful gold eyes reflected the painful battle he fought. "You don't know what you're asking."

"Yes, I do. I'm asking you to trust. To have faith in just one thing. In me." She ran her hands across the precious planes of his face, attempting to erase the harsh lines that cut across his brow. "I was wrong, Flynn. There is something that can't be measured in my lab, that can't be analyzed or reduced to its molecular structure. It's you, my love, and what we feel for each other."

He stared at her and she sensed that he stood on the edge of a final precipice, one he'd spent a lifetime climbing toward. Teetering. Ready to fall into a dark, bottomless pit or tumble straight into sunshine. Straight into her arms.

"Come to me," she whispered. "I'm here for you."

Right before her eyes, he took a deep breath and leapt.

"Jane..." He gathered her close. "Jane. Let me love you. Even if it's only for one night."

"Together, Flynn. We'll make love together."

He clung to her and she anchored him. This time when he surged into her, it was to make them one. He rode with her, not just on top of her, filled and completed her. When he cupped her breasts and ate at the tender tips, he touched *her*, made it unique and special and unlike any woman he'd touched before. The way he stroked her spoke of newness and joy, instead of practiced assurance. And when he finally climaxed, he called her name, shouted it, wound himself deep around her, twining straight through to her core. She burned with him, soared with him, fell from that precipice protected within his grasp.

Together they created a new first. A joining that neither had ever known before.

"I'm not letting you go," he said once he could speak again.

"Will you hold me, like you did in the basement?"

"All night," he promised.

"And will you make love to me again?"

"No worries there. I plan to make a serious dent in your nightstand table drawer."

"Okay, then." Her eyes fluttered closed, exhaustion claiming her. "That's good."

"Very good," he whispered.

He held her as she slept, making promises he couldn't keep, whispering wishes that would never be, sharing the long night with the only woman who'd ever touched his heart. The only woman who'd ever taken the time and trouble to discover that he possessed one.

The only woman he couldn't have.

"IT'S FLYNN."

"Do you have the file?"

"No. I can't get to the lab without her catching on. You'll have to take care of it yourself."

"That wasn't our deal! I agreed to pay you a lot of money, Morgan. Now, get that file."

"Look... I'll be with her all night. I can even keep her busy first thing in the morning. What you choose to do between now and then is your business. No one will be around to interfere."

"If I have to take care of it myself, I'm not paying you a dime."

"I'll cut my fee in half. That'll buy my silence."

"How do I know you won't go back on our deal?" Mick asked suspiciously.

"You know things about me, remember? Past events I'm not eager to have revealed." Flynn closed his eyes. "I'm leaving tomorrow, Barstow. And I won't be back. Put the cash in Jane's lab coat and our business association is at an end."

"Screw me on this and you will pay."

"Don't threaten me, Barstow. Forget to leave the cash and you'll be the one paying."

CHAPTER FOURTEEN

"OH, DEAR. OH, DEAR. JANE? Er...Flynn? There's trouble at the lab, children. Come quick."

Flynn fought to unglue one eye. Jane had more success waking. In fact, she erupted from the bed. "We'll be right there." She reddened. "I mean...I. *I'll* be right there."

"Hurry, my dear. I think this is a police matter. Oh, and good morning, Mr. Morgan."

Flynn sighed. "Yo, Rube."

Footsteps scampered down the hall.

"Did you hear? There's trouble." Jane dragged the covers off him. "*Flynn.* Get up."

"There's no hurry. This particular trouble isn't going anywhere."

"But the lab..."

"We are not going outside naked. Clothes, first. Lab, second. Sheesh." He shook his head in mock disgust. "For a prissy scientist you sure come up with kinky ideas."

She planted her hands on her hips. "Sheesh?"

"I'm making another life change." He butted noses with her. "You have an objection to my sanitizing my vocabulary a bit?"

Jane held up her hands. "Heaven forbid I interfere with any man attempting to evolve past what nature intended."

"Damn right," he growled. "I'm a man on the move, so step aside."

"I'm proud of you, Flynn." She grabbed his arm and

nearly shook it off. "Now can I get you to move outside to the lab?"

It didn't take long for Jane to snatch up clothes and climb into them. Flynn progressed at a slightly slower pace. Opening the bedroom door, Jane followed candy wrappers trailing like breadcrumbs the length of the hallway. They continued down the steps and out toward the back.

Waking Dipstick along the way, she flew from the house and into the yard, the Saint Bernard hot on her heels, barking his concern. To her horror, Sheriff Tucker stood outside her lab along with his deputy, Jimbo. Her uncles were gathered to one side, whispering urgently among themselves.

"Sheriff," she said, greeting him nervously. "Good to see you again."

"Morning, Miss Jane. How are you this fine summer day?"

She lifted a self-conscious hand to her pillow-tousled curls. "Just great. And you and Elva? Were you able to get rid of the ants?"

"Sure were. Sorry I wasn't more specific about the kind of bug spray I needed."

Flynn strolled across the lawn to join them, yawning. She shot him an annoyed glance. "You sure took your time," she muttered beneath her breath.

Of course, he heard. "You didn't want me coming out here buck-naked, did you, sweetheart?" he whispered back. "Think what everyone would have thought. And they'd have been right, wouldn't they?"

A blush mounted her cheeks and she studiously returned her attention to Tucker. "So what's the problem, Sheriff? Is something wrong?"

"We received notice that there'd been a break-in at your lab. It was an automated call that came through in the middle of the night." He shot his deputy an annoyed glance.

"But because Jimbo, here, wasn't familiar with the procedure in dealing with that sort of situation, he waited until this morning to notify me."

Jimbo reddened. "Sorry, Miss Jane."

"That's all right, James," she responded politely. "I didn't even know my lab had an alarm."

"It was a going-away present," Flynn volunteered, hoping it would ease her anger. It didn't.

Jane went to straighten her lab coat and realized an instant too late that she wasn't wearing one. To cover her lapse, she marched over to the cement-block building, flung open the front door and led the way inside. Then she stopped so fast, Jimbo plowed into her.

"Sorry, Miss Jane," he said automatically, before whistling in astonishment. "Well, would you look at that."

Jane was already looking. The foyer remained untouched, as did her office and her uncles'. But the brand-new glass door Flynn had insisted on installing had multiple dings in it, with small starbursts of shattered glass around each impact. To her delight, the door had held. She cupped her hands against the glass in an effort to see into the darkened lab. Two of her chairs lay in fragments on the floor. No doubt they'd been used to ding the door. And sitting with his back against the glass, slumped in an exhausted heap, was Mick.

"Mick, you son of a bitch!" she shouted, pounding on the glass. Jimbo and the sheriff stared at her in open-mouthed disbelief. Flynn chuckled. But Jane didn't care. She was too furious to worry about her reputation. "This is the last straw."

Mick scrambled to his feet and threw himself at the door. "Let me out of here! I've been trapped all night."

"I ought to seal up this door and leave you there until you turn to dust."

"It's not my fault! I came in here to…to— Never you mind." He body-slammed the door again. "Let me out of here!"

Flynn pulled a small remote control from his pocket and handed it to Jane. "Punch in your birth date." She lifted an eyebrow in surprise that he'd even know such a thing and he shrugged self-consciously. "Seemed appropriate at the time. You'll want to change it later—it's so obvious."

She did as he said and the locks on the door snicked open. Mick tumbled through, landing face-first at their feet. "Get me a lawyer," he shouted. "I want to sue somebody."

"Feel free," Jane retorted. "You can sue just as soon as you get out of jail for breaking-and-entering and burglary and whatever else Sheriff Tucker decides to arrest you for." She turned, slanting the sheriff a pleading look. "You are going to arrest him, aren't you?"

"Absolutely, Miss Jane."

"It won't stick! You weren't home and I needed a file I left behind after our breakup. The door locked behind me and the power went out and the phones went dead. I couldn't get out."

"You're not supposed to. That's the purpose of this particular security system. It traps idiots," Jane snapped. "Trust me. I know."

Flynn cleared his throat. "Jane?"

"What?"

"I'm afraid you're going to be annoyed with me."

Uh-oh. "Why?"

"In addition to the new door and other security features, I put a camera in your lab and out here in the foyer."

She turned her outrage on Flynn. "I told you I didn't want a camera."

"I know. And after our little slide into that mudpit yesterday, I can even understand why." He tried to look suitably abashed. "It was very wrong of me."

"Yes, it was."

"It did catch Mick, though, and what he was doing in your lab."

She blinked. Then she smiled. "Flynn?"

"Yes, sweetheart?"

"I forgive you."

"Tape?" Mick croaked. "You got me on tape?"

"Six full hours," Flynn confirmed, "starting when you first walked into the building and—" he took a quick peek in the pocket of Jane's lab coat "—and deposited a small payment. Hell, depending on what time you got here, it's probably still running."

Mick blanched. Then his eyes narrowed and he spun to face Tucker, grabbing at his shirt. "It's all Morgan's fault! He set me up."

The sheriff removed the sweat-dampened fingers and reached for his handcuffs. "That'll be a little tough to prove, Barstow, since he's been keeping me apprised of his plan each step of the way."

Mick turned to Jane next. "You have to listen to me. This is all one of Morgan's schemes. He's an ex-con, did you know that? Burglary, running scams. You name it, he's done it."

She shrugged. "Flynn already confessed about that."

Mick began to babble. "He told me to go to the lab and help myself to the file. I thought it would be okay. I'd never have done it if he hadn't given me permission."

"What about all those other times I caught you in here?"

"I was looking for you!" Mick shouted. "You know that. How can you believe Morgan over me? He preys on women like you. It's his specialty."

She folded her arms across her chest. "Lucky me."

"And has he told you that your uncles bought him at a bachelor auction? Bought him so he'd seduce you?"

"Shut up, Barstow," Flynn growled.

Jane stilled. "What are you talking about?"

"Your uncles bought him because they knew no one else around here would touch you. Morgan was the perfect choice. They bought him to install your security system and be your own personal test subject. Why not use him to keep you happy, too?"

Flynn gathered Barstow's shirt in his fist. "One more word and I deck you."

"Morgan," the sheriff warned. "Turn him loose."

"My God, you've fallen for her." Mick laughed, the sound harsh and jeering. "Flynn Morgan, the man who's seduced more women than he can count, has fallen for an inept—"

"That tears it."

Flynn threw a right hook that would have made Paulie proud. Barstow crashed into the wall behind him and slid to the floor. He clutched this jaw, moaning. "Arrest him! He hit me. I think I lost... I did! I lost a tooth."

"Sorry, Barstow," Tucker said coldly. "We didn't see a thing. Did we, Jimbo?"

"You got that right." The deputy balled his hands into fists. "But if I hear another nasty crack about Miss Jane, I'm throwing my own punch that no one's gonna see. We may not like her experimenting on us, but nobody talks about Jane like that and gets away with it. Nobody."

Tears pricked her eyes. "Thank you." She glanced at Flynn and then away. "If you'll excuse me, I think I'll have a word with my uncles."

Flynn swore. "Jane, wait." She didn't listen. Not that she ever did. He caught up with her outside the lab. He talked fast. "Look, Mick was right. They did purchase me at a bachelor auction. It was to raise money for Lost Springs Ranch. The place where I grew up? It was for a good cause. That makes a difference, doesn't it? Helping homeless kids?''

"They bought you to seduce me?"

Aw, hell. "Not even a little. It just... It just worked out that way."

She charged toward her uncles. "You bought Flynn to seduce me?"

Hickory glanced at his companions and sighed. "Yes."

Dogg nodded morosely.

Candy wrappers exploded around Rube and he sniffed. "It was so you wouldn't go away."

"I don't understand."

"We picked Mr. Morgan because we were certain you wouldn't fall in love with him. He was...safe." Hickory poked at the grass with his cane. "Or so we thought. We didn't want some man tempting you away from here, like Barstow almost did. And since none of the men in town appealed other than as subjects for your experiments, we bought you a birthday gift. Mr. Morgan, here. You could use him to experiment on. Have a little fling, if that's what you wanted, and enjoy life, all without ever leaving home."

"He's an all-purpose present. Yes, he is."

Tears slipped down Jane's cheeks and Flynn glared at the three. "Look what you did! You made her cry."

"Isn't that the sweetest thing you ever heard?" she sobbed.

"*Sweet?*" Flynn lifted his gaze heavenward. "Aw, hell. Why am I even surprised?"

Dogg spoke up. "Barstow told Jane that Morgan loves her."

Jane clasped her hands together and stared at her uncle. "Does he? Does he love me?"

"One hundred percent probability."

Flynn closed his eyes. "Son of a—"

Jane spun around to face him. "You...you love me?"

"Hell, yes."

She shook her head, the tears starting up again. "No, you don't understand. You aren't in love with me. Honestly, you're not."

It took every ounce of self-control to keep from ripping his hair out. "You are something else, you know that? A man tells you he loves you and you tell him no, he doesn't." The tears flooded down her cheeks, melting Flynn's anger like a sack of sugar in a rainstorm. "Aw, honey. Please don't do that."

"It's all a horrible mistake," she managed to say between sobs. "You don't really love me."

"Uh-huh." He turned to Dogg. "Interpretation, please?"

"She cheated on her pheromone experiments."

"I *did*," she wailed. "I didn't try each of the twelve formulas. When I realized number nine was working, I cheated. I kept using just that one so you'd keep doing—" She spared her uncles an embarrassed glance. "Doing what you were doing. It's not love you've been feeling. You're under the influence of my pheromone perfume."

He gripped her shoulders. "How many times do I have to tell you, I'm *not* under the influence of your damn pheromones. Not unless they're part of the normal chemistry between a man and woman. In that case, you've been influencing the hell out of me."

"I know you think you're right, but—"

"I am right. If your perfume worked, all the men we've come in contact with over the past two weeks would have been panting to get their hands on you. And as shortsighted as I think they are—scared is more like it—they haven't acted like lovesick puppies." He thumped his chest. "I'm the only lovesick puppy around here."

Dipstick whined.

"Okay, fine. And maybe your dog. He's pretty darn crazy about you, too."

"You can't argue with science, Flynn," she informed him bitterly.

"Watch me!"

Tucker and Jimbo emerged just then with a protesting Mick between them. Flynn's eyes narrowed and he thought fast. He had to prove their relationship wasn't a result of her perfumes and only one possible way occurred to him. He stomped over toward Mick, who cowered back, fending him off with manacled hands.

"Don't touch me."

"Wasn't planning to." Flynn plunged a hand in Barstow's pocket and retrieved the bottle of pheromone solution he suspected he'd find there. "Stand still," he ordered the three. "And don't move."

"What are you doing?" Jane asked nervously.

"Proving a point." He unstopped the bottle marked LP-9 and upended it over Jane, making sure it splattered on every inch of available skin. Then he caught her shirt lapel and towed her back toward the sheriff, the deputy and Barstow. "Gentlemen, in the name of science, you *will* take this like men."

"What's going on, Morgan?" Tucker demanded.

Flynn shoved the love of his life toward his chosen victims. "Breathe deep, my friends."

Off to one side, Dogg snorted. Hickory paled. And Rube watched with wide, rounded eyes, untwisting one candy wrapper after another and popping a half dozen sour balls into his mouth all at once.

"Please, don't," Jane pleaded. "You don't understand

what could happen. I'm not sure I can handle the repercussions."

"I know precisely what's going to happen, and trust me, you can handle it." Satisfied that they'd all sniffed the hell out of Jane, he tucked her safely out of view. "Now, I know you all suspect you're about to be consumed with irresistible lust. But the truth of the matter is…this isn't a sex experiment."

Jimbo sagged in relief. "Thank goodness," he muttered.

"Nope. She's given up on sex pheromones. Recently your Miss Jane has been working with the government updating her aerosol truth spray." He glanced at Barstow. "You know all about her truth spray, don't you, Mick?"

"You're lying!" he shouted. "They're pheromones."

Flynn shook his head. "You really are gullible, Barstow. That's just what she wanted you to think. It's called a cover story. Since it was government work, she had to keep it all hush-hush." He inclined his head toward Hickory. "Sort of runs in the family, if you catch my drift."

They all stared at the dazzling gold ball topping Hickory's cane. "I'd heard rumors," Jimbo muttered.

Hickory grinned.

Tucker opened his mouth, shot Flynn a sharp look, then closed it again.

"It's working, isn't it, Tucker," Flynn prompted.

"Damn you, Morgan!" the sheriff bit out. "You had no business contaminating me without warning. Do you realize how much confidential information I'm privy to?"

Flynn lifted an eyebrow. "Like what?"

Tucker gritted his teeth, his hands balling into fists. "Like… Like we have an ex-mobster who's living here under an assumed name. He's part of the witness protection program."

"Thank you, Sheriff." Flynn gave the other two men

significant looks. "You see how effective this stuff is. It's even stronger than the formula she developed when she was sixteen. I can assure you the sheriff wouldn't reveal such sensitive information if the spray didn't work."

Jimbo started hyperventilating. "Oh, no. Oh, no. I can't believe this is happening. Truth spray. *Jeez.* Okay, okay. I confess. It's me! I did it. I'm the one who's been eating all the jelly doughnuts."

Tucker sighed. "Relax, Jimbo."

"It gets worse." The deputy's voice rose shrilly. "Your daughter and I are secretly married. We eloped three weeks ago."

"Why, you—"

"I believe Barstow has something to say," Flynn interrupted. "Don't you, Mick?"

Mick sank to his knees with a moan. "It wasn't the pheromone formulas I was after. It was the truth spray. Everyone in town insisted it worked, so I presold it to some very desperate men. I admit it. I needed the money. I have bills. Lots of them. I have a mother in convalescent care. I have an ex-wife. And I have good taste. Really good taste."

"Why didn't you steal the formula when you two were dating?" Flynn demanded.

"I didn't stumble across her formula until right before our relationship ended. I didn't have the opportunity to take a sample, then, and Jane was watching me. But I did manage to incorporate the data in a research file in Jane's computer. I figured she might hand it over since, without the code, it looks like a standard report. The truth formulations are imbedded in the text. I had until the end of the week to pass on the information or return the money. Since I don't have any of the money left..."

"You're up to your ass in alligators?"

Mick shuddered. "Something like that."

"If all you wanted was the truth spray, why did you also take her pheromone perfume?"

"To see if it really worked. That's all there is. I swear I'm telling the truth."

Hickory burst out laughing. "Very good, Mr. Morgan." He hooked his cane over his arm and applauded. "I'm most impressed."

Flynn took a modest bow. "Thanks."

Jimbo looked from one to the other in confusion. "I don't understand."

Tucker turned on his deputy. "You moron! He didn't really use her truth formula. Morgan wanted to prove that Jane's sex spray doesn't work. That he really loves her for herself, not because of some perfume. I played along to see if I could get a confession out of Barstow. Fortunately, he's as much of an idiot as you."

"It's not…? There's no mobster?"

"No mobster."

"I wasn't being forced to tell the truth?" Jimbo closed his eyes and sank to the ground next to Mick. "I'm dead."

"You got that right, Deputy. Now get your ass back to the station. You can call my wife and daughter and tell them to meet us there. Then we're all going to sit down and have a chat. A nice, long, tooth-loosening chat."

"Yes, sir." Jimbo beat a hasty retreat.

"I'll dispose of this trash." Tucker yanked Mick to his feet. "I'll need you to come in, Miss Jane, and fill out a report. You, too, Morgan. You'll have to give me a final update."

"Final update?" Jane asked. She turned to Flynn as the sheriff dragged Mick off the property. "What does he mean by that?"

"He means that we've been planning this sting for a

while. As soon as I found out what Barstow planned, we came up with a way to stop him.''

"The sheriff knew what you planned? He helped? You both did that for me?''

Flynn nodded. "Which is why he was so mad at Jimbo for not saying anything when the call came in about the break-in. Of course, I suspect that's now the least of Jimbo's problems.''

"So, Mr. Morgan,'' Hickory interrupted. "You've now proven that Jane's pheromone perfume doesn't work. Thank you so much for destroying her hopes and dreams. Any other loose ends you care to take care of before leaving?''

"Thought the perfume worked,'' Rube gurgled around cheeks bulging with sour balls. "Worked on Mrs. Motts. How come it worked on her and not on Jane?''

"It never ceases to amaze me how much trouble you can stir up even with your mouth full. We weren't going to mention our little experiment-gone-awry, remember?'' Hickory hooked Rube with his cane and began to tow him toward their house. "I believe this is an excellent time to depart.''

Dogg hesitated in front of Flynn. "Paulie wants to stay. He likes Salmon Bay. He'll start a new business here if you want.''

A half smile tilted Flynn's mouth. "You trying to convince me to stick around?''

"Yes.''

"I'm not the sort of man you want for your niece. You knew that from the beginning.''

Dogg grinned. Leaning closer, he whispered, "I knew. I knew if you came we'd have four more chemists to train.''

Flynn stilled. "Four?''

"Three girls. One boy. Boy will be a lot of trouble. But at least we'll have pollution-free power.''

"What are you saying, Uncle Dogg?" Jane demanded. "I can't hear you."

"Hickory won't be happy if I stick around," Flynn said, trying one more time.

"Will be in nine months, three days. Very happy."

Flynn shook his head, giving up. "Get out of here, Dogg, or your prediction will just be so much talk."

"Use the lab."

Flynn lifted an eyebrow. "Mind telling me why?"

Dogg chuckled while Jane watched in openmouthed astonishment. "No condoms. She forgot to fill the drawers in there." With that, he disappeared across the lawn.

"What was that all about?"

"Guy talk."

She looked as if she intended to pursue the subject, so he stopped her the only way he could. He kissed her until every last thought scattered out of her brilliant curly-topped head.

"Was that a goodbye kiss?"

"It would be the smart thing to do," he muttered.

"Why?"

"You know why."

"Because you're afraid I'll get hurt?"

"Something like that."

She tilted her head to one side. "How were you planning to hurt me?"

"What?"

"Come on, Flynn. Tell me. Were you going to cheat on me?"

"No!"

"Steal my formulas?"

"I'll leave that to Mick," he said tightly. "I've given up my thieving ways, remember?"

She smiled warmly. "I remember. Then maybe you were thinking about lying to me?"

"No! And if you're referring to the auction, I didn't tell you about it because I was afraid it would hurt your feelings. And also because I didn't want you to think badly of your uncles." He glared at her indignantly. "More fool me. You thought it was sweet. *Sweet!* Hell."

"So if you're not going to lie or cheat or steal, how were you planning to hurt me?"

"I—" His mouth opened and closed. Then he sighed. "Knowing me, I'll come up with something."

"That's all right, then." Gold-streaked curls bounced against her temple. "Once you come up with it, just don't do it. Okay?"

He couldn't help laughing. "Good suggestion."

"I thought so."

He filled his hands with the soft, springy curls, then filled his arms with a soft, curvy chemist. "I'm glad for myself that your formula didn't work, but I'm sorry for your sake. If it makes you feel any better, I have every confidence you'll succeed eventually."

"I think I'm just as happy I didn't succeed. Otherwise I'd never have known if you really loved me." She peeked up at him. "Flynn?"

"Yes, sweetheart?"

"The pheromones aren't nearly as important to me as you are." She slipped her arms around his waist. "Will you stay?"

"There's only one way you can convince me."

"What's that?"

He smiled tenderly. "You'll have to make an honest man of me. I'm a changed man, remember? And changed men marry the women they love."

Happiness radiated from her expression, turning her eyes as green as spring-fresh leaves. "You do love me, don't you? It's not the perfume or the pheromones? It's just me."

"It's always been you, Jane." He gathered her close. "And it always will be."

And then he sealed his promise with a kiss, bidding a final farewell to the man he'd once been. Sending another silent thank-you to Lost Springs Ranch. He'd been tossed on their doorstep as an angry child, lost and adrift and headed for ruin. He'd probably set a record for the longest, most difficult success story of all the kids who'd passed through the ranch doors. But he had succeeded. And the future looked bright with promise.

Hell, with Jane at his side, every day would be the sweetest of adventures.

continues with

RENT-A-DAD

by

Judy Christenberry

Why in the world had Melissa Bright bought a bachelor?
Between running a business single-handedly and caring
for her infant daughter, she barely had time to breathe.
And what would Russ Hall do when he found out she had
a baby? He'd expect candlelight and romance. Instead,
he'd find bottles, diapers...and a little girl who would
bring *this* confirmed bachelor to his knees...

Available in May

Here's a preview!

"MANDY IS PERFECTLY capable of holding her own bottle."

"She can?" He stared at the baby. Her hands were on each side of the bottle, but he hadn't realized she could manage without his help. Turning the bottle loose, he watched it sag momentarily before the baby lifted it again. "Well, I'll be. I didn't know you were that talented, Mandy, my girl."

"She can already do a lot of things for herself," Melissa said with a sad air.

"That doesn't make you happy?"

"Oh, of course it does, but...she's changing and growing so quickly. She'll be my only baby and I want to hold on to the sweetness of this first year."

He leaned toward her. "What do you mean, she'll be your only baby? Can't you have more children?"

She seemed startled by his question. "I suppose...I mean physically, I could, but...well, one needs a husband to have children."

His gaze roamed her trim figure, her beautiful face. "I shouldn't think you'd have any trouble finding a husband."

"I'm not looking," she snapped.

"But you should."

"Oh, that's rich," she said wryly. "A confirmed bachelor is urging me to marry?"

"But you have Mandy. She needs a dad."

He could tell he'd hit a nerve. But he didn't want Mandy

missing out on a two-parent family. Considering his only knowledge of a family came from what he'd seen on television, maybe his views were a little unrealistic. But he knew how lonely he'd felt. How different he'd been from the kids in town.

Looking at Mandy's sweet face resting on his chest, he felt a surge of protectivness that was new to him. He'd only been in Casper twenty-four hours, but he could already tell he was forming an attachment to the baby.

And the baby's sexy mother...

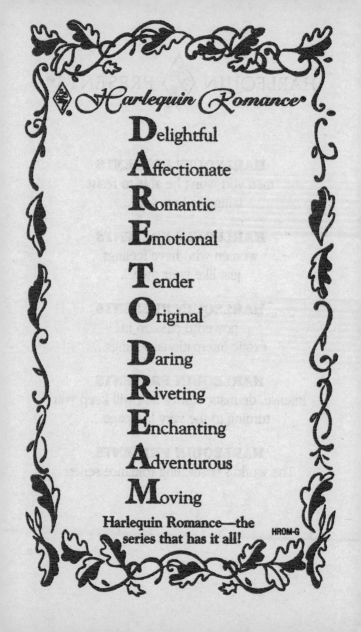

Harlequin Romance

Delightful
Affectionate
Romantic
Emotional
Tender
Original
Daring
Riveting
Enchanting
Adventurous
Moving

Harlequin Romance—the
series that has it all!

HROM-G

HARLEQUIN PRESENTS®

HARLEQUIN PRESENTS
men you won't be able to resist
falling in love with...

HARLEQUIN PRESENTS
women who have feelings
just like your own...

HARLEQUIN PRESENTS
powerful passion in
exotic international settings...

HARLEQUIN PRESENTS
intense, dramatic stories that will keep you
turning to the very last page...

HARLEQUIN PRESENTS
The world's bestselling romance series!

PRES-G

Harlequin® Historical

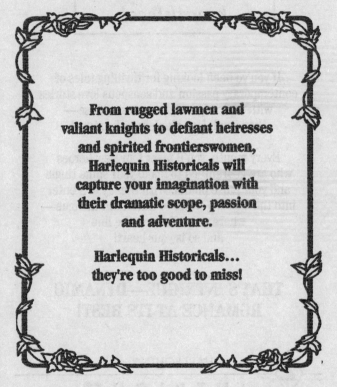

From rugged lawmen and
valiant knights to defiant heiresses
and spirited frontierswomen,
Harlequin Historicals will
capture your imagination with
their dramatic scope, passion
and adventure.

Harlequin Historicals...
they're too good to miss!

HHGENR

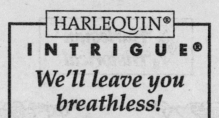

HARLEQUIN®
I N T R I G U E®
We'll leave you breathless!

If you've been looking for thrilling tales of
contemporary passion and sensuous love stories
with taut, edge-of-the-seat suspense—
then you'll *love* **Harlequin Intrigue!**

Every month, you'll meet four new heroes
who are guaranteed to make your spine tingle
and your pulse pound. With them you'll enter
into the exciting world of Harlequin Intrigue—
where your life is on the line
and so is your heart!

THAT'S INTRIGUE—DYNAMIC
ROMANCE AT ITS BEST!

HARLEQUIN®
I N T R I G U E®

INT-GENR

LOOK FOR OUR FOUR FABULOUS MEN!

Each month some of today's bestselling authors bring
four new fabulous men to Harlequin American Romance.
Whether they're rebel ranchers, millionaire power brokers
or sexy single dads, they're all gallant princes—and
they're all ready to sweep you into lighthearted fantasies
and contemporary fairy tales where anything is possible
and where all your dreams come true!

You don't even have to make a wish...
Harlequin American Romance will grant your every desire!

Look for Harlequin American Romance
wherever Harlequin books are sold!

HAR-GEN

HARLEQUIN SUPERROMANCE®

...there's more to the story!

Superromance. A *big* satisfying read about unforget-
table characters. Each month we offer
four very different stories that range from family
drama to adventure and mystery, from highly emotional stories to romantic comedies—and
much more! Stories about people you'll
believe in and care about. Stories too
compelling to put down....

Our authors are among today's *best* romance writ-
ers. You'll find familiar names and
talented newcomers. Many of them are
award winners—and you'll see why!

If you want the biggest and best
in romance fiction, you'll get it
from Superromance!

Available wherever Harlequin books are sold.

Look us up on-line at: http://www.romance.net

HS-GEN